THE ROSE OF THE WORLD

THE ROSE OF THE WORLD

A Hawkenlye Mystery

Alys Clare

Severn House

This first world edition published 2011
in Great Britain and the USA by
SEVERN HOUSE PUBLISHERS LTD of
9–15 High Street, Sutton, Surrey, England, SM1 1DF.
Trade paperback edition first published
in Great Britain and the USA 2011 by
SEVERN HOUSE PUBLISHERS LTD.

British Library Cataloguing in Publication Data

Clare, Alys.
  The rose of the world. – (A Hawkenlye mystery)
  1. D'Acquin, Josse (Fictitious character)–Fiction.
  2. Helewise, Abbess (Fictitious character)–Fiction.
  3. England–Social life and customs–1066-1485–Fiction.
  4. Detective and mystery stories.
  I. Title II. Series
  823.9′2-dc22

ISBN-13: 978-0-7278-8023-9 (cased)
ISBN-13: 978-1-84751-343-4 (trade paper)

All Severn House titles are printed on acid-free paper.

Severn House Publishers support The Forest Stewardship Council [FSC],
the leading international forest certification organisation. All our titles that
are printed on Greenpeace-approved FSC-certified paper carry the FSC logo.

Typeset by Palimpsest Book Production Ltd.,
Falkirk, Stirlingshire, Scotland.
Printed and bound in Great Britain by
MPG Books Ltd., Bodmin, Cornwall.

For Tim and Sandie,
who found each other again,
with much love

Ave, formossisima,
Gemma pretiosa,
Ave, decus virginium,
Virgo gloriosa,
Ave, mundi luminar,
Ave, mundi rosa.

Hail, most beautiful one,
Precious jewel,
Hail, honoured of the virgins,
Glorious virgin,
Hail, light of the world,
Hail, rose of the world.

From Carmina Burana,
Cantiones profanae

Prologue
Early autumn 1210

The woman stood by the tiny window, staring out at the mountains. There was no snow yet on their distant, desolate peaks, but soon there would be. People who knew this place better than she did were already muttering ominously about signs and portents, predicting that a savage, bitter winter was on its way.

She sighed. As if there was not sufficient to worry about already, without the hardships, perils and discomforts of snow that endured for months . . .

Enough, she told herself firmly. She knew she must not allow herself the luxury of a good moan, even in the privacy of her thoughts. They all had to keep cheerful, for in that way they encouraged one another and life did not seem too bad. Their main bulwark was, of course, their faith. It was the reason why they were all there together. The reason for everything that had happened.

Briefly, the woman closed her eyes, detaching from the sparsely-furnished, chilly little room. Very soon her mind soared, up and away, and a slow smile spread over her thin face. It was so easy to find that bliss; to enter in spirit that wonderful realm that was the goal of them all. If she was very lucky – and just occasionally she was – it seemed to her that she could almost catch the vaguest, mistiest glimpse of the heavenly home. More importantly – oh, far more importantly! – once she thought she had *heard* . . . Her physical body forgotten, she gave herself up to the joy that never failed.

Some time later, sounds from the narrow alley below the window brought the woman back to herself. Darkness had fallen. The sounds had been made by her neighbour, closing, locking and barring his door for the night. She wondered if she had locked her own door, and, leaving the room, she went down the steep wooden stairs to check. Yes; all was well. It was not her companions that she feared – of course it wasn't, for those who had endured so much together could never be a threat to one another – but there were other, far greater dangers out there.

They were not yet nearby, or so all those brave spies reported. But one day they would come; of that there was no doubt. If luck were with the community, the painstaking net of eyes and ears that they had created around them would function as it should and those that came hunting would find nothing but empty houses. If luck had turned her back, then . . .

No. She must not think about that.

It was time for bed. She climbed back up the stairs, a hand in the small of her back. Her bones ached at the end of a long day, and already she was anticipating the pleasure of lying down on the hard, straw-stuffed mattress that barely covered her small bed. Compared with what she had once known, it offered sparse comfort, for in her previous life she had lived in luxury. She had been married to a knight who had not been a poor man, but her wealth had been her own; her family name had been – still was – an important one in the region. Twenty years ago her husband had died, and she had given up all that she had, all that she possessed, running joyfully to embrace the life she had dreamed of.

She stood in her small room, unpinning her veil and removing the close-fitting coif she wore beneath it. She had no looking glass in which to peer at her image, but she was sure her once-dark hair must surely be streaked with silver. The shed hairs she found on her pillow and on her garments told her so. She had been a wife; she had borne a son, and he, she knew, had a son. Perhaps more children had come along by now. She did not know, for news was a long time reaching the lonely little village hidden away on the knees of the mountains. A grandmother, she reflected. It would have been good to have held her son's child in her arms.

She turned her mind from the thought. She loosened the laces of her black gown and slipped it off, smoothing down the chemise she wore beneath and feeling her bones protruding through her flesh. She was thin: from grief, from hardship, from fasting. It was difficult to recall the woman she once had been, with the curvaceous hips and the full, generous breasts enhanced by the cut of the gorgeous gowns in colours chosen always to flatter, to bring out the green in her eyes. She had been attractive, beautiful, even, if the men who had danced attendance on her were to be believed. She shook her head, smiling, dismissing a past she neither regretted nor wanted back. It was two decades since she had embraced a man or a boy; were a handsome, naked stranger to appear magically in her bed, she wondered if she would even remember what to do.

She lay down, closed her eyes and made herself relax, hoping to return to the sacred realm she had visited in her thoughts before she prepared for bed. But she could not find it now; other images were intruding, horrible images whose brutality did not lessen even though she had seen them in her mind a hundred times. It was more than a year now since that unspeakable day. She wondered, as she lay in the darkness and endured her memories, how long it would be before the agony faded. If it ever did. In addition to her almost physical reaction to what she had seen, there was also guilt because she had survived where so many had not. Thanks to the spy network, some of them had suspected what was going to happen and had not been there on the Magdalene's feast day. She had been one of them, forewarned and far away when the blow fell. She had tried to make more of her people come away with her, but they had refused to see the danger until it was too late. What a price they had paid. Death by the sword, death by beating, death by burning. Death.

She thought about death. It called to her in sweet, gentle tones, and she wanted very much to answer. Not yet; it was not her time, and such things were not for her to decide.

As if there had been an obligation to recall yet again the awful day when the world had changed, now that she had done so it was easy to let her mind drift. Perhaps it was a reward for enduring her memories and her guilt without protest, for now the horrors had faded away and the blessed realm seemed very close. She gave a deep sigh and gave herself up to the images, dimly making out the angels in their bliss, a vision shot with gold and rose-pink like the sunset. Just for the blink of an eye, she thought she heard the precious, holy sounds . . .

The vision had gone. Once more she lay alone in a cold, stone-walled room, lit only by the distant stars. She strove as hard as she could to recall those sounds, but it was no good: you had to *hear* them even as they issued out of the silence, for they would not remain in the mind once they had ceased.

But there used to be a way, the woman reflected. Before the threat had come, there had been books. Not many, for they were priceless and the knowledge they contained was reserved for those who had proved themselves deserving. But the precious books were all far beyond her reach, some lost forever in the flames, some hidden away so deep that they would never see the light of day again.

She lay in silent contemplation for some time. A memory was stirring, and patiently she waited until it had formed.

At long last she turned on her side and, pulling the thin blanket closer around her, prepared for sleep. She knew what she had to do. Tomorrow she would work out how to get a message out of that besieged land.

ONE

Abbess Caliste of Hawkenlye Abbey paced to and fro across her room behind a firmly-closed door, doing her utmost to control her fury. Her heart was hammering so hard that she felt light-headed, and her fists were clenched so fiercely that her fingernails had cut into her palms.

How dare they! she thought, clamping her lips together to prevent the anguished cry roaring out of her. *As if the abbey and the people we serve were not suffering enough already!*

She indulged her anger for a while longer. Then she drew a couple of deep breaths, walked slowly around behind the wide table where she worked and sat down in the throne-like chair. She drew a piece of scrap parchment towards her and dipped her quill into the ink horn. Then she began to write down the details of the information that had just been issued to her.

Even as she wrote the terrible words, part of her mind was busy trying to work out what she was going to *do* . . .

It was the eleventh year of King John's reign and the second of the interdict imposed on England by Pope Innocent because of the king's refusal to accept Innocent's choice, Stephen Langton, as archbishop of Canterbury. Since then, church services had been suspended. Some of the clergy, braver – or, perhaps, like the Cistercians, more arrogant – than their fellow churchmen, had defied the interdict and were continuing their habitual daily rounds. The majority were not, and most of the bishops of England had fled to France. The interdict had not made the king submit to the pope and, a year ago, King John had been excommunicated. Now, if any good Christian helped or supported the king, that man stood in peril of losing his immortal soul.

Not that any of the king's subjects much wanted to help him. His record was not impressive. He had lost most of England's continental possessions, he had failed in his duel with the pope, and the country was poorly governed. Failure, however, cost as much – or more – than success, for taxes were extortionate already and constantly there were further demands. In addition, John was cruel, he had a reputation for avarice and everyone knew he was no true lover of God. Learned as he was in theology – hadn't he after all spent the formative years of his life with the monks at Fontevrault? – he only studied the great texts of the church so that he could argue points of doctrine with the clergy. Or so people said.

If the pope had hoped that expelling King John from the faith would encourage those with a grievance against him to rise up in rebellion, he was disappointed. The barons had their own reasons for muttering against the king, and these had little to do with the church. As for the mass of the population, they were far from falling into fear and despair at being deprived of the comfort of their church, as the pope had no doubt expected they would. In fact, to the dismay of the clergy, the people of England gave every impression of managing perfectly well. The clergy were beginning to fear that religion would lose its grip, and, indeed, many people were heard grumbling that they didn't see why they should go on having to pay tithes to a church that did absolutely nothing for them.

Nobody could bring their child to be christened, nobody could marry his or her sweetheart, nobody could bring their dead for Christian burial. Far from appearing horrified, the population just shrugged their shoulders and got on with their lives. It was said that people performed secret baptisms according to the old rights, buried their dead in ditches and under hedgerows, and – much as they had always done and always would – bedded each other regardless.

King John's response to the pope's drastic move was, initially, incandescent rage. Those who witnessed it said the king almost went mad, blaspheming against the pope and swearing by God's teeth to banish every last churchman from the realm. If any spy sent to England by the pope were to be discovered, the king would personally tear out the man's eyes, split his nose and pack him off back to Rome as a warning to the rest.

Once he was over his fury, however, John turned the pope's action against him to his own advantage. If the clergy were going to obey their master and cease to do their work, then John would seize their property. There was, after all, little point in a monastery or an abbey if those within were not permitted to support and succour the people. John's officials were dispatched all over England to act in his name, and sheriffs were appointed to administer the properties and, of course, to ensure that the revenues made their way to the king. Those in power in the church were summarily deposed, permitted to return to their posts only if they paid for it; the going rate for a prior was sixty marks.

The king was making a fortune . . .

Now, a year after the excommunication, King John's men had come to Hawkenlye Abbey. Abbess Caliste reflected that, had the abbey not been one of the favourite places of the king's late mother, Queen Eleanor, they'd have come a lot sooner. In the two and a half years since the interdict, Hawkenlye had been kept under observation – a very unsubtle observation at that – and Caliste had been forced to obey the instruction to close up the church and discontinue all services. Nothing specific had been said regarding the shelter down in the Vale, where Hawkenlye's monks and lay brothers administered the holy water from the miracle spring and looked after visiting pilgrims. Abbess Caliste, unshakeable in her conviction that in a time of such hardship people needed the comforts offered in the Vale even more urgently, had taken the decision that the brethren would continue as normal.

They were doing their best. Like the rest of the abbey, they were on short rations, for the new regulations meant that everything from corn to clothing had been seized and locked away in the king's name, doled out with a mean hand at intervals that came far too infrequently. The brethren had tightened their belts and were managing to live on virtually nothing, for this was the only way they could keep food back to give to those who crawled to them on the brink of starvation.

Caliste's disturbing thoughts got the better of her and, putting down her quill, she pictured Brother Saul. He was getting old now, but he still worked as hard as he had always done. He would, Caliste knew, be far too modest to realize it, but the other monks saw him as their unofficial leader, a link to the days when Abbess Helewise had sat in the chair now occupied by Caliste. Brother Saul had been one of Hawkenlye's rocks back then, and he still was.

Caliste's stomach gave a sudden growl. She was hungry, so hungry . . .

Resolutely, she put aside her poignant thoughts on old Saul and her own discomfort. Dipping her quill in the ink, she picked up the thread of what she had been writing.

The king's agents had just left the abbey. Their leader had issued his orders to her as she stood at the gates looking up at them. Since the nuns and monks of Hawkenlye were not called upon to do any work, he'd said, they could not rely on the king's generosity to maintain them in idleness.

The abbey's income was considerable, since Hawkenlye owned large tracts of good land as far afield as the north side of the Weald and the marshlands to the south east. Most importantly, it also had plenty of grazing land suitable for sheep. Sheep provided so much: parchment from their skins, cheese from their milk and, of course, their wool. English wool was in great demand, and Hawkenlye was earning its fair share of the new wealth. Under the current conditions, this wealth now belonged to the king. As his agents had just told the abbess, she was now commanded to record every penny that came in and went out – as if she had not been doing so already! – and keep her accounts ready for inspection at any time. A small amount – *of our own money!* she thought, fuming – would be paid out to the abbey each month.

Standing there, refusing to allow those haughty men on their fine horses to intimidate her, Caliste had raised her chin, looked their leader firmly in the eye and said, 'How, pray, am I to feed my nuns, my monks and those who come to us for help?'

The man had glared at her, and then his face had twisted into an unpleasant sneer. 'Your church is closed, Abbess Caliste,' he said. 'Nobody will come here any more. As to you and your community . . .' He had looked round at the assembled monks and nuns, all of them thin, clad in broken sandals and patched, threadbare habits, and shivering in the chilly October air.

Leaving his sentence unfinished, he had turned back to Caliste and shrugged. Then he and his men had ridden away.

She looked down at her notes, trying yet again to reconcile the tiny allowance with the minimum she knew she needed to keep the abbey alive. It could not be done. Resisting the over-riding urge to drop her head on her hands and howl – a waste of time *that* would be – she closed her eyes, folded her hands together and forced her weary, desperate mind to think.

So many people depended on her, one way or another. She had to find a way to help them. She sat up straight, squared her shoulders and went back to her calculations.

The House in the Woods had a new name: it was officially called Hawkenlye Manor. Few people referred to it in that way. The country people had long memories, and they did not like change. The House in the Woods had been good enough for their parents and their grandparents – probably their great-grandparents too – so why go altering it?

On that late October day, Josse was returning home after a long ride. His old horse Horace had finally died, at an age so advanced that Josse could no longer calculate it, and now he rode a lighter horse that his young son Geoffroi had insisted be called Alfred. Josse and his family had known Alfred from when he was newborn, for he was descended from a golden mare called Honey who had once belonged to Geoffroi's mother, Joanna. Alfred had inherited his grand-dam's golden coat, but his dark mane and the luxuriously long tail were all his own.

As was his intractable temperament; Josse had been riding him for two years now, but his manners still left quite a lot to be desired. Today's excursion had been to remind Alfred who was in control, and Josse was feeling sore and tired. He was also feeling maudlin, for almost without his volition he had found himself riding past the track in the forest that led off to the hut where Joanna had lived.

She had been gone for more than ten years now, but he still missed her. She was the mother of his two children, Meggie and Geoffroi, and also of his adopted son, Ninian. Her death – if, indeed, she really was dead – had left a hole in his life that had never been filled. That line of thought, too, made him sad.

Helewise had come to live at the House in the Woods. After waiting for her for so many years, finally she was there, under his very roof. She had arrived back in June – *Good Lord*, he thought, *was it only four months ago?* – and to begin with he had been so overjoyed that he had not noticed that all was not as he had hoped. She might have left the abbey, renounced her vows and become an ordinary woman, but the problem was – or so he saw it – that in her heart she was still a nun.

It's only to be expected, he told himself as he rode along. She wasn't just a nun, she was an abbess, and of a great foundation at that. Nobody can be expected to leave the religious life and all that it entailed behind in a few months!

It was some five years since Helewise had actually lived within the abbey. Soon after the death of Queen Eleanor back in 1202, Helewise had begun to implement the plans which had long been in her mind. She had quit Hawkenlye in stages, the first one being to stand down as abbess, witness the election and the installation of Caliste as her successor, and then go to live in the tiny little cell adjoining the new chapel on the edge of the forest. The chapel was dedicated to St Edmund and had been built on the orders of Eleanor in memory of Richard, the late king and her favourite son.

The pope's action against King John had effectively closed the abbey to outsiders, and although Josse knew full well that Hawkenlye had done its best to go on being a place of refuge, help and succour, the task had been all but impossible. The attention of the king and his agents had always hovered over the abbey – it was just too important a foundation to be overlooked – and many were of the opinion that John would have robbed the abbey of all its treasures had he not feared the wrath of his formidable mother. Dead she might be, but apparently it made no difference.

The keen glance of the king, however, had slid over St Edmund's Chapel and its little cell without pausing to look properly. Had he done so, he would have seen something quite surprising. The people, finding the church inside the abbey locked and barred, had quietly transferred their devotion to the chapel. Its door was always open, and there was usually a candle burning on its simple altar. Down in its hidden crypt it concealed a treasure known to very few, and it was perhaps the power of this secret that kept the chapel safe from those who wished it ill.

Whatever the truth of it, the people had a place where they could pray. Not only that, for the chapel had its own guardian, and she was a woman whose reputation went before her. She was always there for those in need, providing a smile, a kind word, a simple but nourishing plate of food, a warming drink;

even, on occasions, a blanket on the floor for those too tired to make the journey home until morning. As the years passed, she also began to give remedies for the more common ailments, taught and helped in her work by both Tiphaine, the abbey's former herbalist, and Josse's daughter, Meggie.

In the summer, however, Helewise had implemented the second stage of her withdrawal from the abbey. The House in the Woods had grown in the decade since Josse had gone with his household to live in it, and there had been plenty of room for another resident. However, the sweet hopes that Josse had cherished of Helewise living in any sort of intimacy with him had been swiftly shattered. Quietly, she had explained what she needed: a small room readily accessible to visitors where she could receive and help those who came seeking her, with a little sleeping space leading off it. In effect, he had realized miserably, her desire was to reproduce her cell beside the chapel.

The trouble was, as Josse saw it, that the rest of the world still thought she was an abbess. Or, at least, the whole of the suffering, needy community in and around Hawkenlye did, which, as far as Josse was concerned, was the only part of the world that mattered.

It was all to do with the wretched interdict. Out in the forest, alone except for Alfred and unlikely to be overheard, Josse gave vent to his feelings and cursed the pope, the king, the interdict, the excommunication and everything else that was presently caused him distress.

The echoes of his angry shouts died away. Alfred twitched his ears sympathetically – he was growing on Josse, despite his stubborn nature – and Josse resumed his musings.

To cheer himself up he thought about the beloved people who would be waiting for him at home. His daughter Meggie, he knew, wasn't there. He had actually been quite close to her earlier that day, when he had ridden past the track leading to Joanna's hut. Meggie went over there quite often, and she kept both the tiny dwelling and its herb garden tidy and cared for. Sometimes she would not return for several days. Over the years, Josse had learned to curb his anxiety. She was, he knew, more than capable of taking care of herself and, just like her mother, she seemed to cherish the quiet, secret hut and its almost magical setting.

It was hardly surprising that even someone whose big feet were as firmly planted on the good earth as Josse's should sense the magic, even if he did not understand it. Joanna had been one of the Great Ones of the strange forest people, as had her mother Mag before her. Both Mag and Joanna had left much of their power within the hut and its little clearing, and now Meggie – who, according to her people's predictions, would be the greatest of them all – was adding to what they had so freely bestowed.

Meggie had been absent now for a couple of days. Josse hoped she would soon return. He never dared tell her how much he missed her when she was away but, being the woman she was, he probably didn't need to.

With a happy smile, Josse remembered that Geoffroi would be waiting for him, eager to hear how Alfred had behaved. Geoffroi was now eleven, a strong, robust boy who was tall for his age and already showing the broad shoulders and sturdy build that he had inherited from Josse. Geoffroi loved all living things, and his knowledge of the natural world was wide and profound. For all that there were plenty of people considerably older than Geoffroi living at Hawkenlye Manor and working with its sundry livestock, it was Geoffroi who was the ultimate authority when it came to animal husbandry. Which was quite surprising, his father reflected, considering the boy could barely read or write. Still, as Geoffroi always said, you didn't need book learning to understand why a ewe was limping or to judge which combination of mare and stallion would produce the finest offspring.

Geoffroi himself rode a dark-brown mare called Bruna, the offspring of Horace. It was nice, Josse often thought, that in this way the old horse lived on.

Josse's thoughts rambled on. Everyone else would be home, too. He smiled as he pictured them. Ninian – half-brother to Geoffroi and Meggie, and Josse's adopted son – would be there, his presence all the more treasured because he was so often away. Ninian was in love with Helewise's granddaughter, Little Helewise. She adored him too, and were it not for the interdict, they undoubtedly would have been wed a year or more ago. Little Helewise lived with her family at the Old Manor, the ancestral home of the Warins, which her father Leofgar, being the elder of Helewise's two sons, had inherited.

Ninian spent as much of his time as he could with her and, privately, Josse reckoned the young people had already become everything to each other.

Aye, Ninian. Josse smiled as he contemplated the lad. Others, too, awaited Josse – Gus, Tilly and their children, Will and Ella too, servants in name but more like family to Josse – and their faces flashed one by one across his mind. It would be good to get back.

He realized he was hungry. The household at the House in the Woods ate well, even given the current circumstances, for virtually everything that went on their table came from their own land. Over the year, Josse and his small workforce had gradually cut back the trees surrounding the house, and now several acres were under cultivation. Their sheep grazed on the pastures of New Winnowlands, Josse's former home, with the flock belonging to the manor's present occupants. Given the constant, greedy demands of the king, they were fortunate, Josse well knew, to live in such an out-of-the-way spot. Outside those who lived in the immediate vicinity, only a handful of people knew the House in the Woods even existed.

What would Tilly have prepared for the evening meal? He was almost home now, and he kicked Alfred to a canter. He would soon be finding out.

Helewise was having a lovely day. The autumn weather was pleasantly warm, and she had spent most of the time out of doors, reason enough to make her happy. In addition, for much of it she had had the company of her youngest grandchild, whose father had left her that morning in Helewise's care while he rode on to Tonbridge. He had business with Gervase de Gifford, who was the sheriff.

Helewise didn't enquire, as once she would have done, what that business was. It wasn't that she did not care; it was more that her priorities had changed. The outside world was less important to her now than her family and her loved ones.

When asked by her fond grandmother what she would like to do with their day together, Rosamund promptly said that she wanted to see the Dark Lady. Smiling to herself, Helewise readily agreed and, after the noon meal, the two of them set off through the forest towards the abbey. There was no hurry, so they took their time, chatting as they walked. It was no surprise when, a quarter of a mile or so from their destination, Meggie materialized beside them.

'You're going to see the Lady?' she asked with a smile.

'We are,' Helewise agreed.

'Can I come too?'

'Of course.'

St Edmund's Chapel had been deserted, Helewise's little cell empty. Then there was still no replacement, she observed sadly. Brushing the thought aside, she followed Meggie and Rosamund into the chapel, and together she and Meggie raised the trapdoor cleverly disguised as a flagstone. The three of them descended into the crypt, and Meggie struck a spark, lighting the torch that was set in the wall sconce.

The Black Goddess sat in her niche and, as always, Helewise felt her power. She gave herself up to it for a few moments, then, with a smile to Meggie, slipped away and went back to the chapel above. She went to stand before the simple altar with its plain wooden cross. Without thinking, she dropped to her knees. Soon she was so deep in prayer that she did not notice Meggie and Rosamund come up from the crypt, gently lower the flagstone and leave the chapel.

When finally she emerged into the bright afternoon, it was to discover that the others had found a sunny spot on the slope that led down to the abbey and were crouched on the grass, deep in conversation.

'You'll get cold, sitting on the wet grass!' she scolded, hurrying down to them.

Rosamund turned and gave her a sweet smile. 'We are sitting on our thick cloaks, and mine is lined with fur! Besides, the grass is not wet,' she said. 'Feel! The sun is warm today and has dried it.'

Helewise was about to insist – the child was her responsibility just then – but there was no need. Both of them were already getting up. 'I have just been telling Rosamund about the little bridge I've been trying to build across the stream beside the hut,' Meggie said. 'She'd really like to—'

Rosamund didn't allow others to speak for her. 'I'd love to see it,' she said pleadingly, taking Helewise's hand and giving it a squeeze. 'Can we go with Meggie to the hut, Grandmother?'

Helewise looked from one to the other. *This was meant to*

be my day with my granddaughter! she thought, and then instantly regretted it. Others loved Rosamund too, for the girl was generous with her affections. Why should Meggie not enjoy the child's company as well? She glanced at Meggie and saw understanding in Meggie's brown eyes.

'Perhaps you should go back with your grandmother,' Meggie said gently, 'and we'll go to the hut another time, when—'

'No, go now!' Helewise interrupted her with a smile. 'Just the two of you. I'll see you later, back at the House in the Woods,' she said, giving Rosamund a hug. 'I don't mind,' she added softly to Meggie.

Meggie looked at her intently, the bright golden lights in her eyes that were so like her father's catching the lowering sun. Then she nodded.

The three of them walked together as far as the place where the track to the hut branched off from the main path. There, with a cheerful, 'Goodbye, Meggie! See you later, Rosamund!', Helewise went on alone.

The inhabitants of the House in the Woods knew where Rosamund was, and so nobody thought to worry about her. She was with Meggie, and Meggie was more at home in the forest than anyone else in the family.

Darkness began to fall. First Josse and then Helewise slipped outside to look anxiously down the track that led away under the trees.

'She'll be here soon,' Josse said.

Helewise thought his voice sounded uncertain. 'Yes, I'm sure she will.' She noticed that hers did too.

They waited.

Presently, footsteps sounded, crossing the courtyard behind them. Ninian came to stand beside them, closely followed by Geoffroi. Half-brothers they might be, but there was little resemblance between them, other than an indefinable but unmistakable air of confidence and power. Ninian was tall, slim and dark, like his mother. His brilliant blue eyes he had inherited from his father.

Geoffroi looked worriedly at Josse. 'Maybe Meggie got lost,' he said. 'It's getting dark.'

They all agreed that it was. Nobody said what they were all thinking: that Meggie knew her way through the trees blindfold.

Gussie and Will came out of the house. 'Tilly's making hot soup,' Gussie volunteered. 'They'll be cold when they get here.'

Helewise felt a stab of fear dart into her heart. She put a hand to her chest. 'Josse?' she whispered.

He put his arm around her shoulders. He hugged her very tightly for an instant, then let her go. 'Saddle the horses, Will,' he said firmly. 'Ninian, Gus and I will go and look for them.'

TWO

Ninian left his horse tethered to a tree branch and raced off down the narrow track to Meggie's hut. He had left his father and Gus behind, painstakingly searching the main path and the narrower trails leading off it, while he hurried on to seek out his half-sister. Rosamund will be with her, he told himself over and over again. Meggie will explain that they didn't realize how late it was until darkness was too well advanced to make the journey home. She'll say she's very sorry we were all anxious, but that it seemed safer to keep Rosamund warm and snug with her in the hut overnight. She'll tell me she was planning to set out first thing in the morning to bring her back.

He repeated the words to himself until they were meaningless.

He raced on down the overgrown path, heedless of his own skin, and soon had a bramble tear across his cheek and a lump on his shin where he had run into the outstretched branch of a fallen tree. He was calling silently to Meggie as he ran, and he believed she must have heard him. He would not have said he knew with any certainty exactly where the hut was, yet he made his way straight to it with not a single wrong turn. But there was no time to wonder at his sister's strange powers.

He bounded across the clearing, gasping for breath, his heart pounding so hard that he felt light-headed and sick. He skidded to a halt in front of her door, bending over to ease the sharp pain in his side, then reached out and hammered on the stout wooden planks with his fist.

The door opened instantly, and Meggie's voice said, 'No need to break it down! I heard you coming, and anyway I—'

Then she saw the state he was in. She gasped and, clutching at his shoulders with hands that hurt, rasped out, 'What is it? What's happened?'

He straightened up and looked at her. There was a light burning inside the hut, but she had her back to it and her face was in shadow. Pushing her aside, he stared into the hut. 'Is Rosamund here?' he demanded, eyes darting frantically around the small, tidy space.

He knew the answer to his question even as she spoke. 'No, of course not, she—'

She had understood, as of course she would. She led him inside, closed the door and pushed him down on to the stool beside the hearth. She picked up an earthenware mug and, tipping into it a handful of something from a jar on a shelf, poured on hot water. She stirred it, blew in it and handed it to him. 'Drink.' He obeyed her. 'Now, tell me.'

He did as he was told. He had no idea what she had given him, but he trusted her. Rightly, for the herbal concoction had already calmed him. 'Rosamund hasn't come home,' he said. Then his fear came galloping back, and he burst out, 'It's dark, she's out in the forest and she's barely more than a child!'

'Hush,' she soothed him. He glanced up at her tense face. She muttered something under her breath and then said, 'I walked back to the House in the Woods with her late this afternoon. We were almost there when she saw you and said she'd run on and go the rest of the way with you.'

'You let her go on alone?' Suddenly, he was furious.

'She wasn't alone, she'd just seen you!' she flashed back, her own anger rising alongside his. 'I watched as she caught you up, then I turned round and came back here.'

Realization struck them simultaneously. 'It wasn't you, was it?' she whispered. Her face had gone white.

Mutely, he shook his head.

She sank down on to the floor beside him and reached out for the mug he held. She took a sip, then handed it back. 'It looked like you,' she muttered. 'Are you absolutely sure? Could it be that you didn't hear her hurrying up behind you? You did have your back to us . . .'

He thought hard, running through his movements that afternoon and early evening. There was, however, no real need; he knew full well he'd still been far from home as dusk fell.

'This afternoon I was fishing on the Teise,' he said. 'I was miles away, and it took me ages to get back. I caught a trout,' he added absently.

'So you would have arrived home from the opposite direction,' she said. He watched her fierce concentration as she worked it out. 'Rosamund and I were approaching from the west, and you were coming from the east. It can't have been you she saw.'

He pounced on her words. 'You just said *it looked like you*,' he cried. 'You must have seen this man too!'

Slowly, she nodded. 'Yes, but Rosamund said, *"There's Ninian,"* and I suppose I just took her word for it that it was you.' A sob broke out of her, quickly suppressed. 'I should have looked more carefully! I should have gone on with her and handed her over to you! To him, I mean,' she corrected herself. 'Whoever he was.'

Whoever he was, Ninian thought. Who was he? Oh, dear God, and what did he want with Rosamund?

He twisted around and put his arms around Meggie, pulling her close. 'It wasn't your fault,' he said. He felt her resistance. 'It *wasn't*,' he repeated, 'and you are not to waste any more time on blaming yourself, because that'll take your mind off what you ought to be doing, which is helping me work out what happened and where we're going to find her.' He realized he was yelling. 'Sorry,' he said quietly.

She pulled away from him, pushed back her hair and met his eyes. He saw a flash of humour in hers, there and gone in a moment. 'You're so much the elder brother,' she observed. '*I'm* helping *you*.' She snorted. Then her face clouded and she said, 'Where do we start?'

'Describe this man,' he commanded.

She closed her eyes, and he guessed she was picturing him. 'About your height and build, wearing a dark leather tunic and a short cloak with a hood. You've got a leather jerkin,' she added, her eyes blinking open and fixing intently on his.

'Yes, I have,' he agreed. He waited.

'At first he had his back to us,' she went on, 'and he was walking in the direction of the house.' Her eyes were shut again, the lids screwed up tightly as if by this effort she would make herself remember more. Suddenly, she relaxed, slumping against him. 'That's all,' she said. 'I saw someone, Rosamund said it was you, I believed her. I didn't really study him. He was among the trees and I didn't have a clear view of him, and I—'

Gently, he took hold of her hand. 'Enough,' he said softly.

He had the clear impression she was about to start piling blame on herself again and that wasn't going to help. Still holding her hand, he got to his feet and pulled her up beside him.

'Come on,' he said.

Her eyes in the dim light were huge, the pupils wide. 'Where are we going?'

'I'm taking you to the House in the Woods. Then I'm going to look for Rosamund.'

'I don't need you to take me anywhere!' she snapped. 'I know my way through this forest far better than you do and I won't go astray.' She was reaching down into the corner as she spoke, and he thought she was picking up the bag of provisions and clean linen that she always took with her when she went to stay in the hut.

'Indeed you do,' he agreed, 'but Rosamund is missing, perhaps taken by this stranger who looks like me. I won't risk the safety of another of the family, so I—'

She did not let him finish. She spun round, and he saw that, far from picking up her old leather bag, she had a sword in her hands. It was only a short sword, little more than a long knife, but the candle light glinted off its edge and he could see she kept it very well honed.

He took an involuntary step back. 'You don't—'

Again, she interrupted him. 'I don't know how to use this? Don't patronize me, Ninian. My mother and I lived here in the wilds for years together, and I didn't know about this weapon until long after she'd gone. She would have been able to use it, make no mistake, and I can too.' She held the sword firmly in front of her, the knuckles of her hands white as she gripped the hilt.

She saw his face, and slowly she lowered her blade. He said, so quietly that he was surprised she heard, 'She was my mother too.'

The sword fell on the floor. She was in his arms, and he felt her shake as she sobbed. Then she pulled away, picked up the sword again and said, 'Go. I'll make for the house, and I'll use all my senses to search for any traces of her. Come back when you can.'

He looked at her set expression and realized there was no point in arguing with her. Usually, she looked like Josse, but as she stood there in the little hut there was so much of their mother in her that Ninian felt his heart tear.

He turned away, let himself out of the hut and raced back up the track to where he had left his horse.

Josse could not remember when he had last felt so weary. He and Gus had split up soon after leaving the house, and they had been searching all night. Occasionally, Josse had heard Gus in the distance, crashing through the undergrowth and always calling, calling, her name. Once or twice they had bumped into each other.

Now dawn was beginning to brighten the sky in the east. He and Gus were riding, slowly and with their heads down, back to the House in the Woods. Neither of them had seen any sign of Rosamund.

They were approaching from the forest and, as the area of cleared trees around the house came into view, Josse saw a cloaked figure standing perfectly still on the edge of the path. He did not for an instant believe they had found Rosamund, for he had immediately recognized his daughter. He and Gus drew rein, and Josse slipped off Alfred's back. He was about to run to Meggie and take her in his arms, but something in the quality of her stillness stopped him.

He handed Alfred's reins to Gus, exchanging a warning glance with him. Gus, who, like all the household, was well used to Meggie and her strange ways, gave a brief grin and nodded. Josse turned back to Meggie and waited.

After some moments she said quietly, 'Rosamund was here. I can feel something of her . . .'

'She was almost home, then!' Josse exclaimed. 'She—'

Meggie put up her hand, and he stopped. She smiled at him. 'Of course, you don't know,' she murmured. 'I walked back with her,' she went on. 'When we reached the bend in the path back there –' she pointed – 'Rosamund spotted Ninian, and she ran on to catch up with him. I turned and headed back to the hut.' She drew a shaky breath. 'Only, it wasn't Ninian. He was nowhere near the house at that time.'

Josse was trying to make himself believe the unbelievable. 'So someone was pretending to be Ninian with the purpose of abducting her,' he said slowly. There was a gasp from Gus, quickly suppressed, but Meggie regarded him with solemn eyes and slowly nodded.

'Abducted. Yes,' she said. 'It is terrible, but I believe we will serve her better if we accept the fact and act accordingly.'

'We will return to the house,' Josse began, hardly knowing what he was saying, 'and—'

Gus interrupted him. 'May I say something?' he asked apologetically.

'Of course!' Josse said.

Gus turned to Meggie. 'You just said you could feel her here.' He sounded embarrassed, as if this brush with Meggie's mysterious powers was a little too close for comfort. 'Can you – that is, does this place tell you anything else?'

Meggie looked at him, her head on one side. 'I was completing my examination when you rode up,' she replied. 'Rosamund came running up the path here –' she pointed – 'and someone heavier and with bigger feet was here –' again, she indicated – 'and he had been standing here for some time.'

'That must be the man she mistook for Ninian!' Josse exclaimed. 'You're sure it was a man, Meggie?'

She nodded. 'Yes. I, too, saw him, although only fleetingly, and he was too tall and broad for a woman. Also—' She broke off, frowning.

'Yes?' Josse prompted.

She met his eyes. 'The imprint of this other person is quite different from Rosamund's,' she said shortly. 'Don't ask me to explain –' Josse wouldn't have dreamt of doing so – 'you'll just have to take my word for it.'

'Can you tell anything else about him?' Gus asked nervously. 'Was he – er, was he good?' The light was still dim, but even so Josse could see the blush that stained the younger man's face. 'I mean—'

'It's all right, Gus, I know what you mean,' Meggie said gently. 'You're asking if I think this man's going to harm her. My answer is that I don't know.' She paused. 'I don't feel an immediate threat from the place where he stood, that's for sure, but if a stranger lies in wait and takes a girl away from her family, then that in itself is a threat.'

She reasoned well, Josse thought, although how she knew the things she knew was quite unfathomable. The echoes of her words rang in his ears, and he shook his head to dispel them; standing there in awe at his daughter's powers wasn't going to help Rosamund.

He took Alfred's reins from Gus and, holding out his other hand to Meggie, set off up the track towards the house. Gus fell in behind. 'We shall report to the others,' Josse said firmly, 'and see if they have any news. We shall eat and drink, and then I shall ride down to Tonbridge, find Dominic at Gervase's house and tell both of them that Dominic's child is missing.'

Quite how he would find the words to do that, Josse did not know. He felt Meggie's cool hand squeeze his own. She knew exactly how he felt and was trying to give him comfort. He turned and gave her a smile.

Helewise had not slept. The house seemed very empty – Josse, Ninian and Gus were searching out in the forest and, soon after they had gone, Will and his woman, Ella, had slipped away. As they left, Will murmured to Helewise that they would comb the ground around the house. They had not returned.

Helewise had drifted to the kitchen and, rolling up her sleeves, fixed her mind on helping Tilly prepare food. Sooner or later the search parties would return, hopefully with Rosamund. Everyone would be hungry and cold. Tilly kept the fire stoked, and the kitchen grew almost too hot. When they had cooked everything there was to cook, washed the pans and the utensils and tidied them away, Helewise and Tilly sat on either side of the fire and waited.

As the first light of dawn appeared, Helewise ceased her silent prayers and thought about her son and his wife. Rosamund was their third child, a girl after two sons, and she was just eleven years old. Dominic and Paradisa loved all their children but, with the two boys Ralf and Hugo now living in another household as they trained for their adult roles, Rosamund was very much the focus of her parents' attention. Not that it was spoiling her, for she was an unaffected, affectionate girl with a keen sense of humour that, probably the result of being little sister to two robust brothers, dipped very readily to the vulgar. She was also graceful, gifted with attractive colouring and very beautiful.

Where are you, child? Helewise asked silently. *If you are able, come home to those who love you. If you cannot, hear me now and know that we will find you.*

She sat for a few moments concentrating all her thoughts and all her love on her youngest grandchild. Then she went

back to thinking about Dominic and wondering how they were
going to tell him Rosamund had disappeared.

As they sat round the table eating food for which nobody had
much appetite, Josse summed up everything they knew
concerning Rosamund's disappearance, not that it amounted
to much. He wanted to build up a picture of the previous day
and, quickly understanding, both Helewise and Meggie volunteered information.

'Dominic left her here late yesterday morning,' Helewise
said, 'and we had a bite to eat before going through the forest
to the abbey.'

'I met them on the way,' Meggie added, 'and we all went
into St Edmund's Chapel. Rosamund and I left Helewise
praying and went to sit on the slope above the abbey.'

'Did she say anything?' Josse asked eagerly.

'She said a lot,' Meggie said with a faint smile, 'but then
she always does. Nothing of any relevance, I'm afraid.' She
frowned, clearly thinking. To Helewise, she appeared preoccupied, almost absent, as if whatever was absorbing her so
profoundly was not precisely the same as what they were all
discussing. Then Meggie said, 'No. As far as I recall, our talk
was light and did not touch on anything serious.'

Helewise put out her hand and laid it on Josse's. 'We have
to go down to Tonbridge and inform Dominic,' she said.
'Morning is here, we have found no sign of her and we can
wait no longer.'

'Aye, you're right,' Josse said heavily, getting to his feet. It
was a dreadful prospect, but he knew it would not improve
by being postponed. 'Will's been tending to Alfred, so he'll
be ready to leave as soon as he's saddled up again. Dominic's
staying with Gervase – there was some matter that Gervase
wanted to ask him about – so I shall be able to inform both
of them at the same time.'

There was a short silence, and then Helewise said, '*I* shall
be able to inform them?'

He looked down at her. He knew what she was suggesting,
and for a moment his heart leapt with relief. But her place was
here. 'No,' he said. 'You should stay here, where you can—'

'Make soup?' she said spiritedly. 'Josse, Tilly and I have
prepared an ocean of soup. Dominic is my son,' she went on

softly, 'and he left Rosamund in my care.' She raised her chin,
and an expression spread over her face that he knew of old.
'I will not have it that this frightful news is broken to him by
anyone but me.'

She, too, had stood up. She stood before him, straight and
tall, and he knew there was no more to say. He held out his
hand, and she took it. 'Come on, then,' he said.

They rode down the road to Tonbridge in silence. Josse was
trying not to think about what lay ahead: it was something
that had to be done, and he dreaded it, but it would not be
improved by dwelling on it. Instead, he let his mind ramble,
and presently he found himself recalling other journeys he and
Helewise had made together. *I used to have to slow old
Horace's pace,* he mused, *but now our mounts are more evenly
matched.* He glanced over to Helewise's grey mare, another
of Honey's descendants. Her name was Daisy.

Too soon they were at the bottom of Castle Hill and the
town was before them. The river curled through the valley,
and swirls of fog hung over the marshy ground to the east.
The town was already about its business, and Josse had to
shout out several times to clear their passage along the narrow,
crowded streets.

They turned off to the left, and the crowds quickly thinned.
Gervase de Gifford's house was some distance out of the town,
and Josse, who had visited many times, led the way unhesitat-
ingly. They rode into the courtyard, and almost immediately
a lad emerged to take their horses.

'Morning, Sir Josse,' he said with a grin. Then he saw
Josse's expression and the grin faded.

'Is the sheriff at home?' Josse asked as he dismounted.

The lad nodded, then jerked his head in the direction of the
steps leading up to the house. 'Him and the mistress are having
breakfast,' he said.

Josse nodded his thanks and then gave Helewise a swift,
questioning look.

'Ready,' she whispered.

Together they mounted the steps and went into the hall.

Helewise looked around her at the home of Gervase and Sabin
de Gifford. The hall was generously sized and well furnished.

The rushes on the stone floor were fresh and sweet-smelling, and the table at which the family were sitting to eat was sturdy oak.

Gervase was on his feet, greeting his guests and calling to a servant to bring more food. Helewise paused briefly to respond to his welcome, but her eyes were on her son.

Dominic had also risen. Unlike Gervase, he stayed where he was at the table. He was staring at her, and she recognized that even in that first moment he was aware something was wrong.

Josse was muttering something to Gervase, who turned to stare at Dominic. Helewise, hardly noticing, walked steadily across to her son.

'Rosamund is missing,' she said. 'She was last seen yesterday at dusk and we have had been out all night looking for her. We believe she was taken away by a young man who was lurking close to the House in the Woods.'

She watched Dominic's face. She saw doubt and anger and, finally, agony so severe that instinctively she reached out to him.

He pushed her hands away. 'She is eleven years old, Mother,' he said, and his voice was like ice. 'Could you not have taken better care of her?'

Helewise felt as if she had been stabbed through the heart. She dropped her head, fighting tears. She sensed a swift movement beside her, and Josse's arm went round her shoulders. She heard his words as from a great distance – he was saying it was not her fault, it was the result of mistaken identity, and that Dominic should take back his harsh comment – but she did not take them in.

He blames me, she thought. *He blames me and he hates me.*

A tear slid down her cheek.

She was ushered to a chair, Josse holding her as if he feared she would fall, Sabin disentangling herself from her children and rushing to take Helewise's hand. Then Dominic was before her, his face stiff as he said curtly, 'I apologize, Mother. Apparently, I was wrong to put the blame on you.'

She met his eyes. 'She was, as you say, in my care,' she said. 'I will do my utmost to help you find her.'

He studied her for a moment longer. Then he turned away.

THREE

Josse sat with Dominic and Gervase as they worked on how best to hunt for Rosamund. Helewise, still looking so stunned that Josse longed to comfort her, sat alone and silent at the end of Gervase's long table. Gervase had already summoned a group of his most reliable men and, when Dominic had asked if somebody could ride over to the Old Manor to ask his brother Leofgar to come to help, Gervase had readily agreed. Now, as they waited for the others to assemble, the three of them divided up the terrain and decided who should lead the hunt in which sector.

'We should each concentrate on the areas we know best,' Gervase said. 'This means you, Josse, concentrate on the forest between Hawkenlye Manor and the abbey.'

'We have searched the ground there all night!' Josse exclaimed impatiently. Although he knew it was sensible to sit here and organize the search so as to make best use of the available men, in his heart he felt they were wasting time and he longed to be out looking for Rosamund.

Gervase looked at him, sympathy in his light eyes. 'I know, old friend,' he said, 'but it was dark. You may well have missed something important.'

'I'll take the area east of the forest, centred on New Winnowlands and covering the roads and tracks to the coast,' Dominic said. Josse glanced at him. His face was pale, and a muscle worked constantly at the point of his jaw. His pain and his anger were palpable. I would not, Josse thought, like to be the man who has taken Rosamund when her father finds him.

'Good,' Gervase was saying. 'You are confident that your brother will join us, Dominic?'

'I am.'

'Very well. We will assign to him the area to the north and north-east of the town. I propose to put my most able deputy in charge of Tonbridge, and I will concentrate on the lands to the west, taking a band of men out towards Saxonbury, Hartfield and the Ashdown Forest.'

'The forest is a royal preserve,' Dominic said, frowning. 'Is it not a waste of time to search there?'

'Indeed, the king often rides there and would like to make it his own private hunting ground,' Gervase replied, 'but as yet there is nothing to prevent access.'

'Providing you don't hunt the deer,' Josse muttered.

'Yes, but where does that not apply?' Gervase countered. 'They say there are plans to fence in the whole forest, but for now it is as good a place to hide as any.'

'I do not know it,' Dominic said. 'It is a forest, yet you speak of good hunting?' He shook his head. 'I cannot reconcile the two.'

'You are thinking, perhaps, of the Wealden Forest that surrounds Hawkenlye,' Josse said. 'Aye, you'd be hard put to chase and fell a deer there, for the trees and the undergrowth grow so densely that the very tracks disappear in the spring. The Ashdown Forest is in truth a heath,' he went on, 'and quite different in nature from the woodland around Hawkenlye. You—'

But Dominic put up a hand to silence him. The question answered, Dominic had more pressing matters on his mind. 'My mother should go to the abbey,' he said decisively, sending a glance in the direction of the silent figure at the end of the table. 'People come and go there all the time. Basing herself there, she will be in a good position to keep her ears open for any whispered rumour of – of where my daughter may be.'

Josse felt the onset of an agonizing conflict. Dominic's suggestion was astute, for Hawkenlye was the closest sizeable community to the place where Rosamund had last been seen and, as Dominic had implied, had always been a centre for gossip and rumour. But he did not know, as Josse did, Helewise's attitude to the place where she had lived and ruled for so long.

She avoided it. She had explained to Josse that she did not wish her presence to undermine the new regime led by Abbess Caliste. Josse suspected there was more to it than that: he feared that part of her regretted her decision to leave and wished she was still Hawkenlye's abbess.

Either way, she would not take kindly to a curt order from her son that she should go and stay there . . .

Helewise had bowed her head, and she had not uttered a word. It was up to Josse to say so.

'Your mother will not return to the abbey,' he said quietly. 'Abbess Caliste is in charge now, and Helewise does not wish to remind the community that once they were led by someone else.'

Dominic's face twisted into a grimace. 'She will surely not allow such a consideration to outweigh the present emergency?'

'I think she will,' Josse said.

There was a brief, tense silence. Then, turning to Helewise, Dominic broke it with a single, icy word: 'Mother?'

Josse watched as slowly she raised her head and met her son's eyes. 'I will not return to the abbey,' she said.

'But you—' Dominic began furiously.

Now it was his turn to be silenced. Helewise said, quietly but with infinite authority, 'Dominic, I will not be persuaded. What you suggest is not possible.'

Dominic opened his mouth to protest again but, eyes fixed to his mother's grim face, he subsided.

'Thank you,' she said calmly. 'I will not go to the abbey, but I do agree that what you suggest is sensible. I will lodge close by, and I will send someone to be my eyes and ears within the community. That will serve as well.'

Dominic snorted. 'It rather depends who you send.'

'Leave me to worry about that,' Helewise flashed back. Then, regret filling her face as if suddenly she had recalled why they were all there, she added gently, 'I promised to do my best to help, son, and I will.'

He looked at her for a long moment. Then he nodded.

There was a sudden commotion in the courtyard outside, and a group of a dozen men erupted into the hall. While they were still settling down to hear the sheriff's instructions, there was the sound of a horse's hooves clattering across the yard, swiftly followed by the arrival of Leofgar Warin.

He went to greet his mother. Then he spotted his younger brother and, without a word, went across to take him in his arms in a tight embrace. Breaking away, he turned to Gervase and said, 'What do you want me to do?'

Josse was heading for the House in the Woods. He planned to gather his household around him and tell them that they were to search every track, path and animal trail until they found some trace of Rosamund. She had stood in the place that Meggie had pointed out, he reflected, and someone had taken her away. Unless they flew, Josse thought, they must have left a mark of their passage and, however small it is, we must find it.

He was riding as hard as he could, given that he was leading a second horse. Where Helewise was bound, she had no need of Daisy, and Josse was taking the mare back to the House in the Woods. He and Helewise had ridden back up the hill from Tonbridge, and he had left her at the point where the track to Hawkenlye Abbey branched off the main road that circled the forest. She had not told him what she planned to do. When they had parted, she had done her best to reassure him, but she had failed.

'I shall be perfectly safe, Josse dear,' she had said, looking up at him as he struggled to control both Alfred and her mare, the horses excited from the hard ride and restless to be moving again.

'How will I know?' he asked. He heard the pleading tone in his voice.

She smiled. 'You will have to trust to God and the good spirits of this place to make sure that I am.'

'But—'

'Josse, what else would you have me do?' she demanded. 'Dominic blames me for Rosamund's disappearance, and he is right to do so for she was left in my care. Do you think I could wait back at home, helping Tilly prepare endless soup, while everyone else searches? *Do you*?' she insisted, when he did not answer.

'No,' he said gruffly.

'Well, then.' She reached up and took his hand. 'Don't worry. I'll be all right. I'll keep in touch.'

Then she had slapped Alfred hard on the rump and, before Josse was aware, he found himself cantering away.

The only tiny spot of comfort in the whole exchange, he now thought as he slowed his pace for the final approach to the house, was that she had referred to his house as home.

That, in this terrible day, was something . . .

As soon as Josse was out of sight, Helewise stepped off the road and entered the forest. She knew the tracks well, and it was worth the risk, for she was in a hurry. Furthermore, if she stayed on the road there was always the possibility that Josse would double back and come after her. He was, she knew, deeply unhappy about leaving her.

She walked fast, stopping now and again to get her bearings. She did not habitually cross the forest from north to south, but she knew where she was heading and at this time of year the trees were all but bare, allowing her to be guided by the sun. It was faint today, obscured by high, thin cloud, but she could tell where it was. The air was cold; she huddled deeper inside her thick cloak and tightened the strings of her hood.

She had not enjoyed parting from Josse when he was so very anxious about her. She knew what he felt for her, and her love for him was equally strong, even if she had no idea how to express it. But it was not the time to dwell on her failings there, she reprimanded herself. Not when there was another, far greater, failure to deal with.

Dominic's coldness towards her had been perfectly understandable but, oh, how it had hurt! She turned her mind from that, too. Nothing short of returning Rosamund to him would alter his dark mood, and she would just have to suffer. She did not even dare to think what Paradisa was going through.

It was heartening that Leofgar had raced to offer his support. Helewise knew, however, that her elder son would not be able to go on helping indefinitely. Leofgar was a man of importance now, with connections to the fringe of court society. Whatever he might privately think about the king – he was careful not to say, but Helewise did not need to hear it in words – he gave every appearance of being a loyal, responsible subject. The king had announced he was going to pay a visit to Leofgar and Rohaise in the very near future, and Helewise was sure that, much as Leofgar would like to go on searching for his young niece, his brother would understood that he had to put his own family first.

It helped her, a little, to be doing something positive to help the search. What she had said to Josse was the truth: she could not have borne returning to the House in the Woods to sit waiting for news. In her old life, she reflected, her conscience would have made her do just that, since it was the hardest thing. Now, once more a woman in control of her own comings and goings, she was free to do what she chose.

She strode on, ignoring her fatigue and the ache in her

legs. She was used to walking – they all were – but now the demands she was making on herself were extreme. To take her mind off the pain, she thought about where she was going.

The abbey was out of bounds to her, for the reasons that dear Josse had so eloquently given. It was not that the community would not have welcomed her, and that included Abbess Caliste, for there was a great depth of understanding and love between the former abbess and the present one. It was that the abbey would not be best served by Helewise's return, since, despite their best efforts not to do so, the nuns and the monks would not be able to help a very understandable tendency to remember – and undoubtedly talk at length about – how life used to be in Helewise's day. Were there to be some emergency, there could very well be a few of the older ones who turned to Helewise and not Abbess Caliste for guidance. That would not do.

Helewise did not feel that she could take up her abode in the little cell next to St Edmund's Chapel, no matter how much she longed to, for much the same reasons. The chapel and its attendant accommodation were outside the abbey walls but, all the same, everyone would know she was there. You just couldn't help that sort of news spreading in a place like the abbey.

No. What she had in mind was somewhere a great deal more remote from the Hawkenlye community. It depended on two things: whether she succeeded in finding it, and whether the person who had very recently been living there would permit her to stay.

She found the place quite easily, only missing her way once. The question of whether or not she would be allowed to stay did not arise, for there was nobody there.

As Helewise unfastened the intricately-twisted knot of rope that fastened the door of the little hut, she wondered where Meggie was and when she would be back. Then she put aside her speculation and set about the tasks she had to do. She collected water from the stream and several loads of kindling and dead wood from the surrounding woodland. She got a fire going in the hearth inside the hut, for it would be cold that night. She checked on Meggie's food supplies, relieved to discover that, although she would very soon be hungry unless

she foraged for more, she would not starve. Once she had seen
to the practicalities, she went outside into the little clearing
and turned her mind to the reason that she had come.

Being much closer to the abbey than the House in the Woods,
the hut made a more convenient base for her task. But there
was more to her choice than that; much more. She needed an
intermediary who could slip in and out of the abbey without
arousing interested comment, someone who did it all the time
and who people were used to seeing coming and going, and
this was the best place to find her. The person she had in mind
had once lived mostly within the abbey walls as a nun, although
it had been common knowledge that she had close allegiances
with the strange forest people who had once frequented the
area. Now they were gone, or so it was said, or perhaps they
had become better at remaining hidden. The wildwood was
steadily shrinking as the population grew and men nibbled
away at its fringes, bringing more and more land under cultivation. In addition, the old tolerance of those who lived a
different life and worshipped God in another guise was fast
becoming nothing but a memory. In lands far away to the
south, the church had taken up arms against those it accused
of heresy, and it was only a matter of time before the same
harsh and narrow rule was applied everywhere.

It was no wonder they had gone, Helewise mused.

Yet she was one of the few people who suspected that they
had not all deserted the Hawkenlye wildwood. She knew for
certain of two who remained. One stayed out of love for
Hawkenlye's abbess, for she was her sister. The other had her
own unfathomable reasons, and it was she whom Helewise
was waiting for.

She stood quite still in the centre of the clearing. The little
stream sang its bubbling song away to her right, and somewhere a blackbird protested at her presence. She wondered
if she should venture out into the forest and start looking for
the woman she sought, but quickly she dismissed the thought.
They always knew when an outsider was in their domain. If
Helewise was patient, by some mysterious method word
would be passed and the one she was mentally summoning
would come.

'Helewise.'

She had no warning, and when the quiet voice spoke right

in her ear, Helewise jerked round so violently that she felt a stab of pain in her neck.

'That'll need a rub with some oil and some warming herbs,' the voice went on. 'You never have taken enough care of yourself, have you?'

Helewise stared into the watchful eyes and studied the weather-beaten, deeply lined face. The newcomer opened her arms, and Helewise walked into her firm embrace. Then she took a step back, and she and Tiphaine, former herbalist of Hawkenlye Abbey, exchanged a warm and loving smile.

It was neither woman's habit to waste time, for years spent in an abbey had cured them of that. Tiphaine was first to speak. 'I know why you are here,' she said. 'The little girl.'

'Yes, my granddaughter,' Helewise agreed. 'Her name is Rosamund and she's—'

'I know,' Tiphaine interrupted gently.

Helewise wondered how she knew, but almost instantly answered her own unspoken question. 'Meggie,' she breathed.

'Meggie, aye,' Tiphaine said. 'She and the child were here together yesterday. She's a pretty little thing, and she has a generous heart.'

'Yes, she—' But Helewise's eyes had filled with tears and she could not trust her voice.

Tiphaine stepped closer. 'She is alive and as yet she is unharmed,' she murmured.

Hope flared in Helewise's heart. 'You know this? You have seen her?'

Tiphaine shook her head. 'Not since she and Meggie left this place to return to the House in the Woods.'

'Then how can you be so sure she's not—' Helewise could not say the word *dead*. 'How do you know she's unharmed?'

Tiphaine looked at her for a long moment. 'Such a death would have been so far from the natural ways of the woodland that we would have felt it,' she said. As Helewise opened her mouth to protest, Tiphaine stopped her. 'Do not ask, Helewise. I cannot explain further. You will just have to believe me.'

'You do not know where she is,' she said instead. She was sure Tiphaine had no such knowledge for, had she done, she would have acted upon it.

'No,' Tiphaine agreed.

'I need to know if anyone inside the abbey mentions her,'

Helewise said. 'People always gossip, and it's possible some visitor to Hawkenlye has seen or heard something of her. I—'

'You want me to find out,' Tiphaine finished for her.

'You should see Abbess Caliste and explain what I need to know.'

'She is already aware of what has happened. Selene has been to see her.'

Selene. Caliste's twin. Helewise had seen her once and believed she was Caliste. But that was long ago; with a shake of her head she brought herself back to the present. 'I would dearly like to speak to Abbess Caliste, only I cannot—'

'You cannot go yourself. I understand.' Tiphaine had turned and was already walking away.

'Where are you going?' Helewise cried.

Tiphaine stopped and looked at her over her shoulder. She smiled quickly. 'Where do you think?'

He did not know what to do.

It was the day after he had taken her. At first it had been so easy; far, far easier than he had thought possible. Right from the start, once the audacious, brilliant plan had slipped into his head, events had played straight into his hands.

He did not understand the impulse to creep away from the others and follow his lord when he had gone off under the trees. His lord had said, clearly and firmly: 'Wait for me here.' Usually, all the men obeyed his instructions automatically. They knew what he was capable of when he was in a temper, and his temper was all too easily aroused nowadays when, like all the wealthy and important men in the land, he had a sackful of problems to deal with. It had been as if a secret voice had spoken inside the young man's head: *Go after him. See what he's up to.*

Whose voice had it been? The young man did not know. He heard voices quite frequently. Often they issued warnings concerning the other men: *That one doesn't like you. That one is whispering behind your back. That one means you harm.* At first he hadn't known whether or not to believe the voices, but lately he had begun to think that they – whoever they were – were his only true friends. When the voice had told him to creep after the lord, he had obeyed without question.

He had watched carefully, and he had seen what the lord

was looking at so intently. It hadn't taken him long to come
up with his brilliant idea. Everyone knew about the lord. The
men exchanged the stories freely amongst themselves, always
making sure the lord wasn't in earshot, and it was thrilling to
sit there and hear all about the things he had done. What a
man he was! He was afraid of nothing and nobody, and he
dismissed the boring old greybeards of the church and all their
thou-shalt-nots with a snap of his fingers and a cruel laugh at
their gullibility.

He did just as he pleased, their lord.

The young man wanted more than anything to be recognized,
welcomed, taken into that precious inner circle of the favoured.
It is my right, he told himself. *Very few of the others are to
him what I am.*

The lord knew his identity, of course he did, but it did not
seem to make any difference. The lord did not know what the
young man was really like, so he would just have to show
him. *I am clever enough to know what pleases the lord*, the
man thought, *and I am resourceful enough to find it for him.*

Find *her* . . .

Yesterday he had stayed carefully concealed as the lord
watched the two figures walk away, only emerging from
his hiding place once they were gone. The young man had
remained hidden as the lord strode off, out from under the
trees and away to where the other men were waiting for
him. He had heard the lord's shouted command and the jingle
of harness metal and stirrups as the party had ridden away.
He had hesitated for an instant – he would be in trouble when
they discovered he hadn't mounted up and gone after them
– but he had decided that the lord would readily forgive him
once he knew what he had been doing.

Once the lord and the men had gone, the young man had
set about finding her. It had been quite hard at first because
she and the other person had gone to sit out in the open, in
full view of the great abbey that sprawled on the edge of the
forest. They were joined by an older woman, and for a while
he believed that his wonderful plan would come to nothing.
Then they all came back towards the trees and he had to hurry
to hide. He followed them, always staying out of sight.
Although the dark-haired young woman with the lights in her
eyes sometimes stopped and stiffened, listening intently as if

she sensed the presence of someone or something that should not be there, she did not see him.

Then the older woman left, and he stayed close to the other two. Later, he followed them right across the forest – he had been frightened then – and over to where the trees began to thin out on the far side. He heard them chattering to each other and realized they were about to part, and he had to hurry on ahead so as to intercept her.

Then that amazing thing had happened. She caught sight of him, and, although he swiftly turned his back, he believed the game was up. But she thought he was someone else. Someone she knew and trusted. He heard her say goodbye to the dark-haired one – 'Goodbye, Meggie!' she called – and he risked a quick glance to watch as this Meggie turned away, back the way they had come.

The girl came right up to him, calling out to him: 'Hello, Ninian! Thank you for waiting – shall we walk home together?'

He would not have believed he could think so fast. He was extremely proud of his resourcefulness. He said swiftly, 'Not Ninian, I'm afraid, but he sent me to come and meet you. We're not going home; we're all going to meet up at Meggie's hut.'

She looked up at him. 'That's where I've just come from,' she said uncertainly. 'Meggie didn't say anything about us all meeting there.'

'That's because it's a *surprise!*' he said, smiling broadly.

'A surprise?' Still the doubt clouded her wide, dark eyes.

'Yes! Ninian and the rest are taking food and wine over there, we're going to make a big fire, and there'll be singing and dancing!'

Then she smiled. 'I love dancing.'

'So do I! Let's dance together, shall we? I'd like that.' As he spoke he was hurrying her away, back towards the western fringe of the forest, although not along the same track that the other woman had taken. That would not do, not at all.

They went on chattering together, just as if they were old friends, and at last they emerged from under the trees close to the chapel.

The girl looked anxious. 'We've missed the path to the hut,' she said. 'We'll have to go back into the forest and I'll see if I can find it. It'll be easier coming from this direction, because the path is clearer and—'

He had to stop her. He said winningly, 'I've got a horse and he's really fast. Shall we go for a ride? We've got time. It'll be ages till the food's ready.'

She stared at him, and he realized she was beginning to have her suspicions. 'He's jet black and his name's Star because he's got a star on his brow,' he said. 'You can ride behind me and I'll show you how he goes. You really love horses, don't you?'

It was a gamble, but the voice in his head suggested it and the voice knew what it was about. Her face brightened into an eager smile, and she said, 'Come on, then!'

He took her little hand and hurried on to where he had tethered his horse earlier in the day. His horse was standing half-asleep, grass trailing from its mouth. He tightened the girth strap and helped her up, settling her behind the saddle, then he mounted. 'Put your arms round my waist,' he said and felt two slim, strong arms snake round him. 'Ready?'

'*Yes!*' she cried.

It was some time before she told him to turn back. When he refused, she became first upset, then angry, then, finally, afraid. 'Where are we going? Where are you taking me? I want to go home!' she cried, over and over again until he thought he would go mad.

He found a desolate spot where a stand of trees grew in a bend of the river. He drew rein, dismounted and helped her on to the ground. He kept a firm grip on her wrist.

He looked down into her face. Night was advancing fast, and he could only just make out her features.

'I'm afraid we're lost,' he said, with some truthfulness since, in the darkness, he only had a vague idea where they were and he knew he would be lucky to find his destination if they rode on. 'I'm really, really sorry.'

She studied him, her eyes narrowed in concentration. He sensed she half-believed him. 'What should we do?' she asked.

'We'll stay here,' he said decisively. 'I have a thick blanket in my pack and you can have that. I'll put on my heavy cloak. We'll light a small fire –' if he made sure to stay within the trees, nobody would see – 'and we'll have our own little camp. How does that sound?'

She looked at him dubiously. 'Is there any food?'

He had some dried meat and a couple of apples in his pack. 'Yes.'

She sighed. 'Very well, then.'

That had been last night. This morning it had been much, much harder. In the end, he'd resorted to telling her where they were really going. She was both excited and afraid, but most of all worried because her family didn't know where she was and what she was doing.

He had to lie about that, too. He had told so many lies that his head was spinning. She was clever, too clever, and once or twice she had caught him out. That had led to more lies, all of them echoing around in his mind and competing with the voices that were *shouting* at him now.

He would have liked to pull his head off and throw it away. In a rare moment of rational thought, he wondered what on earth he was doing. Sometimes he thought he was quite, quite mad.

Now he really did not know what to do . . .

Finally, he made up his mind. They would go on, just as he had planned.

They were about to set off when he heard the sound of fast hoof-beats drumming on the ground. His head shot round, and he saw a hard-ridden horse pounding towards them. The rider was shouting and wildly waving an arm.

He looked at the girl and read alarm in her face. 'Hide in the trees with Star,' he said urgently, and to his surprise she obeyed. Perhaps she had already made up her mind that he was not going to harm her, whereas whoever was approaching in such a hurry was an unknown quantity. There was no time to dwell on it.

He put his hand on his sword hilt and turned to face the horseman.

FOUR

Tiphaine had spent the night in the herbalist's hut at Hawkenlye Abbey. It was dry, fragrant and adequately comfortable. She had arranged some sacking on the wooden work bench and slept as soundly as she usually did.

The hut had been her workplace for many years. She still went there regularly. Abbess Caliste knew about her discreet visits and did nothing to prevent them, for Tiphaine was a herbalist with a rare gift and without her hard-working hands those who visited the abbey in need would have been greatly the poorer. Nobody, including Tiphaine herself, was exactly sure of her present status. She had asked to be released from her vows but, unlike Helewise, she had not felt the need to have her departure from the abbey formally recognized. Besides, also unlike Helewise, Tiphaine was still involved in its day-to-day affairs. She just did not want to be a nun any more, for the church was changing and, even if she still loved the Lord who had come to earth as a man to save the world, she no longer cared for the mortal men who were in charge.

Her status, Tiphaine had decided, really did not matter. It was immaterial to her and, as for the men of power, they had far greater things to worry about in this time of interdict than a half-pagan woman who wished to return to her true self . . .

There was no real hurry to quit her night's lodging, for it was unlikely that anybody would visit the herbalist's hut that morning. As Tiphaine knew only too well, there was not the same demand for medicines and remedies because people did not flock to Hawkenlye now as they always used to. Tiphaine did not bother her head with the intricacies of the political debate that raged through the land. She simply saw two great men, one of them a king and one of them a pope, who ought to be able to do better than plunge a whole nation into confusion, uncertainty and hardship.

Tiphaine got up, stretched, tidied away her makeshift bed and put more wood on to the small fire that smouldered in the brazier. She filled a pot with water and set it to boil, then reached up to the shelves with practised hands and mixed herbs for a drink. She set out a dry crust of bread and a strip of salted meat, eating the food slowly while she arranged her thoughts. When she had finished, and the herbal concoction was coursing through her body, she made sure the fire was dying down, packed up her bag and left the hut.

She moved swiftly and silently and kept to the shadows. Dressed in black as she was, with her hood over her head, anyone glancing at her would have taken her for a nun. She crossed the cloister and walked along to Abbess Caliste's room, tapping softly on the door. Invited to enter, she went in and shut the door behind her.

'Tiphaine!' Abbess Caliste's face lit up. The big table in front of her was, Tiphaine noticed, strewn with pieces of vellum, each covered in tiny rows and columns of figures and what Tiphaine assumed were words. 'How good it is to see you. Is there any news? Will you sit down?'

Tiphaine shook her head. 'Thank you, no. It is possible that some visitor to Hawkenlye may have heard or seen something concerning Rosamund's whereabouts, and—'

'And you wish to go among them and ask,' Abbess Caliste finished for her. 'Of course you must! Oh, Tiphaine, the family must be beside themselves with anxiety!'

Tiphaine nodded. 'Aye, for she is young and vulnerable.'

Abbess Caliste looked down with a frown at the work spread before her. 'I would help if I could, but the king's agents were here yesterday and I have a great deal to do.' She sighed. 'Their demands are all but impossible.'

'It is a heavy burden that you bear, my lady abbess,' Tiphaine said.

Caliste looked up at her. Tiphaine did not often address the abbess by her formal title – there were old and profound ties between the two of them that made their relationship unique – but just then she had done so deliberately, intending to remind young Caliste exactly who she was and encourage a little confidence. 'You can do it, if anyone can,' Tiphaine added, her voice so low that she was not sure Caliste heard.

Caliste closed her eyes and her lips moved in a silent prayer, then, looking at Tiphaine, she said, 'Tell me if you discover anything. May God help you all in your search.'

Tiphaine nodded. Then she turned and quietly let herself out of the room.

Next, Tiphaine went to the infirmary and spoke to Sister Liese. Sister Euphemia had at last acknowledged her years and now spent her days in Hawkenlye's home for aged monks and nuns. Although she was always willing to offer help and advice, her legs and feet were swollen from decades of hard work and she found standing painful. She liked to sit in her chair by the door or, when the weather was warm, outside in the sunshine, watching and thinking. Sister Liese was a woman of middle age who had come to Hawkenlye on the death of her husband and had quickly proved to be a dedicated healer with a particular gift with the young. She had calmly acknowledged that taking over from Sister Euphemia was a hard task and, during her early years in the abbey community, she had been modest and self-effacing. Now that Sister Euphemia had finally retired, Liese had stepped into the role to which she had been appointed and, in her own quiet way, she was proving to be almost as firm a rock as her predecessor.

Tiphaine told her briefly about Rosamund. Sister Liese nodded. 'We have few patients at present,' she said. 'All have been here for at least two days, so it is unlikely that they can offer any helpful information. I will, however, be sure to ask anyone who comes in.'

Next Tiphaine went down to the vale, where the monks were tending to the needs of a handful of hungry-looking pilgrims. Brother Erse, Hawkenlye's carpenter, was performing old Brother Firmin's task of fetching holy water from the shrine. Brother Firmin had been dead for some time.

She broke the news of Rosamund's disappearance to Brother Saul and, horrified, he promised to ask the visitors if they could offer any information. 'Some of us might go out and join in the search,' he offered. 'The dear Lord knows, we've little enough to do here.' He stood with Tiphaine, looking at the lean faces of the visitors. 'They're all close to starving, but we've so little to give them,' he added softly.

Tiphaine glanced at him. 'You don't look exactly tubby yourself,' she murmured. 'Don't forget to eat, Saul. If you give it all to them, who'll be here to help the next lot?'

He bowed his head. 'You're right,' he sighed. Then, as if it were just too distressing to dwell on the sorry state of them all, he said, 'Could the child simply have wandered off into the forest and got lost?'

'I pray you're right,' she replied. She didn't see any need to tell him about the stranger who looked like Joanna's son. The poor man had enough to worry about already.

Helewise spent the morning making successive forays out from Meggie's hut, steadily covering all the ground in its immediate vicinity. She found nothing. She returned to the hut to prepare a simple meal, wondering how soon Tiphaine would be back. Perhaps Meggie would come over. It would be good, to sit down with both of them to eat.

Tiphaine came back around noon and made her brief report. 'Nobody's got anything to offer,' she concluded, 'but then it's early days yet.'

'Yes,' Helewise agreed. Not even a full night and day had passed, she reflected. It was not very long, really.

'Where's Meggie?' Tiphaine asked suddenly.

'She hasn't come back,' Helewise answered. 'Since she's not here, I imagine she's with Josse at the House in the Woods. She was there yesterday.' She hesitated, then, since it was Tiphaine to whom she spoke, went on: 'She seems to be able to pick up a – a *sense* of people, from the very ground itself,' she said slowly.

Tiphaine reached across her and helped herself to an apple. 'Of course she can. She's Joanna's child and Mag Hobson's granddaughter.'

'Yes, I know.' Helewise smiled briefly. 'What I was saying was that I guess she will be searching around the place where Rosamund was last seen, using whatever faculty she has that the rest of us lack to try to see what happened.'

Tiphaine nodded as if that made perfect sense. 'Let's hope she succeeds,' she said.

Helewise sighed. There seemed nothing more to add, but she made herself think of the practicalities. 'Tiphaine, I'm going to stay here, if Meggie doesn't mind,' she announced. 'I need to be here, so that if anything happens at the abbey, or if there's any news, you can come and tell me immediately.'

'I'll do that,' Tiphaine said.

'But we've got to eat, so I'm going over to the House in the Woods to fetch some supplies.' Although she did not say

so, she also wanted to see Josse. Her excuse to herself was
that she needed to find out if there was any news. The truth,
if she could admit it, was that she missed him. In this time of
such anxiety, he was the one person she wanted to be with.

Tiphaine stood up. 'I'm going back to the abbey,' she said.
'Something may turn up.'

Helewise tidied the little room, banked down the fire in the
hearth and followed her out of the clearing.

Early as it was, Josse had already organized two search parties.
Gus and Ella had gone with Will in a wide circle to the south
of the house, and Geoffroi was with him, covering the ground
to the north.

Ninian had not yet returned. It was now many hours since
he had been gone, and all Meggie had been able to say was
that he had said he was going to look for Rosamund. Josse
wondered where he was. Ninian was a grown man and well
used to looking after himself, but there was a streak of reckless-
ness that ran through him and he had a temper as hot as any
of his infamous paternal relatives.

Now, slowly and painstakingly covering the ground with the
son of his blood close by, Josse sent up a silent prayer for
the adopted son whom he loved as dearly.

Perhaps Ninian was with Meggie. She was now absent too.
According to Will, she had slipped out of the House in the
Woods during the time that Josse and Helewise were down in
Tonbridge. She had not told Will where she was going, although
Josse suspected she was at the hut in the forest. She would
probably have met up with Helewise there. He said a prayer
for them, too.

He stopped and straightened his back. Being tall, it
was a strain to spend so long bent over studying the ground.
He put both hands to the base of his spine, kneading the
aching muscles with his knuckles. Geoffroi, noticing, called
out, 'What's wrong?' Then, quickly: 'Have you found
something?'

'No, nothing,' Josse replied. 'Backache,' he added tersely.

Geoffroi's shoulders slumped. He resumed his searching.

They pressed on northwards through the dense woodland and
presently came to the place where the trees began to thin out.

Ahead was the road that curved around the northern border
of the forest. To the left it led to Hawkenlye and, if you
branched off it to the right, down to Tonbridge. In the opposite
direction, the track led away to the east and the south-east,
circling the forest and heading off into open countryside.

Side by side, Josse and his son emerged on to the road.
Josse looked both ways, but there was nobody in sight. He
glanced down at Geoffroi. 'What should we do now?' he asked.
The question was rhetorical; it was hardly fair to expect an
eleven-year-old boy to supply the answer to a question that
had his father stumped.

Geoffroi frowned, an unaccustomed expression on his round,
cheerful face. 'We could follow the road for a while,' he
suggested. 'We might find somebody working in the fields
who was there yesterday and saw her – them – pass by.'

It seemed to Josse a pretty vain hope, but he had nothing
better to suggest. They fell into step and set off westwards
along the road, keeping a lookout for any distant figure in the
open ground to their right.

It was Geoffroi who heard the sound. He stopped, caught
at Josse's sleeve and said, 'Father, stop.' He screwed up his
face in concentration. Then: 'Listen! I can hear horses.'

Josse strained his ears, and soon he, too, caught the faint
sounds. A horse – no, two horses – coming towards them from
the west. Travelling fast.

Josse stepped to the side of the road and pulled Geoffroi
with him. If the riders were out on business of their own, they
would pass straight by. If not . . .

Josse and Geoffroi waited.

The horses came into view around a bend in the track.
Visibility was poor there on the fringes of the forest. The trees
were almost bare now, but those lining the road were vast,
their huge trunks and wide-spreading branches blocking the
light. Nevertheless, as Josse peered at the riders, he thought
he recognized one of them. He was, unless Josse was mistaken,
one of Gervase de Gifford's men.

He stepped in front of Geoffroi and, as the riders approached,
raised a hand in greeting. The man in the lead pulled his horse
violently to a halt, and the man behind, taken unawares, almost
rode into him. When they had recovered, the first man said,
'You are Sir Josse d'Acquin, aren't you?'

'Aye.' Josse's heart was pounding. He stared into the man's face. He had brought news, of course he had. Was it good news? Oh, God, was it bad?

The man had slid off his horse and thrown the reins to his companion. Now, approaching Josse, he made a sketchy bow and said, 'Sheriff Gifford sent me to find you. I've been trying to find Hawkenlye Manor, but it's too well hidden for me, even though I'd have said I knew the lands well hereabouts . . .' He paused, frowning.

'What do you want with me?' Josse said, barely managing to control his agonizing impatience.

The man must have picked up something of Josse's mood. 'Forgive me, sir,' he muttered. Then he said, 'They've found a body. The sheriff wants you to come with us, quick as you can.'

Josse felt as if his legs would collapse under him. A wave of nausea took him, and he saw black spots before his eyes. *A body.* Geoffroi was beside him, clutching at his hand, seeking reassurance.

Josse made himself stand upright. Fighting to keep his voice level, he said, 'Whose body?'

The man had had time to realize his mistake. 'I'm sorry, sir, that I am, really sorry.'

I'm sorry . . .

'Who is it?' Josse shouted.

'It's not the little girl. It's a man, sir.'

Not the little girl. Josse put up his free hand and covered his face, for a moment shutting out the world and simply praying silently, over and over again, *Thank you.* Then, recalling Geoffroi beside him, he composed his expression and dropped his hand.

'I will return to the house to leave my son there and to fetch my horse, then I will go with you,' he said. He was quite surprised at how calm he sounded. 'Will you wait here for me?'

The men glanced at each other. 'I should return,' the first man said dubiously. 'Sheriff said not to be too long about it, as I was leading one of the groups looking for her.'

'I'll stay,' the other man said. 'My horse is blowing hard from the ride over here. She's not as young as she was.' He gave the mare an affectionate pat.

'There's water in the stream that passes under the road, just down there,' Geoffroi said helpfully, pointing along the track. 'If you loosen her girths and give her a breather and a good drink, she'll soon be better.'

The man smiled at him. 'That's good advice, young lad,' he said. 'I shall do just that.'

Relieved that he had avoided having to take either man back to the house – although he was not entirely sure why – Josse grabbed Geoffroi's hand and hurried away.

The mare had indeed recovered by the time Josse rode Alfred out on to the track. He had left a message with Tilly to say what had happened and where he was going, and he knew she would deliver it efficiently as soon as any of the others came in. Geoffroi would add any necessary details. The most important thing was to make sure none of them experienced the same shocking moment that he had done, when the man broke the news.

Now Josse followed his companion – whose name, he told Josse, was Tomas – down the road. They rode fast, pushing the horses as hard as they could. On, on, they went, round the great bulge of the forest and the curve that swept past the abbey. A narrow path led off to the left – Josse had ridden that way and knew it led to the forest hamlet of Fernthe – and the main track went on to dip down into a shallow valley. Ahead, Josse knew there was a turning up to the right that led, via a steep-sided and ancient road, up to Saxonbury, but that was not where they were going. Before they reached it, Tomas indicated a trail that led off to the west, quite soon veering to the north-west.

Tomas turned in the saddle and gave Josse an encouraging grin. 'Not far now,' he said. He waved a hand to the right. 'River's over that way. The body's on the edge of a little copse of trees beside it.'

The land on either side of the track was flat and few trees grew. Soon Josse was able to make out the stand of oaks. He could see five or six horses, their reins held by a lad scarcely older than Geoffroi, and a group of men stood huddled together. Several of them were banging their arms across their bodies to keep warm.

Josse nudged his heels into Alfred's sides and the horse

took off, passing Tomas and taking the long, gentle rise up to the oak trees at a gallop. He pulled the horse up and, as soon as Alfred was approximately at a standstill, slipped off his back and threw the reins to one of the men.

He had spotted Gervase, crouched over something that lay on the ground, covered by a cloak. He ran up to him, and Gervase, turning to face him, slowly stood up.

'Who is he?' Josse demanded. 'Has he—' *Has he anything to do with Rosamund?* he almost said. But that was foolish. However would Gervase be able to tell?

'I do not know his name,' Gervase said. His eyes on Josse's were full of compassion. 'It is possible that you may.' He bent down and folded back the cloak.

Josse stared at the dead face. The body lay on its back, arms outstretched, the right leg bent beneath the left, which was extended. It was that of a young man in his early twenties, with long, light-brown hair and a clean-shaven face. His clothes were of good quality, the tunic bound with a rich brocade trim in shades of yellow and gold. There was a large pool of caked blood beneath his left nostril, extending down over his mouth and chin and dribbling on to the tunic, and he had a black eye. A bruise darkened the left side of his jaw.

'He's been in a fight,' Josse said, kneeling down beside Gervase.

'He has, and he gave as good as he got.' Gervase uncovered the hands, placed side by side on the corpse's belly. The knuckles of the right hand were grazed, reddened and swollen. It looked as if one of the punches that the dead man had landed had broken a small bone in his own hand. The left hand was bruised over the first and middle finger knuckles.

'Not quite as good,' Josse observed.

'What's that?' Gervase demanded. He sounded tense.

'You said he gave as good as he got,' Josse said. 'He didn't, for he is dead and his opponent, whoever he was, has fled.' He straightened up, feeling another twinge in his back.

'Do you think the blows to his face were enough to kill him?' Gervase asked.

Josse stared down at the body, trying to bring to mind all that he had ever learned about violent death. 'I would not have said so,' he stated eventually. 'I would guess that he suffered those fists in his face while he was still on his feet and fighting back, for his nose has bled a great deal and the bruising has come out on his face and his hands. Men don't bleed much once they are dead,' he added. Sister Euphemia had told him why, once, but he wasn't sure he remembered the details.

He turned to face Gervase. 'I'm wondering why you waited here with him until I came to join you,' he said. 'It must be quite some time since you found him, and the day is chilly.'

Gervase raised an eyebrow. 'You are always so insistent that you must be allowed to see a body where it fell, Josse,' he replied, 'and I for one do not dare to risk your scorn and your wrath by going against you.'

'My scorn and my—' Josse began, and then he realized that Gervase's tone had been ironic. 'Aye, well, that's as maybe,' he muttered, embarrassed.

He heard Gervase give a soft laugh.

'I will have a look around,' Josse announced firmly, choosing to ignore it. He bent down to the body again. 'There's little to learn from the spot where he fell –' gently he lifted one outstretched arm – 'and I'd say he went over backwards, perhaps as a result of one of those heavy blows.' He touched the bare flesh of the throat and then slid his hand inside the costly tunic. 'His garments are fine quality . . . and his body is very cold.' Slowly, he stood up. He looked around, taking in the surroundings. Narrowing his eyes, he stared up into the stand of trees. With a soft exclamation, he hurried up the slope and began a close inspection of the ground.

'I believe someone camped here,' he said when Gervase hurried to join him. 'Look. A horse stood there, and for some time, I would say. There are some oats scattered, and about a horse length away, a pile of droppings.'

'A single horse,' Gervase murmured.

'Aye, and a sizeable animal.'

'The dead man's horse?'

'Perhaps.' Josse had seen something else and, slowly and carefully, he was moving across to look. 'There was a camp fire here,' he said, pointing to where cut turfs had been laid over a patch of burned earth. 'And one – no, two people lay beside the fire.' He indicated the areas of flattened grass.

Gervase frowned. 'Two men camped here but with only one horse. What, they're Templar Knights, sharing their mount for the sake of brotherhood and poverty?'

Josse grinned briefly. 'Maybe, but I would suggest rather that the killer rode away on his horse.'

'What of the victim's horse?'

'If, indeed, both victim and murderer rode to this place, then presumably the killer took the dead man's horse away with him.' Josse was searching again, slowly circling the trees, but soon he gave up. 'I can't read the hoof prints. You and your men have walked and ridden all over the ground, and it's impossible to say if a mounted man rode away leading a second horse.'

'So what—?'

Josse held up both hands as if fending Gervase off. 'No more!' he exclaimed. 'I need time to think about what we have found here.'

Gervase held up his hands. 'Yes, of course.'

They walked side by side back to where Gervase's men stood around the body.

Josse glanced down at the dead man, whose face was now covered by a piece of sacking. 'We will take him to Hawkenlye Abbey,' he announced. 'The new infirmarer is acquiring quite a reputation, and if she can't tell us what killed this man, I will personally go to fetch Sister Euphemia out of her well-earned retirement and ask her.'

He watched as Gervase's men put the body on a makeshift stretcher, made out of the man's cloak fastened around two heavy branches cut from one of the oak trees. The procession formed up and – with Gervase and Josse in the lead, and Tomas and his old mare at the back – they began to wind their way slowly back to Hawkenlye.

When they had gone only a short distance, Gervase cleared his throat a couple of times and then said, 'Josse, as you know, Dominic Warin came to see me.'

'Aye,' Josse replied. 'Some matter you wanted to discuss with him, I understand.'

For some moments Gervase did not answer. Sensing his discomfiture, Josse turned to look at him. Gervase's usual air of amused detachment appeared to have deserted him. 'Well?' Josse prompted.

'There is a band of robbers in the area,' Gervase said, the words emerging in a rush, as if he disliked having to utter them. 'I am spreading the word to all men who have large manors and houses, for to be forewarned may afford some protection.' Again, he hesitated. 'I asked Dominic to tell me what valuables he possesses, suggesting he make certain that they are safely hidden or locked away,' he hurried on. 'I propose that you do the same, Josse, and I am happy to come to the House in the Woods to check on your security.'

'That's good of you, Gervase,' Josse said, surprised, 'although I can't bring to mind much that any of us possess that's worth locking away.'

'Oh, you'd be surprised.' Gervase gave an awkward laugh. Before Josse could reply, he added, 'I have some experience with thieves, Josse. I know what they look out for; I can help you, if you are willing.'

'Well, I suppose I am . . .' Josse said slowly. His mind was working busily. Why on earth was Gervase discussing this unlikely suggestion of his, when there was another, far graver issue preoccupying them all?

Because he is my friend, he realized, *and he thinks in this way to take my mind off my fears.*

He turned to Gervase with a smile, about to thank him for his kind concern. But Gervase's expression stopped the words before he could speak them. Whatever this was about, it was a great deal deeper than a sympathetic gesture from a compassionate companion.

Then he knew.

Feeling the same fear-induced nausea that had flooded him when Tomas had told him about finding a body, he said in a hoarse whisper, 'You fear that these thieves may not stop at stealing property. You believe they may have taken Rosamund.'

Gervase's eyes widened in horrified protest. 'No, Josse!' Violently, he shook his head. 'No, my friend. Believe me, I have not the least reason to suspect such a thing.' He muttered something, but Josse could not make it out.

Josse was not convinced. 'Then why do you mention these robbers at all, when you must know that concern for any valuable possessions I might have is the last thing on my mind?'

He had spoken far more fiercely than he had intended. Gervase hung his head, as if accepting the rebuke. Instantly sorry, Josse reached out a hand. 'I am sorry, Gervase,' he said. 'You were trying to distract me, I know.' He took a couple of breaths, and he felt his heartbeat slow down. 'I promise I'll think about what treasures I own, and when next you are at the House in the Woods I'll show you where I hide them and seek your advice as to how to keep these robbers' filthy hands off them.'

Gervase nodded, but did not reply. In silence, they rode on to the abbey.

FIVE

Josse stood beside Gervase, watching Hawkenlye's infirmarer work her way all over the dead man's body. It had been taken to a curtained recess, then stripped and washed by two young nuns working under the close eye of their superior. Josse had studied the infirmarer as she stood there, her full attention on what her nurses were doing. He did not know her well, and his first impressions were favourable. When one of the young nuns – nervous, perhaps, under the infirmarer's unwavering stare – dropped a bowl of dirty water all over the clean sheet on which the body was lying, Sister Liese had issued no sharp reprimand, but quietly told the girl to fetch another sheet and then mop up the mess.

Now, observing her as closely as she had watched her nuns, Josse's tentative admiration for her grew. She handled the body as if it still lived, he observed, touching the wounds to the face and the hands as if the man could still wince at the pain. She was modest, too, and after a quick inspection of the torso, groin and legs, she had pulled up the sheet so that the body was covered as far as the waist.

'He has been hit over his ribs.' Sister Liese's soft voice broke into his reflections. 'There is bruising. See?' She beckoned to them without turning round, as if she knew they were watching. Josse and Gervase stepped forward, and Josse saw the dark discolouration over the lower half of the man's rib cage.

'Left side again,' he muttered.

Sister Liese turned to look at him. Her eyes – light, and halfway between blue and green – fixed on his. 'Yes,' she agreed, 'and the damage to the face is worse on the left. The man who punched him favoured his right hand.'

She turned back to the body. Now she raised the head with one gentle hand while she slipped the other beneath it. She felt around for some moments, and Josse knew what she would find.

He waited and, after a short time, Sister Liese smiled briefly and said, 'Ah, yes.'

'He fell flat on his back,' Josse said. 'There must have been a stone, or a rock, that his head struck.'

'Yes, I agree.' Sister Liese reached out and took Josse's wrist in a surprisingly firm grasp. She raised the dead man's head again and placed Josse's fingers on the base of the skull. He felt a deep dent, and over the spot the thick hair was sticky with blood.

'Not, strictly speaking, murder,' Gervase said. 'What do you say, Josse?'

Josse was thinking. 'He and the other man were fighting ferociously, exchanging hard punches, and we know from our man's knuckles that he landed several hits. Then his opponent struck a particularly effective blow – perhaps the one that damaged our man's nose – and he staggered backwards.'

'He might have been knocked out,' Sister Liese suggested. 'Even if it does not kill him, a hard blow can render a man unconscious.'

'Unconscious or driven back by the blow, either way he tripped or fell, landing flat on his back and striking his head on a stone.'

'A rock.' Sister Liese spoke with conviction. 'The wound is a hand's breadth across, and so too large for a mere stone.'

Josse suppressed a smile. Such precision, he thought. 'His head hit a rock,' he amended, 'and the force of the impact shattered his skull and killed him.' He looked at Gervase. 'Whether or not that is murder is not for me to say.' He turned back to Sister Liese. 'Thank you, Sister. We are most grateful for your help.'

She bowed her head. 'It is what I am here for,' she said. She looked down at the body. 'Will you wish to visit him again?'

Once more, Josse noticed, she had spoken of a man, not a corpse. 'We will,' he said quietly. 'There is the question of identity. Somebody knows who he is, and we shall—'

But she had understood. 'I will brush down his garments and dress him,' she said. 'Lying on his back, his visible wounds are not horrifying, and if he is clad in his habitual tunic, he will look much as he did in life.'

'You wish to spare this somebody further distress,' Joss murmured.

She met his eyes. 'The knowledge that he is dead will be sufficient,' she agreed. 'Now, if you will excuse me . . .'

'Aye, of course.' Josse nodded to Gervase, and the two of them left the recess and walked away down the long infirmary.

'We should speak to Abbess Caliste,' Josse said as they emerged into the cold, clear air. Helewise always used to come to witness old Euphemia's inspection of a victim's body, he thought before he could stop himself. Abbess Caliste, he knew, would have her own good reasons for not being present, and it was not for him to judge her. Cross with himself, he increased his pace. 'Come on.'

Gervase tapped on the door of the abbess's room, and her soft voice bade them enter. Observing her, Josse felt even guiltier over his brief disloyal thought. Her table was groaning under its load of heavy, bound ledgers and piles of vellum, and her eyes were bloodshot and ringed with the grey of extreme fatigue.

'Sir Josse, my lord sheriff, I deeply regret that I was not able to be there when the poor man was brought in,' she said, getting to her feet to greet them. 'I have been praying for his soul, and a mass will be said for him.'

She did not, Josse observed, give any excuse to exonerate herself, as well she might have done. 'You are busy, my lady,' he said, indicating the table.

'The king's agents were here two days ago,' she replied tonelessly.

There was no need for her to explain. 'Will the abbey survive?' he asked.

The lines of anxiety in her lovely face deepened, and she shrugged. Then, with a lift of her chin, she said, 'If I have anything to do with it, yes.'

Touched, Josse went forward and briefly took her hand. 'We have a little surplus at the House in the Woods,' he murmured.

She looked up at him with a smile. 'You have your own people to think of, dear Sir Josse. They are your responsibility, just as the abbey is mine.'

But I am not subject to the iron fist of a greedy and selfish king, Josse thought. Nobody has come to Hawkenlye Manor to demand we hand over all our produce and all our income, to be given back to us if we do as we are told.

He could not, of course, say it aloud. Gervase was an old friend, and Josse would have trusted Caliste with his life, but such a comment was treason and walls had ears. Even – or perhaps especially – abbey walls.

He leaned closer to the abbess. 'We have enough,' he whispered. 'If you ever reach your wits' end, we are there.'

He was still holding her hand, and now she gave his a firm squeeze. 'Thank you,' she breathed. 'I know.'

He let go of her hand and, embarrassed suddenly, stepped back to stand beside Gervase.

'So, the dead man,' Abbess Caliste said, sitting down in her great chair. It seemed to Josse as if she had briefly stepped out of her role as head of the abbey and now had re-entered it, for all at once it was undoubtedly she who held authority in the little room. *Helewise, your successor was wisely chosen*, he thought. Abbess Caliste was speaking, and he made himself pay attention.

'You do not know who he is, I imagine, or else you would have called him by his name,' she said.

'Correct,' Gervase said. 'We can say, however, that he is a man of quality, judging by his clothes and his general appearance.'

'I understand that he was found out to the west of here, close by the river.'

'Yes, my lady,' Gervase said. 'There is a track that leads along the river valley and then on to the hamlet of Hartfield, where the ground begins to rise up to the open heathland of the forest. It appears that the dead man made camp in the place where he died, although of course it is impossible to say in which direction he had been travelling.' He glanced at Josse. 'He rode a good-sized horse and he had someone with him, for there were signs that two people had lain beside the little fire that he made.'

Abbess Caliste did not reply. Her elbows were on the table, and she had propped her chin on her clasped hands. Her expression was serene, but Josse had the impression that, behind the calm features, her mind was working fast.

He was right. After a short time, she said, 'Two people and a horse spent the night in that camp. One is now dead. The horse and the other man have disappeared. It seems there are two possible explanations: one, the second person killed the man and rode away on the horse. Two, someone else arrived, fought the man in the camp and, having laid him out, left him for dead and rode away with the other person who was in the camp.'

Gervase was looking puzzled. 'Why should there have been anyone there besides the two who fought?' he demanded. 'There was only one horse there overnight and, if two people had rested there, surely there would have been a second one?'

'The pair might have ridden on one horse,' the abbess said.

Gervase muttered under his breath and Josse caught the words *blasted Templars again*. Addressing the abbess, Gervase said, 'As I said, why raise the possibility of a third person? I—'

Josse understood. He flashed an anxious glance at Abbess Caliste and said, 'She's thinking of Rosamund. Aren't you, my lady?'

Slowly, the abbess nodded. 'I am. Somebody took her away, but we know she did not have her own horse with her. Unless her abductor brought along a mount for her, then he must have borne her on his own horse. They rode off westwards, heading for some unknown destination, and, overcome by darkness, they stopped to rest for the night. Some time during the night or the next day, someone else came across them. He attacked the man and the two of them fought. The man was killed, and – and—' She stopped, her face pale.

'And took Rosamund?' Josse asked softly. 'If, indeed, it was she who slept beside the camp fire that night, then where is she now?'

Abbess Caliste held his eyes. 'I do not know, Sir Josse,' she said. 'It is little enough to go on, but it would seem we have nothing else. If we agree that it may have happened in that way, does that not give us a focus in our search for her?'

'Of course it does!' Gervase said eagerly. Josse could sense the energy building up in him, bursting for release. 'We must gather all our men together and head out to the west, towards the Ashdown Forest. We—'

But Josse interrupted. '*He* was taking her in that direction,' he said gently. 'The man who abducted her. It does not neces-sarily follow that whoever now has her has the same objective in mind.'

The horror that lurked beneath his words overcame him briefly. He put a hand to his face, hoping to hide his expression. He was too slow. Abbess Caliste's voice said calmly, 'Sir Josse, we must maintain our strength and go on trusting that she will be found safe and unharmed. We are praying for her constantly, and God will hear us.'

He looked up. There was such certainty, such absolute faith in her expression that for a moment he believed her. Then he thought of that lonely, desolate spot where the dead man had been found, and of the miles of empty countryside that stretched away all around it. It was the end of October, and the nights were cold. Rosamund was little more than a child.

He managed a smile. 'I am comforted, my lady. Meanwhile, we must do everything we can to help ensure this happy outcome.'

Gervase's impatience had got the better of him. 'You must excuse me, my lady,' he said, bowing to Abbess Caliste, 'for I have much to do if we are to pick up the trail while there yet remains any freshness in it. Now, in addition, there is the problem of how we are to discover the identity of the dead man.'

'Of course,' she said. 'Go, my lord.'

'I also must leave you,' Josse said, backing out in Gervase's wake. 'I wish to break the news of this death to my household before they hear it from others and – er, and fear the worst.'

'I understand,' the abbess said. 'Give them my love and tell them they are in my thoughts and in my prayers.'

He bowed. 'I will.' Then he hurried away.

Josse watched as Gervase shouted instructions to his men. Then they all rode off, the ground vibrating under the pounding hooves. He mounted Alfred, hurried out through the abbey's main gates and, setting a good, fast pace, took the slope up towards the dense woodland at a canter and headed off beneath the trees. Very soon the track became too narrow and overgrown to ride, and he dismounted, leading Alfred behind him.

He met Helewise on the path that led from the hut in the clearing. She was walking towards him and drew to a halt as he came into view.

'Josse!'

He was gratified that she looked both relieved and, he thought, happy to see him. 'Aye. I've come from the abbey.' He told her about the discovery of the body, explaining, as delicately as he could, Abbess Caliste's theory concerning Rosamund.

She took in his words without speaking. She squeezed her eyes shut at one point, and he feared she would break down, but she regained control. 'Thank you for coming to tell me,' she said after a moment. 'Tiphaine has returned to the abbey – she was heading for the vale, so that's probably why you missed each other – and she may have more to report when she comes back.'

'Would you like me to stay with you till she returns?'

He watched her as she considered the offer. It was hard to read her expression, but eventually she shook her head.

'No. Thank you, but no.' She took a step closer to him and reached up to touch his cheek. 'Dearest Josse, there is nothing I would like better than for you and I to walk hand in hand along the track and settle down together in the little hut, fastening the door against the wildwood and all the threats of this world, but it would be selfish in the extreme because everyone in the House in the Woods looks to you for guidance and leadership and they *need* you.' She paused. 'Besides, they know no more of this latest dreadful event but that a man's body has been found, for, indeed, that was all you knew when you left Geoffroi at the house and collected your horse.' Absently, she patted the horse's sweaty neck. 'You've been riding hard,' she observed.

Josse sighed. 'Aye, and I'm not done yet,' he said heavily. He knew she was right, and he must hurry on to the House in the Woods.

There was sympathy in her eyes. 'Poor Josse.' Then, brightening, she said, 'Perhaps there will be news at home! Many resourceful and determined people have been searching for her, and why should not one of them have found some clue as to where she is?'

'Because—' He stopped.

'Because?'

'They're all looking in the wrong place!' he blurted out. His frustration and his anger boiled over. 'Everyone who has gone out from the House in the Woods, Dominic's party out to the east and Leofgar's to the north, they'll find no trace of her because the accursed, bloody *bastard* who took her rode off to the west!' he shouted. Then, hearing the echo of his furious words: 'I apologize, Helewise.'

'For calling the man who took my granddaughter an accursed,

bloody bastard?' she asked spiritedly. 'Josse, I could not have phrased it better myself.'

He opened his arms, and she stepped into his embrace. For a moment they stood pressed together, and she was holding him as tightly as he was holding her. But it was their common distress that united them, and he knew it.

It was he who broke away. He dropped a kiss on her forehead – he was tall, but so was she – and said, 'Farewell, Helewise. I will return soon, and sooner if there is any news.'

'I, too, will come to find you if I learn anything,' she replied. 'Please explain to Meggie why I'm using her hut.'

He was surprised. 'You mean you haven't told her yourself?'

'No. I haven't seen her since you and I set out for Tonbridge –' she paused – 'yesterday morning.' Her face fell. 'Dear Lord, is it only a day? It seems like months.'

But he hardly heard. 'She has not been to the hut?'

'No, Josse.' She smiled. 'Don't worry, she'll be back at home. Where else would she be?'

'You're right,' he muttered, turning Alfred and pulling on the rein to get him to move off. He tried to squash the twitch of unease that was coursing coldly through him. 'Come on, Alfred, lift your feet.'

The horse reluctantly got going. Josse turned to look at Helewise, standing alone on the path.

'Don't worry,' she repeated. Then she gave a small wave, turned round and walked away.

The afternoon was drawing to a close as Josse led Alfred into the stable block at the House in the Woods. Will came out to meet him and silently took the horse's reins from his hand.

'He'll need a deal of attention tonight,' Will observed lugubriously. He glanced at Josse. 'Like his master,' he added.

'I'm all right,' Josse snapped, twisting round to scowl at Will. The movement tweaked his sore back, and a pain like a red-hot needle flashed right up his spine. 'Ouch,' he moaned.

Will watched him sympathetically. 'Tilly'll do you a hot poultice for that,' he said. 'Good at hot poultices, is Tilly.'

'Yes, Will, I know.' She ought to be, Josse reflected, since Meggie was teaching her. 'Thank you for your concern,' he

added, 'and I'm sorry I snapped at you.' His face as impassive
as ever, Will nodded an acknowledgement.

Then Josse understood the implications of what Will had
just said. *Tilly will do you a hot poultice.* Tilly was the appren-
tice; Meggie was the teacher. So why hadn't Will said *Meggie*
would do it?

He spun round to face Will, sending another knife point of
fire through his lower back. 'Where's Meggie?' he asked
urgently. 'Is she here? *Is she*?'

Will did not meet his eyes. 'No.'

'But she's been here, hasn't she? She's come and gone, along
with the rest?'

Now Will looked at him. 'No, sir. She left some time yesterday
morning.'

Anxiety burning through him like fire, Josse grabbed Will's
arm. 'When did she leave?' He felt Will wince and let go of
him, muttering an apology.

Will's deep eyes were screwed up tightly as he tried to
think. 'Well, it was after you and the abbess – you and the
lady Helewise, that is – had ridden off to find the sheriff and
the lady's son.' His frown intensifying, he added, 'Reckon
she was still here after you came back, though I couldn't
swear to it.'

Had she been at the house when he returned? Josse tried
to think. So much had happened yesterday, and they had all
been beside themselves with worry. Meggie had definitely
been there before Josse and Helewise left for Tonbridge – he
remembered her saying how Rosamund had been happily
chattering to her. But he did not think he had seen her when
he got home.

He tried to take it in. Meggie had left the House in the
Woods yesterday morning and, according to Helewise, she had
not gone to the hut. Nobody, it seemed, had seen her for well
over a night and a day . . .

Will cleared his throat and said tentatively, 'Sir?'

Somehow Josse knew he wasn't going to like whatever it
was that Will was preparing to tell him. 'What is it?' he asked
tersely.

With a visible effort, Will met his eyes. 'The lady's mare's
missing.'

'Daisy?' It was a stupid and totally irrelevant question.

'Daisy,' Will confirmed.

'She's been stolen?' It was not all that likely, since the House in the Woods was well hidden and some distance from the road. But then Gervase had said something about robbers . . .

Will sighed. 'Reckon Meggie came for her,' he said.

'Why? What grounds do you have to say that?' Josse demanded.

'Because I'd put the mare's bridle aside on my workbench ready to repair a bit of loose stitching, and whoever took the horse knew where to find it. So . . .'

'So it could only be one of us,' Josse finished for him.

There was a painful pause. *Where are you, Meggie?* Josse asked silently.

Somebody must know where she was.

He ran from the stables, across the yard and took the steps into the hall at a couple of bounds, the exertion giving rise to another groan of pain. He flung open the heavy wooden door and burst into the hall. A fire was blazing in the hearth, and around it sat Geoffroi, Gus and Tilly. Tilly's younger children, subdued for once, sat in a corner quietly playing with their toys. The eldest child, a boy, sat close to his father, and Gus had an arm around the lad's thin shoulders. Ella, presumably, was in her habitual place in the kitchen.

Just as Will had said, Meggie was not there. Josse repeated his question: 'Has Meggie been home today?'

Gus looked up at him, surprised. 'No! We thought she'd be over at the hut.'

'She's not. She hasn't been there at all.'

'Oh, no! Then where is she?' Geoffroi looked wildly around, his expression anguished.

'Will thinks she's taken Daisy,' Josse added. 'Where can she have gone?'

'She's probably met up with one of the other search parties and gone back with them,' Gus said reasonably. 'Dominic was here earlier. He found nothing,' he added quickly, in response to Josse's unspoken enquiry, 'and he said he was going to make his way slowly back to New Winnowlands and aim to be there as darkness fell.'

Dominic. Oh, Dominic. 'How is he?' Josse said gruffly.

Gus shrugged. 'He's holding up.'

Poor Dominic had to go home to Paradisa this night, Josse realized, and tell her the child is still out there somewhere. Dear Lord, help them both.

Tilly got up and went to stand beside Josse. 'Come and eat,' she urged. 'Ella's got hot food all ready, and there's a jug of spiced wine just waiting for the hot poker to make it steam.'

Food. Wine. Josse realized how hungry he was. He subsided on to a bench by the fire and, looking gratefully at Tilly, said, 'Aye, I like the sound of both of those.'

Tilly hurried off to fetch the food, and Gus prepared the wine. Josse took a deep draught – he felt the warmth and the alcohol hit his empty belly and for a moment his head swam – and he emitted a long, 'Aaaah,' of satisfaction. Presently, Tilly returned with a platter of mutton stew in rich gravy, with chunks of root vegetables and a generous hunk of bread, and Josse ate as if he hadn't seen food for days. It did not take him long to clear the platter and, putting it down, he said, 'I have some news. Not much, but I wish to keep you all informed. Gus, would you please fetch Will and Ella?'

While they waited, Josse wondered idly how many other knightly households included their servants in family discussions. He smiled wryly to himself. His no longer felt like a knightly household – if, indeed, anywhere he had lived fitted that description, whatever it meant – and he had never been entirely sure where kin ended and kith began.

Geoffroi got up and came to sit beside him on the bench. Josse put his arm round the boy, just as Gus had done to his own son. It felt good.

When Will and Ella had settled – the diffident Ella so far to the back of the little group that Josse could hardly see her – he told them everything that had happened since he had been summoned that morning by the sheriff's man, Tomas, and ridden off with him. His listeners made no comment beyond a few soft muttering among themselves, so Josse went on to outline Abbess Caliste's thoughts on what might have happened.

It was Gus who spoke first. 'It's either a falling out among the two people who slept in the camp, then, and in that case probably nothing to do with our Rosamund.' A frown creased his brow. 'It could be that the man who took her was challenged by someone, who he fought with and who was killed in the fight. Or else maybe it was the dead man that took her, and somebody objected to that and went to try to take her back.' His frown cleared. 'I reckon that's the most likely way of it.'

'Aye,' Josse said thoughtfully. 'Aye, it's possible.'

'This other man got the better of the abductor,' Gus went on, 'and as a result of a particularly good punch, the man fell backwards and crushed his skull.' He looked around the company. 'So, assuming that if this other man attacked the dead man because he didn't hold with him taking a little girl, what did he do?'

Josse had been wondering the same thing. 'He might not know who she is and where she belongs,' he said slowly. 'He might even now be trying to take her back home, but unable to because he doesn't know where home is.'

'She'd tell him, surely?' It was Tilly's voice, and Josse looked at her in surprise. She had come a long way, he reflected absently, from the skinny, nervous, shy little tavern girl she once was . . . 'Rosamund's not slow to speak up, is she? When someone rescued her and asked where he ought to take her, she'd say, *I live at New Winnowlands*, and she'd be able to tell him where that was.'

'Even if she couldn't,' Geoffroi put in, 'and I could, and she's the same age as me, she'd have said something like *I know them at the abbey so you can take me there.*'

Josse nodded slowly. 'You'd think so, wouldn't you?' he said vaguely. Something was troubling him. It had begun earlier as a small, dark suspicion right on the edge of thought, and he had been able to push it away without too much effort. Now it was back, insistently demanding his attention. And it wasn't small any more.

Gus was looking at him. 'What is it?' he asked quietly. It was as if he already knew . . .

Josse let his eyes roam around the circle of faces lit by the flickering firelight. Will, and Ella crouched back in the shadows. Gus and Tilly, all three children now sitting close to their parents, as if they had been drawn there for security. Geoffroi, his round face turned up to Josse so full of trust.

Josse knew he had to tell them. 'I have been thinking,' he said heavily. 'There is one set of circumstances I can envisage that would explain everything.'

'What?' Tilly asked nervously. Gus dropped his eyes.

Josse took a deep breath, exhaled and then breathed in again. 'Let us suppose that, indeed, the person who caught up with Rosamund and her abductor by the trees above the river had gone to fetch her back. He challenges the man who has her. They fight. The abductor strikes his head and he dies. The man who has come to rescue Rosamund sees what he has done and knows he will be judged a murderer. He has struck and killed a man, and he will probably hang.' Josse's voice broke on the word, but he made himself go on.

'Who could this man be?' he demanded roughly, staring round at the others. 'Someone who cares about Rosamund, obviously, someone who will not sit by while evil is done to an innocent child. Someone who, having rescued her, cannot bring her back because he'll be arrested and charged with murder.'

'Is it Dominic?' asked a small voice beside him. 'You would kill a man who took me, Father, I know you would.'

Josse hugged his son to him. 'Aye, Geoffroi, I'd do so willingly if it was the only way I could get you back,' he agreed. 'But it can't be Dominic, can it? He was here earlier, you told me?' He looked enquiringly at Gus, who nodded.

'He's called in more than once in the course of the day,' Gus confirmed. 'I don't think he'd have let the rest of us go on searching and worrying if he knew the little lass was safe.'

'I agree,' Josse said. 'So, who else could it be?' With the exception of Gus, they were all looking stunned. 'Gus?'

Gus shook his head. 'I don't want to say, sir. It's murder, in the eyes of the law. I – no.'

Josse sighed. 'Very well. We have not seen Meggie since yesterday, although I do not for a moment think that, strong as she is, she could have inflicted those punches on the dead man's face. Who else is missing?'

They all looked round. On every face but Gus's, puzzlement slowly gave way to realization, and then to deep dismay.

Geoffroi whispered, 'Oh, no!'

Josse hugged him tightly. 'We do not know for sure, son,' he said. 'But I fear we must prepare ourselves to face the possibility that the man who fought the dead man is the one person who ought to be here and isn't. Who, if I'm right, none of us has seen since the evening we discovered that Rosamund was missing.'

He looked round at them all. In case anybody was still in doubt, he told them. Softly, he uttered the name: 'Ninian.'

SIX

Gervase had almost run through the list of people he was summoning to the Hawkenlye infirmary to see if they knew the identity of the dead man. None of the nuns recognized him, and Gervase had no more success with the monks from the vale. Brother Saul had helpfully brought a party of visiting pilgrims with him but, to a man, they had briefly gazed at the dead man's face and mutely shaken their heads.

The parties out searching for Rosamund were regularly reporting back to Gervase – and the long succession of: 'Nothing yet, sir,' was becoming extremely frustrating and very worrying – and he had paraded each and every one of his men past the body. Nobody recognized him.

The victim was a man of some means; that was evident by his clothing and the fine leather of his boots. Studying him now, Gervase looked at the hands. They were well shaped, reasonably clean and nicely kept. The dead man was no peasant dressed up in stolen garments. Gervase looked at the neatly-cut hair. That, too, indicated a man with the money and the time to look after himself.

Who are you? Gervase asked him silently. *What were you doing out there by the river? Did you abduct the missing girl? If so, who fought you, killed you and took her from you? Where were you taking her? Where has he gone with her?*

So many questions. So many uncertainties. Suppressing the urge to punch something, Gervase left the recess and strode out of the infirmary.

He decided to ride down to Tonbridge to see if his deputy had anything to report. The day was drawing on towards evening, and the light was fading fast. He wanted to speak to his deputy before it became too dark to search and everyone went home for the night. Another day had passed, he reflected anxiously, and Rosamund was still missing. And, always lurking behind all his pressing preoccupations, there was that other matter; he must not leave it too long before making the journey out to the House in the Woods to inspect Josse's valuables . . .

He was entering the abbey's stable block when he heard the sound of hooves. Turning, he saw Leofgar Warin riding towards him.

'What news?' Gervase demanded.

Leofgar held up a hand. 'None. I am sorry, that is not why I have sought you.'

Gervase felt himself sag. Just for a moment, he had hoped . . . He looked up at Leofgar and said, more sharply than he had intended, 'Why are you here, then?'

Leofgar's expression suggested that he understood Gervase's mood. 'I have to go home,' he said. 'I'm sorry, I wish with all my heart that I could get out there again now, sleep here tonight and return to the search in the morning. She's my niece, and I cannot imagine what my brother and Paradisa are going through. But I cannot stay. I have pressing concerns of my own.'

'What's more important than a missing child?' The question burst out of Gervase before he could stop it. 'I apologize,' he said instantly. 'I have no right to question your movements.'

'No, you haven't,' Leofgar agreed, with the ghost of a smile. 'But I'll explain anyway.' He slid off his horse and, coming to stand close beside Gervase, said quietly, 'My wife and I are expecting an important guest. The king is on his way back to his palace at Westminster, and he is to honour us with a visit as he progresses north.'

Gervase was stunned. 'You – King John is to stay with you? At the Old Manor?'

Leofgar's smile held genuine amusement now. 'Don't sound so surprised,' he said mildly. 'We do have a bed or two to offer, and my household can rise to a grand occasion and turn out quite acceptable fare.'

'I did not mean to imply otherwise,' Gervase said stiffly.

'No, I know you didn't,' Leofgar replied. 'Between you and me,' he added, lowering his voice still further, 'I wish he was returning to London via a different road. I'm not looking forward in the least to entertaining a demanding king and however many hangers-on he happens to have with him. As my wife so perceptively remarked, it's nothing to be proud of as he's only staying with us because our house happens to be conveniently situated.'

'I am sure it is more than that,' Gervase said politely.

Leofgar looked at him, his mouth twisted in an ironic grin. 'You are?'

'I – er, I—'

Leofgar waved a hand. 'It is of no matter.' He gathered up his horse's reins and put a foot in his stirrup, preparing to mount.

'Wait!' Gervase exclaimed, remembering. 'Can you spare me a moment longer before you leave?'

Leofgar glanced up at the twilight sky and nodded. 'Yes, if you're quick. What is it?'

'We have an unidentified body in the infirmary.'

Leofgar tethered his horse and, as the two men hurried over to the infirmary, Gervase explained how and where the dead man had been found. 'So nobody knows who he is?' Leofgar asked.

'No,' Gervase replied in a low voice, leading the way to the curtained recess. He stood back, letting the curtain fall behind him, and Leofgar approached the body.

After a moment he said, 'I do.' He turned and met Gervase's eyes. Very quietly he went on, 'His name is Hugh de Brionne. His father was close to the king's brother and very readily changed his allegiance to John as soon as Richard died. Josse, I believe, is acquainted with the father, although clearly he did not recognize the son.' He glanced back at the still face. 'This death will sorely grieve Felix de Brionne.'

'Hugh was his only son?'

'He – Felix's wife bore him a daughter and two sons. This is the younger son.' He put a hand on the dead man's shoulder.

Something about Leofgar's manner did not seem right. 'What else?' Gervase asked in a whisper. 'What is it that you do not tell me?'

Leofgar shot him a glance, then looked away. 'Nothing,' he said firmly. 'It's gossip, no more, and I do not believe it is right to spread rumours.'

'Rumours?' Gervase demanded.

Leofgar expelled his breath in an angry sound. 'It is to do with the brother. It is said by those with nothing better to do than wag their idle tongues that he is not Felix's child.'

'Ah. I see,' Gervase murmured.

Leofgar spun round. 'Do you?' he hissed. He parted the

curtains, looked out and, apparently finding that nobody could overhear, said urgently, 'I have met Felix de Brionne and his wife several times. Béatrice is a very lovely woman and she was only thirteen when she was wed. Felix was more than twenty years her senior. Her first child was a girl and Felix was not pleased.' He paused. 'I tell you this not because it satisfies me to discuss the intimate dealings of another man and his wife, but to make you understand,' he went on. 'If indeed Béatrice took another man to her bed – and I am by no means convinced that she did – then the affair was short-lived, for when later she bore Hugh, her second son, there was no doubt who had fathered him for he is the image of Felix.' He stopped, looking down at the body. 'He was,' he corrected himself. He sighed. 'Poor Felix. Poor Béatrice.'

'Where do they live?' Gervase asked. 'They should be informed that their son is dead.'

'Their manor is to the east of Tonbridge, on the slope of the North Downs,' Leofgar said heavily. 'Felix is old now and his comprehension comes and goes. He will not, I think, understand. It will be Béatrice on whom the blow falls most cruelly.'

Béatrice who has another son who is probably not the offspring of Felix, Gervase thought, *in whom it is hoped she will take comfort.* But he did not say it aloud.

Tiphaine was heading back to the hut deep in the woodland. She had observed the sheriff and Helewise's elder son speaking together by the stables and, unseen by either, she had slipped into the infirmary after them. She had heard Leofgar identify the dead man, although the name meant nothing to her. It might to Helewise, however. She increased her pace. Darkness was falling fast and she still had some way to go.

Helewise heard someone approach. She was outside fetching water from the stream, busy preparing vegetables and beans in a stew for supper. She had returned from the House in the Woods earlier with generous supplies of food, which Tilly had helped her carry. But she was not in the least hungry. The ongoing, gnawing anxiety had quite taken away her appetite, but she knew she must force herself to eat. Besides, there were others to consider.

She looked up to see who was coming. It was probably Tiphaine, although she could not help hoping it might be Meggie. Or, even better, Josse . . .

Tiphaine stepped out from beneath the shadow of the trees and into the clearing. She gave Helewise the low, reverent bow that she had always performed before her superior and, approaching, said, 'Your son's given a name to the dead man. He was called Hugh de Brionne.'

Helewise repeated the name to herself. She did not think she had ever heard it before. 'Who is he?'

Tiphaine shrugged. 'Some lord's son. His old father's close to the king, or was when he had any wits left.'

Helewise thought about that. Then she said, 'Has his identity had any bearing on the hunt for Rosamund?'

Tiphaine came to stand beside her, and Helewise was grateful for her solid, strong presence. Tiphaine was a woman who was very close to the earth, and strength emanated from her. 'I don't know, my lady,' she said gently. 'Reckon they're still thinking about that.'

Helewise studied the lean, weather-beaten face. Tiphaine looked tired. 'Come and eat,' she said, taking the older woman's arm. 'It's nothing special but at least now we've got enough for the next few days.'

With dismay, she heard what she had just said. *The next few days.* Dear God, was it going to be as long as that before they found Rosamund? The familiar guilt seared through her again.

They were stepping inside the little hut, and Tiphaine was watching her. 'She'll be found, my lady,' she said. 'I am quite sure of it. She's not dead.'

Helewise stared at her. 'How can you be so sure?' she cried sharply. 'She's only a girl, Tiphaine! She could be—' Horrible images flashed before her eyes, but with an effort she shut them off. Tiphaine was trying to comfort her, she realized, and she had just shouted at her. 'I'm sorry,' she whispered. 'It's just that I'm so desperate to accept she's all right but I don't know if I can believe you.'

Tiphaine went on looking at her. Then she said, 'You can, my lady,' and turned to set out the wooden bowls for supper.

They sat down close by the hearth to eat their supper. It had grown much colder once darkness had fallen, and the warmth was welcome. Helewise was quite pleased with her bean stew, which was greatly improved, she thought, by the addition of some of Meggie's dried herbs. She tried to eat slowly – if she ate beans quickly her stomach tended to bloat – but she was too hungry, and she wolfed down her bowlful. Beside her, Tiphaine ate her stew mechanically, her thoughts clearly elsewhere, occasionally emitting a grunt of satisfaction.

'I'd have thought we would have had a visit from Meggie before now,' Helewise ventured, trying to suppress a belch. Her pleasure in the taste of the herbs had brought the girl to mind.

'She'll return here when she's ready,' Tiphaine said calmly. Then, her eyes narrowing, she added softly, 'She'll be on the little girl's trail, like as not.'

Helewise spun round to look at her. 'How do you know that?' she demanded.

Tiphaine looked up from mopping her bowl with a piece of bread, her expression registering surprise at Helewise's sharp question. 'Stands to reason,' she replied, swallowing a mouthful. 'Joanna knew how to follow a person's footsteps across many miles. Meggie's her daughter. I expect Ninian can do it too, since he's her son. They've both inherited many of her gifts, so why would that not be one of them?'

Helewise was torn between a sudden glow, because she was sure Tiphaine was right, and a stab of pain.

Josse had loved and lost Joanna, and he did not often speak her name. To have Tiphaine refer to her so readily and easily, as if she had just stepped out of the hut and it was not ten years and more since she had gone, was a shock, and not entirely a pleasant one.

Helewise had to admit that she did not much care to hear Joanna's name.

She commanded herself not to be so selfish. What Tiphaine had just said was *good*. It gave them hope. 'You really think they can do it, Tiphaine? You believe that we'll get Rosamund safely back?'

Tiphaine reached for more bread and nodded. 'Aye.'

Her assent, Helewise reflected with a private smile, could have been to either of the questions. It was probably to both.

She bent down to pick up the jar of small beer that Tilly had lugged across the forest that morning and, filling two mugs, handed one to Tiphaine. Raising her own, she said, 'To Rosamund, wherever she is. May God keep her safe.'

There was a muttered *Amen* and the sound of Tiphaine slurping up her beer.

Helewise had hoped that Josse might have called in before nightfall and, even better, might have stayed in the hut over-night, but she had not really expected him to. As she lay up on the sleeping platform, drifting into sleep, she pictured Josse's face. In her imagination, he was standing on the edge of the clearing outside the hut and he turned to look at her. There was just sufficient light to see his face, and his expres-sion as he met her eyes brought a smile to her face.

She would go to look for him in the morning, if he did not turn up at the hut first. She had to tell him that the identity of the dead man was now known. It would, she reflected drowsily, give her a fine excuse to seek him out.

Ninian had gone to settle the horses for the night. The saddles and bridles were safely concealed back in the sleeping place, and he had fashioned rope head-collars and tethered the horses to the trunk of an alder. They would have hobbled them and set them to wander, but they were both afraid the animals might be seen.

That must not happen.

He checked once again to make sure the knots were firm and then dipped under the low branches of the pine trees where he and his sister were going to spend the night.

Meggie looked up at him. She had lit a small fire, contained within a circle of stones from the shallows of the river. 'All well?' she asked softly.

'Yes.' He lay down on his blanket and gave a deep sigh.

Meggie watched him. She could tell how tired he was. She was wrapped up warmly in her cloak and blanket, leaning comfortably back against her saddle. 'Go to sleep,' she said. 'You look as if you can't keep your eyes open any longer.'

He yawned widely. 'Very well. Call me when it's my turn to watch.'

'I will.' She smiled at him, but he had already shut his eyes. He turned on his side, away from her, and wound his cloak around him. He would get a decent sleep before his turn came, she reflected, since she felt wide awake, despite her bodily fatigue. Her mind was racing, refusing to shut off. It was no use fighting it, and so she let her thoughts roam back over the hours and the miles since she had set out from the House in the Woods.

She had been surprised at the ease with which she had picked up Rosamund's scent. Well, she corrected herself, it was not exactly a scent, because that implied that it was something you could detect with your sense of smell. It was more a sort of feeling, a certain knowledge that Rosamund had stood *just there*. Meggie remembered how it had felt to stand with her eyes shut absorbing Rosamund's essence, concentrating so intently on the strange sensation that she had barely registered her father and Gus coming up behind her. She had believed that was going to be all she could manage, but then she had realized there was more. She found the direction in which Rosamund had set off and, once she became used to interpreting what her senses were telling her, it was relatively easy to follow where Rosamund and her abductor had gone. Provided she went quickly – she had a strong suspicion that this weird effect would not be long lasting – there was a chance that Rosamund might be found.

Meggie had barely heard the others agonizing over where Rosamund could be and how they would set about finding her. She had volunteered the small amount of information she had – Helewise, she had noticed, had been watching her keenly, as if she'd known Meggie's thoughts were not entirely on the discussion – but in the privacy of her own head she had been struck with wonder at her newly-discovered gift and longing to begin testing it. As soon as her father and Helewise had set off for Tonbridge, she had slipped away from the house and almost instantly she had discovered Rosamund's trail. Already, the essence had been fading; she'd known that she was going to have to hurry.

She had also understood that she needed a horse. She waited until her father returned, riding Alfred and leading Helewise's mare, and as soon as she could she went into the stables and tacked up Daisy, apologizing to the mare for having to take her out again so soon. For a desperate few moments she had not been able to locate the bridle; it had been on Will's workbench, waiting for him to mend a fraying stitch. Typical of tidy-minded, painstaking Will, the strong needle and the thick thread were on the bench beside the saddle, and Meggie had quickly done the repair. It was not as neat a job as Will would have done, but the stitching would hold.

She made herself ignore her guilt over setting out without telling her father. It was an unbreakable house rule, imposed on them all from Josse himself to the smallest child of Tilly and Gus: *always let someone know where you're going and when you expect to be back.* It was quite right and made total sense, living as they did in the depths of the wildwood and in the middle of hard times, when there were desperate men about who would attack and harm you for the price of your boots.

I'm sorry, dear, dear Father, she said to him silently as she led Daisy away, looking over her shoulder all the time in case someone spotted her. *I know you'll worry, because, although you try to hide it, you get twitchy even when I stay over at the hut for a few days, and it's pretty safe there.*

She knew she had to go alone. The presence of anybody else – even someone she loved as profoundly as she loved her father – would have altered the balance and might have obliterated that small, clear voice that seemed to be calling out to her: *Follow me. Follow me.*

She had ridden on for all the rest of that day, sometimes quickly, when there was only one obvious direction to take and she did not have to keep dismounting to check that she had not gone wrong, and sometimes agonizingly slowly. Once, out to the west of Hawkenlye Abbey, she had become confused by many sets of hoof prints and boot prints and it had taken her almost till dusk to find the trail again. By then it had faded so much that it was barely detectable . . .

The awareness that she was cold broke across her thoughts. She reached out to poke the fire, and the sudden, leaping flames sent a wave of warmth out to her. Ninian had collected plenty of firewood, so she put a couple of lengths on top of the blaze.

Ninian. She glanced over at his sleeping form. It had been quite a surprise to discover that she had not been the only one on Rosamund's trail . . .

She had spent her first night on the high ground to the west of the Hawkenlye vale. Although the mighty woods of the

Wealden Forest ended to the south-west of the abbey, there were still occasional wooded rises, and she had made her meagre camp at the top of one of them. She had come well prepared, making fire with her flint and steel and cooking a simple supper. The hot drink had been very welcome, and she had dosed herself with her own herbs. Wrapped in her heavy cloak and a couple of thick wool blankets, she had not fared too badly.

In the afternoon of the next day, she had spotted a rider ahead. Tensing, she had studied him. Her first instinct had been that it was Ninian, but then Rosamund had seen her abductor at quite close quarters and believed him to be Ninian. Meggie had forced herself to wait, testing out her first impression, and realized that she had no reason to doubt it. She put her heels to Daisy's sides and hurried to catch him up.

His expression as he turned to look at her had been unreadable, even to her, and it had crossed her mind that he was deliberately keeping her out, shutting away whatever he was thinking so that she did not pick it up.

Then he smiled. Smiling too, happy to see him, glad that she would not have to pursue the trail alone, she said, 'So you can do it too.'

He replied simply, 'Yes.'

He told her he had found the spot where Rosamund and the man who had taken her had spent the previous night. 'At least, I'm pretty sure I have,' he added. 'Two people lay there, and there was a fire, although only one horse.'

'She's only small,' Meggie said. 'She'd have ridden behind him.'

She suggested returning to the camp site so that she, too, could inspect it, but Ninian said there was no need. 'The trail's already faint and there's no point,' he went on. 'Anyway, I think I know where he's taking her.'

She had been so excited at his words that she hadn't pursued the matter of the camp site. 'Where?' she demanded.

He stared at her, his blue eyes brilliant in the soft autumn sunshine. *Not our mother's eyes*, she remembered thinking absently, *for hers were dark, darker than mine, which are just like Father's. Ninian, too, must have his father's eyes.*

She did not know for certain who had fathered her half-brother, although she had a pretty good idea.

He said, after teasing her with a pause so long that she had been about to thump him, 'I believe they're heading for the Ashdown Forest. They've been going west,' he went on quickly when she opened her mouth to interrupt, 'and for miles that way there's little but heathland.'

'Then what is his destination?'

'There are hunting lodges out on the forest,' he said eagerly. 'They were built for the great lords, so they don't have to waste valuable hunting time riding to and from whatever grand house they're staying in. It's like camping, I suppose,' he added thoughtfully, 'only far more comfortable, and I expect there's a gang of servants to cook the deer the lords have just killed and to warm the beds.'

She hardly heard the last part. 'Do you know where these hunting lodges are, then?' she asked.

He grinned. Raising his arm, he pointed. 'There's one about five miles ahead.'

They had found it. As soon as they had it in sight, it was obvious that it was inhabited. There were horses tethered outside, and the sounds of human activity could be heard coming from the small yard behind the lodge. Men were hurrying to and fro – the gang of servants, no doubt, Meggie had thought – working to fulfil the orders of an exacting master and make everything ready for his arrival.

There were people within, too; the sound of their voices floated out on the still air.

Was one of them Rosamund?

Meggie, stiff with tension at knowing the child might be so near, wanted to creep up and look, but Ninian grabbed her and threatened to tie her to a tree if she tried. 'If they see you, they'll either take you too or have you arrested for trespass,' he hissed.

'What do you suggest?' she hissed back, equally angry.

He loosened his hold on her. 'We wait,' he replied. 'We'll make camp over there, among the trees –' he pointed – 'and the gorse will hide us well enough. Then we watch and work out who's in there, what they want with Rosamund and—'

'And how we're going to get her back,' she interrupted.

He smiled at her. 'My thoughts exactly.'

Careful not to disturb Ninian, Meggie got to her feet and crept over to the edge of the secluded spot where they had made their camp. She could see the lodge quite clearly, for it stood out as a rectangle of denser black in the darkness. Everything was quiet now, and only one small light burned.

Earlier, a group of horsemen had ridden up, the horses lathered and the men loud-voiced and exuberant; the hunting, it seemed, had been good. Meggie and Ninian, watching from their hiding place in the gorse, had counted ten men. Meggie could have sworn that Ninian recognized one of them, but when she asked him, he shook his head.

The sounds of a very good party had floated out to them from the lodge. There was singing and laughter and, at one point just after the hunters had arrived, a furiously angry voice shouting harsh but inaudible words. The men, it appeared, had fallen to arguing even before they'd had time to drink more than a couple of mugs of wine.

Meggie stood in the darkness for some time, concentrating so hard that it made her head ache. She was trying to sense if Rosamund was in the lodge, or whether this long, chilly vigil was a complete waste of time. She did not let herself dwell on that for long. If it was, then Rosamund would be far away now and out of reach, even to two people who had inherited their mother's strange gifts.

Rosamund had to be there. Surely, it could not be that both Meggie and Ninian were wrong?

She arrested that thought too, replacing it with a positive one. Tomorrow the men would set out again, either to resume the hunt or to return to wherever it was they came from. She and Ninian would be ready and, whoever had Rosamund and wherever they went, the two of them would follow.

It seemed as good a thought as any on which to go to sleep. She returned to her bed, stoked the fire again and lay down. She knew she was meant to wake Ninian so that he could take his turn on watch, but she was all but sure that everyone in the lodge had retired for the night. Nobody would go anywhere until morning, so Ninian might as well sleep too.

She rolled on her side, her back to the fire's warmth, and very soon fell asleep.

SEVEN

The man felt as if his head had been invaded by other people's thoughts. They were in there, the voices, inside his skull. They ordered him to do things, and when he got it wrong, they grew angry. Lying in the darkness, he gave a low moan, quickly suppressing it. The others had mocked and laughed at him quite enough for one day, and he would not give them the satisfaction of starting all over again.

He did not understand. It was all so confusing.

It had been late in the day when he and the girl had reached the hunting lodge. He would have gone in earlier, but he dared not do so until his lord arrived. He had taken the girl back to the river, and they had played a game, making a dam out of driftwood across a little stream that wound down the bank to join the main current. She had enjoyed that, and so, he had to admit, had he.

He *liked* the girl. She was pretty, she was quick-witted and she made him laugh.

Then the self-doubt had returned and the silent questions had started up again. Was he doing the right thing? Ought he to return her to her family? Oh, but he had to go on! The voices told him so. They said it was the only way to get what he so desperately wanted.

He and the girl had been mounted on his horse, waiting on a low rise above the lodge, when his lord finally arrived. The lord was in a good mood, laughing loudly and joking with the men. They all went inside, and the man knew he could wait no longer. He said to the girl, 'We can go in now!'

She looked at him brightly. 'Is the party going to be soon?'

'Yes, yes! Very soon.'

She had paused to fluff up her pretty hair and brush the dust off her cloak. The little gestures had gone straight to his heart. Before emotion could undermine him – *remember why you are doing this!* – he tightened his hold around her waist and kicked his heels into Star's sides.

He went first into the lodge, holding her hand and drawing

her in after him. Nobody noticed them to begin with. The lord
was sitting in a fine leather-seated chair beside the fire, and
two of his body servants were pulling off his boots. The boots
were caked in mud. More servants had heated wine, and the
aroma of spices was heavy on the air. The lord's men all had
mugs in their hands and were drinking greedily. As the man
watched from the fringes of the group, the lord reached out a
hand and took his own fine silver goblet from the servant who
bowed low beside him.

'To the chase!' he roared, and all the others joined the toast.
'To Madame Roe and Lord Fallow! Long may they thrive—'

'And long may we hunt them!' the men yelled back.

Then the lord caught sight of him. 'There you are!' he
exclaimed. 'We missed you on the hunt today. Where have
you been?'

A narrow path opened up between the men crowding around
the lord. His heart hammering in his chest, slowly the man
walked along it. The girl's small hand in his was hot and
sweaty with nervous excitement.

The lord's eyes fell on her and for an instant opened in
recognition.

'I have brought you an unexpected guest, my lord,' the man
began, 'for I know that—'

He did not have the chance to explain himself. As if his
lord saw everything that had happened in the past two days
in the blink of an eye – he probably did, for he was very, very
clever and his mind worked as fast as quicksilver – he turned
to the man and fixed him with eyes that blazed with fury.

Into the hush that had suddenly descended, he said in an
icy voice, 'So you bring me a girl?'

'I thought – I—' the man stammered.

The lord, as if aware of all the ears straining to hear, flung
out his arm in a wide gesture. 'Get out, the lot of you,' he
shouted. 'Go and hurry those blasted cooks. I want my dinner!'

One by one the others shuffled away. The man and the girl
stood side by side before the lord. 'You were saying?' the lord
prompted silkily.

The man sidled closer. Speaking almost into his lord's ear,
he whispered, 'We – I know that your preference is for young
women, my lord. Why, your good lady wife was scarce more
than this girl's age when you wed her, and she—'

The lord flung out his balled fist, and it was only the man's quick reaction that saved him. 'Do not dare speak of my wife!' the lord hissed. His face was scarlet with fury, the bright eyes swelling alarmingly above the puffy cheeks. 'She was young, yes, when first I laid eyes on her, but she was precociously mature and already a woman!' He paused, panting. 'What do you think I am?' he demanded, the low, controlled voice almost worse than the awful shouting. 'You have brought me a *child*!'

The man wanted to weep. Everything had gone amiss. He had got it wrong, as so often he did. Already, the voices were starting up their clamour inside his head, jeering at him, accusing him, calling him a fool.

His lord had beckoned to the girl, and she was slowly walking up to him. He held out a hand, and she took it. He was speaking to her; the man knew he must be because he could see the lord's lips moving. He told the voices to be quiet so that he could listen.

'—your name, child?' the lord was asking.

'Rosamund Warin.' The girl spoke up clearly, causing the lord to smile.

'Rosamund,' he said. 'Rose of the world. Warin . . . Yes, I know the name. Who is your father, Rosamund Warin?'

'He is called Dominic and he lives at New Winnowlands.'

'I know that name, too,' mused the lord. He frowned in concentration for a few moments, and then, his prodigious memory coming to his aid, he said, 'The abbess of Hawkenlye was called Warin.'

'Yes, she's my grandmother, only she's not abbess there any more. She—' Rosamund did not go on. The man wondered why. It was not that the lord had stopped her; more as if she herself had elected not to say any more.

The lord did not appear to have noticed.

The man watched him intently. As if the lord felt his eyes on him, he looked up and stared right at him.

The man bowed his head to receive whatever furious invective the lord chose to hurl at him. He did not even dare to think what his punishment would be. It would be severe and it would be painful, that was for sure.

The lord's voice said calmly, 'Look at me.'

Slowly, the man obeyed. To his huge surprise, the lord was smiling. 'You are a fool,' he said, quite pleasantly, 'but then

I expect you already know that, for people no doubt tell you all the time.'

'Yes, my lord,' the man muttered. He very much wanted to lower his eyes, for the lord's hard stare was paining him, but he did not dare.

'A fool, but it may yet be that in your folly you have unwittingly done me a service,' the lord went on. He paused, frowning. 'Yes,' he said softly, more to himself than to the man. 'Yes, I believe that would work very well . . .'

The man waited. Between him and the lord, Rosamund stood quite still, like a slender statue. The lord turned to her. 'Why were you brought here, child? Do you know?' he asked her kindly.

'He said there was to be a party,' she said, nodding her head towards the man. 'He told me I would meet you, lord, and he said it was a surprise.' She stopped, and it seemed to the man, watching her back, that her shoulders drooped a little.

The lord must have noticed, too. 'Would you like to go home?' he said gently.

Her head shot up. '*May* I?' Then, as if she remembered her manners: 'I mean, after the party, of course.'

'Of course,' the lord echoed. He leaned towards her. 'Tomorrow I shall take you back to Hawkenlye Abbey,' he announced.

'But my grandmother—' The girl bit off the rest of whatever she was going to say. If she had been about to point out again that her grandmother was no longer abbess of Hawkenlye, she must have thought better of it. Perhaps, the man reflected, she had decided that being taken to the abbey was as good an offer as she was going to get and she had better accept it. 'Thank you, my lord,' she said instead. 'That would be most convenient.'

'Good,' the lord said. Then, his eyes dancing with light as if he were contemplating some wonderful event: '*Good*!' He clapped his hands, yelled to the others that they could come back and told them to bring the food with them.

The remainder of the evening had passed in a blur. Everyone had drunk a lot, and the shouting and the singing had all resonated inside the man's head, competing with the voices that alternately cajoled, threatened and, very occasionally, praised him.

The others made him the butt of their mocking jokes, and it had hurt him. He had done all this, conceived his brilliant plan, to stop them treating him like an idiot. He had truly believed that bringing the girl would please his lord so much that the lord would turn to him, thank him and announce that he was to be advanced to the post of one of the lord's close guard. That would have shown them, all of them, for at long last he would have been in his rightful place at his lord's side.

Where he, of all men, surely belonged. Even if nobody ever seemed to remember it.

It was late now, and everybody was sleeping. The girl had been accorded a corner to herself, and the lord had made sure that she was snug and comfortable. He had commanded that the men respect her privacy, and the man knew that nobody would dare to disobey. The girl was safe now.

Somehow, despite the fact that his plan had gone so badly awry, he could not help being glad about that. It had never been his intention to hurt her. He'd just had to use her as a means to an end, in much the same way that people used him.

Tomorrow they were taking her back to the abbey. The lord had seemed very pleased about that. The man tried to think why. He was quite good at thinking, or at least he was when the voices gave him a bit of peace. They were quiet now – perhaps, like the others, they, too, were asleep – and the man frowned as he thought about why the lord might be happy to go to the abbey.

An image began to firm in his mind. It was misty and vague at first, but then it solidified and he knew what he was seeing. *Of course.*

A slow smile spread across his face. He drew up his cloak, made himself comfortable and very soon, against all his expectations, he fell asleep.

Helewise woke very early the next morning, worrying about Rosamund and trying to puzzle out whether the death of this Hugh de Brionne could be connected with the girl's disappearance. She got up quietly – Tiphaine was still asleep – and built up the fire in the hearth. She knelt beside it to say a heartfelt prayer for her granddaughter's safety: 'Please, dear Lord, let her be waking in warmth and safety this morning. Let her find her way back to we who love her.'

She prayed for a little longer, then stood up and, with quick, decisive movements, put water on to heat and set about making the breakfast porridge. The Lord could not bring Rosamund home by himself, and it was up to Helewise to do whatever she could to help. She did not know quite why, but she had the growing conviction that she must tell Josse the dead man's name as soon as she could. She ate her bowl of hot food standing up, swallowing it so fast that she burned her throat. Then she shook Tiphaine gently, told her where she was going and set off.

The morning was still young as she strode along. In the weak sunlight the grass by the track was glistening with frost; the first frost of the autumn. *Hurry*, she told herself. She increased her pace.

By the time she reached the House in the Woods, she was out of breath and glowing. She ran up the steps and opened the door, finding Josse and Geoffroi eating at the big table by the hearth. Ignoring their surprised expressions, she said, 'The dead man's name was Hugh de Brionne. Tiphaine overheard my son Leofgar identify him last night.' She pulled up a bench and sat down on it, only then realizing that she felt quite exhausted.

Josse was staring at her, repeating the name under his breath. 'Hugh de Brionne. Aye, I know the family. His father Felix and I both saw service with King Richard.' He narrowed his eyes, clearly concentrating hard. 'Aye, now that I know the man's identity, I can see that he did indeed look a little like his father, although his face was badly—' Belatedly, he recalled his son's presence. 'Er, his face had suffered some wounds, and so I did not see the resemblance yesterday.'

'It is easier to detect similarity between two people when you are looking out for it,' she said. 'You had no idea who the dead man was.'

He gave her an affectionate smile. 'Kind of you to say so,' he murmured. Then, speaking so softly that he merely mouthed the question: 'Has Meggie turned up?'

She shook her head. So Meggie was not here at the house either . . .

Josse had turned to Geoffroi, who was listening wide-eyed to the conversation about the dead man. 'Son,' he said, 'I have to go to speak to Gervase. Somebody must go to inform the dead man's parents what has happened and, since I know Felix de Brionne, I think it ought to be me.'

Geoffroi nodded. 'Can I come too?'

Josse put his arm round his son's shoulders. 'You could,' he said, 'but, if you are willing, I have a much more important job for you.'

Geoffroi's expression brightened. 'What is it?' he asked eagerly.

'Son, Helewise has to get back to the hut, and neither Ninian nor Meggie has yet returned. I need someone here who can come and find me if anything happens, and, since Will, Ella, Tilly and Gus all have a full day's work ahead of them, the obvious person to ask is you.'

For a moment Helewise thought the boy would see through the ruse. Josse was right: the house of a mother and father being informed of their son's death was no place for anyone who did not have to be there, especially one of such tender years as Geoffroi. The boy's expression was at first doubtful, but then, as he thought about the suggestion, his face cleared. 'I'll ride like the wind and by the most secret ways,' he said excitedly. 'I'll—'

Gently, Josse stopped the eager flow of words. 'If you need me, go to the abbey. I will leave word there of where I am bound.'

Geoffroi looked at him solemnly. 'I will.'

Josse reached over to embrace him briefly then, with a glance at Helewise, led the way out of the hall. 'I'll go and get Alfred,' he said as they hurried across the courtyard. 'Will you ride with me?'

'As far as the path to the hut, yes,' she replied.

He looked at her. 'You still will not come to the abbey?'

She shook her head. 'No, Josse. Abbess Caliste has quite enough to cope with in these dreadful times without her predecessor turning up uninvited.'

'Very well.'

Will was busy in the stable block and swiftly helped Josse prepare his horse. 'I'm going first to Hawkenlye, Will,' Josse told him, 'and then on from there. I don't know how long I shall be.'

Will nodded. 'Gus and I will take care of the place in your absence,' he said.

Josse got into the saddle and reached down his hand to Helewise, pulling her up so that she sat in front of him, sideways across the horse's withers. Then he kicked Alfred and they set off across the forest.

Riding through the abbey gates some time later, Josse wished, not for the first time, that Helewise was not quite so stubborn. He understood her reason for avoiding Hawkenlye, but surely this was an emergency and she should have made an exception to her own rule.

Still irritated, Josse left Alfred in the stables with the young nun who had taken over from old Sister Martha and hurried to the abbess's room. If Gervase was at the abbey or expected soon, she would know. He knocked and went in.

Gervase stood just inside the door. 'I was about to come and seek you out, Josse,' he said. A slight frown creased his forehead.

'Good morning, Gervase.' Josse turned to bow to the abbess. 'My lady abbess.'

'As always, you arrive when we need you,' she murmured. She inclined her head towards Gervase. 'The sheriff has a task for you, if you will accept it,' she said, her voice grave.

'You want me to inform the dead man's parents of his death,' Josse said quietly. 'Aye, I guessed as much. That's why I'm here.'

'Leofgar believes you know the family,' Gervase said.

'I know Felix, or I did,' Josse replied. 'He may not remember me, for they say his mind wanders.'

'Shall you and I ride there together?' Gervase said. 'It is not far, I believe. We can be back here later today.'

'Aye, I'd be glad of your company,' Josse said. 'It's a grim task.'

As he and Gervase left the room, he sensed the abbess's sad eyes on them. Listening carefully, he could just make out the soft words of her prayer.

They made good time to the manor of the de Brionnes. The day was cold and bright, and the ground was hard. Even the descent into the low lands around the river did not slow them, as it usually did, for the weather had been dry recently and the rise in the water level that regularly came every winter had yet to happen.

They followed the track as it rose from the valley towards the North Downs, and presently Josse indicated the turning that led off it towards their destination. It was years since he had visited Felix de Brionne – back in the early days of King Richard's reign, he recalled – but he found the way without mistake.

They knew as soon as they rode into the well-kept yard that the sad news they brought had already reached the household. It was evident in the total absence of cheerful, everyday sounds and in the red-rimmed eyes of the lad who came out to take their horses. As they walked towards the impressive, iron-studded oak door, it opened and a grim-faced servant looked out at them.

'The family is grateful for your condolences,' he began, with the air of a man who had said the same thing many times already that day, 'but Sir Felix and Lady Béatrice are not receiving visitors today.'

The door was already closing when Gervase put his foot in the gap. 'I am Gervase de Gifford, sheriff of Tonbridge,' he said. 'This is Sir Josse d'Acquin, an old friend of your master.' He leaned closer and said very softly, 'We are the ones who attended the dead man's body and took it to Hawkenlye Abbey.'

The servant shot them a swift, inquisitive look. Then he nodded and, opening the door widely, ushered them inside.

A woman sat by herself in an elaborately-carved oak chair beside the wide hearth. She was dressed in a tight-bodiced, wide-skirted gown of dark velvet, and a veil covered her head and much of her face, held in place by a gold circlet. Hearing their footfalls, she raised her head and turned to look at them.

'I said no visitors, Stephen,' she said in a low voice made husky by grief.

'Beg pardon, my lady, but this is the sheriff and this is Sir Josse d'Acquin, a friend of the master,' the servant muttered. He added something in a whisper that sounded like *they found the body*.

It was not strictly true, but it was no time to quibble.

Lady Béatrice stared at them. She pushed back the veil, and Josse saw that she was perhaps in her late thirties. He also observed that, haggard with sorrow as she now was, she was still very beautiful. Her smooth brown hair was drawn back from a centre parting, and her large eyes were almost black. Her skin

was good, her nose straight and delicate, and her mouth wide
and shaped for laughter.

She was far from laughing now.

Greatly affected, Josse approached her and, bowing, took
her cold hand in his. 'You have my deepest sympathy, lady,'
he said. 'You and I have not met before, although, as your
man here says, I know your husband from our service together
under King Richard.'

She nodded. Josse was about to go on, but Gervase interrupted. Stepping forward to stand beside Josse, he said, 'I
apologize for my abrupt manner, my lady, but it is my duty
to discover how your son died. May I ask how you know of
the tragedy? Sir Josse and I came here to tell you, but it seems
to me that you have already been informed.'

She studied him. 'Leofgar Warin came and broke the news
last night.'

'Leofgar,' Gervase breathed. Turning to Josse, he murmured,
'He did say he knew the family. I would have asked him to
come and tell them, only I understood he was in haste to return
home.'

It had been a kindness, Josse reflected, for Leofgar to put
aside his own pressing needs in order to perform such a sad
task. He wondered how Felix had taken the news.

He considered how best to ask her. He said, 'Lady Béatrice,
is your husband not with you? Has he, perhaps, retired to bed
to nurse his grief?'

The dark eyes met his. 'You would ask me, I believe, if my
husband is able to comprehend what has happened. If his
fast-failing wits have grasped the fact that his son is dead. My
answer is that I do not believe so.' She dropped her head.

Then you face this tragedy alone, Josse thought. *You poor
woman.*

'My lady, may we speak to Sir Felix?' Gervase was asking.

'You may,' came the quiet reply. 'He is in the chamber
through there.' She pointed to where an arched doorway gave
on to a passage.

'Come with me, Josse,' Gervase hissed. Josse bowed again
to the still figure in the chair and followed him through the
arch.

Felix de Brionne lay in a high bed under heavy covers. He
had aged greatly in the years since Josse had seen him. His

face was a yellowish-grey colour, the cheeks so sunken that the large nose stood out like the prow of a ship.

Josse stepped up to the bed, bent over the old man and said softly, 'Felix? It's Josse.' The eyes fluttered open and Felix looked up at him. Josse smiled, and Felix's dry lips stretched in an answering smile.

'Josse,' he breathed. 'I remember you.'

Gervase, close beside Josse, leaned down and said, 'Your son is dead, Sir Felix, and we are very sorry. I am sheriff of Tonbridge, and I will do my best to discover how he died.'

The old man's brows drew together in a frown. 'My son,' he said. He stared at Josse, reaching out to grasp his hand. 'Hugh is my son. The other one, no.' Straining forward, he beckoned Josse nearer and said in a cracked whisper, 'I forgave her, long ago. I love her, you see, and she's young, much younger than me.' He lay back on the bank of pillows, panting slightly from the brief exertion. He closed his eyes. Josse exchanged a glance with Gervase and was about to suggest they tiptoe away and leave the old man to sleep when he spoke again.

Quite clearly, he said, 'There is something wrong with the other one.' Then his breathing deepened and presently he emitted a soft snore.

Josse led Gervase out of the chamber and back to the hall.

'Well?' Lady Béatrice asked as they came to stand before her.

Josse, embarrassed, was about to make some innocuous comment and nudge Gervase into taking their leave. Gervase, however, was not ready to depart.

'My lady, I am sorry if this is painful and appears to you insensitive,' he said, 'but, as I said, it is my duty to discover all that I can about your son's death. In pursuit of that, there are questions that I must ask.'

Josse watched her reaction. She gave a faint sigh – perhaps of resignation, as if she knew what was coming – and nodded. 'Ask your questions,' she said quietly.

'Can you suggest any reason why Hugh would have been in the area in which we found him?' Gervase asked. 'It was out to the west of Hawkenlye Abbey, on a rise above the river.'

'No.'

'Does he have friends who live nearby? Kinsmen, perhaps?'

She looked at him levelly. 'Our family is small. My husband

has one elderly cousin, but she is unmarried and childless. I am an orphan and have no brothers or sisters. I have three children: Hugh, a daughter who lives with her husband close to Canterbury, and another son.'

There was a long pause. Then Gervase said, 'And where does the other son live? Could Hugh have sought him out or gone to visit him?'

Her gaze did not falter. 'He lives here with Felix and me. He is not here at present. He is a grown man and keeps his own friends. It is not for his mother to question his comings and goings. As to whether Hugh was seeking him out, I doubt it. The brothers are not close.'

She closed her lips very firmly, as if determined to say no more. But Gervase was not satisfied. 'Will you elaborate, my lady?'

She gave a small sound of exasperation. 'Brothers are natural rivals, my lord sheriff. From childhood, sibling boys will always wish to be the first in the affection of their mother and their father.' She gave a brief shrug. 'My sons are no exception.'

Josse watched as, slowly and inexorably, her stiff face dissolved and the tears formed in her eyes. 'My sons . . .' she whispered. Then, squeezing her eyes shut, she said, 'Now I have but the one.'

Josse went to her, sensing from a pace away her struggle to hold on to herself. 'My lady, we will leave you,' he said. He glanced around for the servant, but the man was already hurrying over to his mistress. 'Look after her,' Josse said.

The servant's expression implied very clearly that he did not need Josse to tell him.

Josse had expected Gervase to head straight back to Tonbridge, or possibly the abbey, for his duty was surely to resume the search for Rosamund and, now, the hunt for who was responsible for Hugh de Brionne's death. With a painful effort, Josse turned his mind away from that. To his surprise, however, Gervase suggested they go to the House in the Woods. 'We are quite near,' he said, 'and perhaps I may impose on you for some food and drink.'

'Aye, of course,' Josse replied. It made sense, he supposed, although something in Gervase's manner was disturbing him.

Did the sheriff share Josse's awful suspicions about Ninian? Was his strange, abstracted air because he knew he would have to arrest Josse's adopted son and charge him with murder?

With a shiver of dread, Josse put his spurs to Alfred's sides and hurried after Gervase.

They rode hard, covering the miles swiftly and without speaking. At the House in the Woods, Josse asked Will to tend the sweating, blowing horses, and he led Gervase inside the hall, where a very welcome fire burned in the hearth. He was about to call out to Tilly to bring food and drink when Gervase, with a hand on his shoulder, spoke.

'Josse, while I am here let me do as I said I would and check on your valuables,' he said.

'I don't care about my valuables!' Josse burst out. 'Dear God, this is no time for that, Gervase!'

Gervase's face hardened. 'I am doing all I can to find the girl, Josse,' he said coldly, 'but please remember that I have other obligations, one of which is to prevent theft. It may be a minor matter to you, but it is not to me.'

Josse waved a hand. 'Oh, very well,' he said grudgingly. Gervase was right, and he knew it. Forcing himself to concentrate, he looked around the wide hall, and his eye fell on the big oak chest that stood beside the door leading to the kitchen. He strode across to it and flung back the lid, revealing some tarnished silver vessels that had belonged to his mother and a wickedly-curved blade that his father had brought back from Outremer. 'Hardly worth a thief's trouble,' he remarked as Gervase knelt to look into the chest.

Gervase did not speak for a few moments. Then he said, 'Your daughter has a jewel.'

'Aye,' Josse breathed. He had forgotten the Eye of Jerusalem, the great sapphire that had also accompanied his father home from crusade. 'Follow me.'

He strode across the hall and, twitching aside a heavy hanging on the opposite wall, revealed a small wooden box set into the stonework. He reached inside his tunic and withdrew a small but heavy key, unlocking the little door. 'We keep the stone in here,' he said.

Gervase was right beside him, staring over his shoulder into the dark recesses of the box. 'The jewel is your daughter's, yet you have the key?'

'Meggie has her own key,' Josse said shortly.

'How many people know about this hiding place?'

Josse shrugged. 'Most of my household, I suppose, *might* know, although I don't think—'

Suddenly, Gervase stiffened. 'What was that?'

'What?' Josse felt alarm course through him.

'I heard voices . . .'

Josse didn't hesitate. Spinning round, he ran across the hall and down the steps into the cold air. Seeing nobody, he hurried on to the stable yard, where Will was calmly rubbing down Alfred's damp coat while Gervase's horse, its nose in the water bucket, awaited its turn. Other than Will, there was nobody there either.

'Has anyone just arrived?' he panted.

'Not since you and the sheriff,' Will replied, not turning from his task.

Puzzled, Josse trotted back to the hall. Gervase was still standing by the secret box, arms folded, a frown on his face. 'Seems you were mistaken,' Josse said.

Gervase raised an eyebrow. 'Really? Perhaps it was your servants, back there.' He nodded towards the door to the kitchen. Then, before Josse could reply, he went on, 'This seems reasonably safe, Josse, although since you say most of your household know of its existence, I suggest you get a stonemason to make a new one and this time keep its location to yourself.'

'I trust my people,' Josse said shortly.

'I'm sure you do.' Gervase's tone was terse. 'Nevertheless, a secret known to many is no secret.'

'But I—' Josse began.

Gervase put up a hand to stop him. 'I must go back to Tonbridge,' he said. 'I need to speak to my deputies and learn if they have anything to report.'

'You will not stay and eat?' Josse was surprised at his sudden decision to leave.

'No, thank you. I will return to the abbey later today, and I hope to see you there, Josse.'

With the briefest of bows – a mere nod of the head – the sheriff turned and strode away.

The woman sank to her knees, her joints cracking and protesting as they made contact with the cold, hard stone. She closed her eyes, shutting out the view of the snow-clad mountains through the small window.

News had come to the lonely village; terrible news. When, she reflected bitterly, was there any other kind? Another stronghold had fallen, one they had all believed would stand for ever, unassailable as it was but to the nimble-footed goats. That devil in armour who led the enemy had somehow managed to bring a siege engine within range, and the usual brutal result had swiftly followed. Hangings, burnings, mutilations, terrible deaths.

The woman pressed her fists into her eyes, trying to blot out the vivid images. People bled when they burned. She hadn't known that . . .

She began to pray, at first saying the words silently, then gradually moving her lips until finally she was speaking out loud, her voice waxing in strength. Slowly, as if it were some grace given to her because of the fervour of her prayer, she began to feel comforted. At first, it was no more than the softest of touches, as if an angel's wing had brushed in a loving gesture against her cheek. She thought she heard a tiny snatch of music. Keeping her eyes closed, maintaining the fierce concentration, the sensations intensified, and suddenly it was as if a brilliant arrow of rich, golden light flashed across her vision.

Deep within her grieving heart, hope was born.

She opened her eyes and slowly turned her head to face the north.

EIGHT

Meggie and Ninian began their vigil early. Concealed in the gorse bushes and intent on the hunting lodge, Meggie reflected that the men within must be wealthy. In that time of privation, the feasting had gone on late into the night and, this morning, the servants had been up and about soon after first light, lighting fires and preparing yet more food and drink. Smoke curled lazily up from the roof of the lodge itself, and from the smaller building beyond, which must surely be the kitchen, a veritable blaze appeared to have been lit. Whatever was for breakfast – and Meggie's mouth watered as she thought about food – was going to be tasty and, more important, abundant.

She and Ninian, when they woke, had eaten exactly the same meal they had consumed last night: some strips of dried meat and half an apple.

Presently, men started to emerge from the lodge. In ones and twos, they went round to the back of the lodge, presumably to where some servant had dug a latrine ditch, and then crossed to where the horses had been tethered overnight in a lean-to. Even the horses were well cared for, Meggie observed. There was a generous layer of straw between them and the cold ground, and the hay nets were stuffed to bursting. The sound of metal clinking on metal floated out from the lean-to as the men tacked up their mounts.

Halfway along the line of horses there was a big chestnut gelding with two white socks on his forefeet. Even from the distance that separated them, Meggie could see he was a wonderful animal, with the gracefully arched neck, small ears and slightly concave nose that told of Arab blood. He would go like the wind. Beside him was a big black horse with a star on its brow. He, too, had the exotic look that came when an English bloodline had been infused with the fast, deft-footed horses that the crusaders had brought back with them.

As if he knew her attention was lapsing, Ninian nudged her.

'They'll be off soon,' he said into her ear. 'They'll leave
the servants to clear up and bring the kit.'

He seemed very knowledgeable about the habits of the
great. She smiled to herself. Well, he'd spent the years between
eight and fourteen in the house of a knight, learning how to
be a squire, so it was hardly surprising. 'I'm ready,' she
whispered back. 'The horses are packed, and we can be away
in a moment.'

He nodded. They went on watching.

When all the other men were mounted and ready, the leader
came out of the hunting lodge. He stopped in the doorway,
took a deep breath of the clean forest air and looked at the
rolling country all around.

Meggie's eyes were drawn to him. He was a strongly-built
man of medium height and looked to be in his early forties.
His thick hair sprang in waves and curls from his head, dark
reddish-brown in colour and tinged with grey at the temples.
He was barrel-chested, perhaps running to fat, although it was
difficult to tell his true shape beneath the heavily padded tunic.
It was a gorgeous garment, Meggie noticed, made of expensive
russet-coloured cloth and with costly embroidery at the neck.
He wore a wide belt of beautifully tooled leather, and from it
hung a jewelled scabbard that bore a sword. He also carried
a short knife.

He called out something to the men, and they all laughed.
Then he turned and spoke to somebody behind him, still within
the lodge. Meggie clutched Ninian's hand, but he had seen,
too, and together they watched as Rosamund stepped daintily
out into the soft morning sunshine.

'She is – oh, I truly believe she is unharmed,' Meggie whispered. 'Ninian, she's smiling.'

He nodded. 'Yes, I can see,' he whispered back. 'She must
be—'

Whatever he had been about to say, he stopped. Following
the direction of his eyes, Meggie watched as another man
emerged from the lodge. He was about Ninian's height and
build, and he wore a brown leather tunic, and over it a short
cloak with a hood.

She stared at him. Seeing him now, she understood exactly
why she had let Rosamund run after him in the woods near
to Josse's house. He really did look very like Ninian.

She dug her elbow into her brother's ribs. 'See?' she hissed. 'Do you wonder that Rosamund and I both mistook him for you? Especially when he was where we were expecting to see you, near to the House in the Woods.'

Ninian was watching the man. 'He's younger than me,' he said.

'Yes, but not by more than three or four years.' The man was now helping Rosamund up on to the black horse. Once she was secure, he sprang up behind her. 'He even moves like you,' Meggie added.

Ninian turned and grinned at her. 'I never blamed you anyway for Rosamund's disappearance, but if I did, I wouldn't any more. All right?'

She grinned back. 'All right.' Then, her eyes on Rosamund: 'Ninian, can't we just ride over to them and take her back?'

'I've been wondering the same thing.' He frowned. 'I've no idea why the man who looks like me abducted her, but for some reason he's now joined up with all those others, and I can't believe that they're all in it. It seems most likely that the – that their leader would see by Rosamund's reaction that she knows us and would readily let her go with us. But, Meggie, what if that didn't happen? What if they were determined to hold on to her?'

'We'd fight!' she hissed. 'I have my sword, and so have you, and we've got our knives!'

He sighed. 'I appreciate how you feel, but there are just too many of them. We can't fight ten well-armed men, and that's not counting however many servants there are milling around over there.'

The hot blood was racing through her, and for an instant she wanted to ignore him and rush out to rescue Rosamund all by herself. She took a deep breath and then another, deliberately calming herself. He was right. Tempting as it was to act right now, the risk was too great.

'Very well,' she said. 'We'll follow at a safe distance and see where they go.'

He did not speak, but the sudden hard hug he gave her was answer enough.

Josse was down in his habitual place with the Hawkenlye monks in the vale. When Gervase had so abruptly hurried

away from the House in the Woods earlier, he had felt guilty
about remaining there doing nothing but working his way
through a platter of Tilly's excellent cooking, so without
pausing for food he had fetched a disgruntled Alfred and ridden
back to the abbey. His stomach growling with hunger – for
the day was now well advanced and he had eaten nothing
since early morning – he had sought out Brother Saul and
asked if he could spare something to eat.

As if he, too, were recalling so many previous occasions,
Brother Saul appeared with a hot drink and a bowl of thin,
watery gruel and commented, 'Just like old times, eh, Sir
Josse?'

Josse took the wooden bowl, setting the mug carefully down
beside him on the ground. He smiled at the old lay brother.
'Thank you, Saul. Aye, it is. There's many a morning I've
scrounged a meal from the monks.'

He did not say so, but he could not recall a time when the
gruel had contained quite so little oatmeal. Nevertheless, he still
felt guilty about eating it, when there were so many far needier
than he.

Brother Saul watched as he ate and drank. 'Anything more
I can do for you?' he asked.

Josse shook his head. 'No, Saul, thank you.' Realizing that
Saul was undoubtedly hovering for another reason than tending
to Josse's needs, he said, 'No news yet, I'm afraid.'

Saul's face fell. 'The dead man's kin were not able to provide
any clue in the little girl's disappearance?'

'No. We still do not know that there's any connection between
Hugh de Brionne's death and Rosamund's disappearance.'

He had finished his meagre meal, and Saul took the empty
vessels from him. 'I'll go and pray for the lass,' he said. He
smiled briefly. 'If dear old Brother Firmin was still with us,
he'd be doing the rounds with his precious holy water to keep
our hopes up. Set a store by that water, did Brother Firmin.'

Josse watched him walk away. He was, Josse mused, far
too thin . . .

It was no good sitting here lamenting everything that was
wrong with the world. Standing up, he brushed the worst of
the dust and the creases out of his tunic, tightened his belt
over his hungry stomach and strode out of the monks' quarters.
Gervase had promised to return later, he recalled, once he had

seen his deputies to hear their reports and issue the day's orders. Josse decided he would suggest they resume the search for Rosamund by heading off to the north-west. It would save time if Josse was ready for Gervase when he arrived. Leaving the vale behind, he strode off up the path to the abbey.

In the hut in the forest, Helewise could not settle. She moved restlessly about, first inside, then out in the glade, striding to and fro, always straining to hear the slightest sound that might indicate Meggie was coming back. Despite Tiphaine's calm reassurances of the night before, she was increasingly worried about her.

Tiphaine made a simple noon meal for them. Helewise found it hard to eat. The food was not very appetizing, and anxiety had taken away her appetite. She wondered how she was going to endure another day and, when Tiphaine put on her cloak and announced she was off down to the abbey, Helewise went with her as far as the edge of the woodland.

'Will you come down with me, my lady?' Tiphaine asked.

'No, Tiphaine,' she replied. 'I think, however, that I shall stay here, by St Edmund's Chapel. I—' She shrugged. There was no need to explain.

'Your prayers will be heard,' Tiphaine said. Very quietly, she added something else, which sounded like *the Lady will hear you*. Then she turned and headed on down to the abbey.

The group from the hunting lodge set off along a track going roughly north-east. Meggie and Ninian found it easy to follow them, for the men were understandably confident of their safety, riding as they did in a large group, and nobody bothered about keeping a watch on the road behind.

On the road to the west and above Hawkenlye Vale, the party drew rein and halted. Meggie and Ninian swiftly left the track and, dismounting, lead their horses into the trees and hurried back to the road to observe.

'They're separating,' Ninian said. 'Look, one lot are heading off north, and the others seem to be going down towards the abbey.'

'The young man who has Rosamund is in the second group.' Meggie was watching closely. 'The man in the russet tunic is going with them, and a couple of others too. They've stuck close by him all the way,' she added. 'They look like his bodyguards.'

Ninian did not comment. She turned to him, a question framed, but he leapt up and hurried back to their horses. Soon they had remounted and were following the smaller group on the road to the vale. After a couple of miles, it became clear they were not going down into the vale, for they had taken a narrow track that swung round to skirt it to the south.

'I think,' Ninian said, 'they intend to go round to the east of the abbey and enter through the main gates.'

'Too grand to trot up the path that leads to the little west gate?' Meggie suggested.

'More likely because the main gate's more suitable for horsemen. Come on –' he kicked his horse to a canter – 'they're getting too far ahead. Even if we're fairly sure where they are bound, we don't want to lose them.'

They hurried on. Meggie could make out the members of the group quite clearly now. The leader, in his russet tunic. The man who looked like Ninian, Rosamund sitting in front of him on the black horse. The two burly men who she thought were bodyguards. What were they going to do? Would they ride into the abbey and say that they had found Rosamund wandering and so had brought her to that place of safety so that the nuns could look after her until she could be reunited with her family? It seemed likely. Perhaps the man in the russet tunic had been angry with the young man who'd taken Rosamund – Meggie recalled the furious, shouting voice last evening – and wanted to put a wrong to rights as quickly as he could. If he was the young man's lord, as he seemed to be, then it would be up to him to inflict punishment and—

The group had split again. The bodyguards were riding away northwards along the track to the abbey gates. The man in the tunic and the man who looked like Ninian, with Rosamund still sitting in front of him, were heading off to the east.

They were not heading for the abbey at all.

Meggie felt sick with dread. A loud warning alarm was ringing inside her head. Something was about to happen, something terrible. She knew it was, and she did not know how to prevent it.

The two horses were cantering up the gentle slope towards the dense woodland. Just up there, directly ahead of them, was St Edmund's Chapel. Filled with horror, Meggie looked at Ninian.

There was no time to explain, and, indeed, she had no idea what she would have said. All the strange skills that she had inherited from her mother and her grandmother seemed to coalesce, and she felt as if her skin were tingling. She did not know if Ninian felt it too; just then it did not matter. She kicked her horse and yelled, '*Hurry*!'

Rosamund was worried. They had told her they were going to Hawkenlye Abbey, and she had been very relieved because she knew lots of the nuns and the monks there and they would look after her. She did not understand what had happened. The man – his name was Olivier – had been kind to her and she quite liked him, but he had told her quite a lot of lies. He'd said there was going to be a party, and that she must not tell her family because it was meant to be a surprise. Well, that amounted to a lie because although there had been a sort of party at that lodge place last night, none of her family had been there, so it wouldn't have mattered if she'd told them after all.

She did not know what to make of the lord. He was kind, too, and he had made her laugh. He'd made sure she had a nice private place to sleep – as private as possible, anyway, in a lodge full of men – and he had come over himself to make sure his orders had been carried out. Rosamund thought he was quite a grand lord. For one thing, he had been hunting and stayed at that lodge, and for another, it seemed to her that he was used to issuing a lot of commands and having them instantly obeyed. Olivier and the other men called him *my lord* and most of them seemed really in awe of him.

Rosamund was worried because now it looked as if they were not going to the abbey after all. It might still be all right if instead they were going where she thought they were . . . She felt Olivier kick his heels into Star's sides to encourage him up the long slope, and, looking to her right, she saw the lord's lovely chestnut gelding cantering easily along beside them. The horse was so light on his feet that he almost looked as if he were flying.

They reached the place where a semicircle of land jutted out from the dense woodland, almost opposite the abbey gates below. Olivier drew Star to a halt, and the chestnut stopped close beside them. Olivier was talking to himself. It frightened Rosamund, and she twisted round to look at him.

His eyes looked odd. They were wild and darting from side to side as if he was trying to watch several people all at once. That was peculiar too, because Rosamund could not see anyone in the clearing except the lord on the chestnut horse. She listened, trying to make out what Olivier was saying.

'I did it,' he whispered. 'Yes I did, and you can't tell me I didn't. This time I got it right and I haven't made any mistakes.'

Whoever he thought he was talking to must have replied. He was quiet for a few moments, as if listening, then he hissed, 'I did! I *did* do it right!'

She did not know what to do. Every instinct told her to get away from him. He scared her. He still had an arm around her waist, but it did not feel as if he was holding her very tightly. Without giving herself time to think too much – she knew her nerve might fail if she did – she wriggled out of his grasp and slid down to the ground, landing with a thud and jarring one ankle.

'Ow!' she cried.

Olivier leapt down after her and was just about to grab her when the lord said curtly, 'No.'

He, too, was off his horse. He walked across to her and, bending down, smiled at her. 'You know this place, do you not, Rosamund?' he asked.

She eyed him warily. 'Ye–es,' she said slowly. There seemed no harm in agreeing.

'You've been here before,' he went on. He reached out and took her hand, clasping it lightly in his. 'I would guess that you come here quite frequently.'

'It's St Edmund's Chapel,' Rosamund said. Everyone knew that. 'It was built by Queen Eleanor, and it's where people go to pray for the soul of King Richard.' Everybody knew that, too. She wasn't giving anything away.

There was only one thing that was secret. Rosamund swore to herself that nothing on earth would make her reveal it.

He still held her hand. There was a pause while he looked right into her eyes. His were so blue, so very blue. She waited. 'I think you come here with someone else,' he said. He was panting, she noticed, as if he had been running hard.

'Sometimes I come with my grandmother,' she said. Was that what he wanted to know?

'No, not your grandmother!' For an instant he sounded impatient and the nice smile vanished, but then quickly it was back. 'You come with a much younger woman, a very pretty girl with brown, curly hair and eyes that dance with light.' His mouth was open, and his thick tongue came out like a darting snake and licked his lips.

Rosamund knew who he meant. She did not understand why this man with the hungry eyes and the wet mouth wanted to find Meggie, but she knew enough to realize that it would not be good if he found her.

She opened her eyes wide and said, 'I come here with the nuns. Some of them are young but, of course, you can't see what colour their hair is because they're veiled.'

He let go of her hand. His arms shot out, and he grabbed her by the shoulders. His fingers were hard, pushing into her flesh, and they hurt. She knew then how dangerous he was.

She was not without courage. She said, very clearly, 'You are hurting me.'

Instantly, his grip relaxed. He gave a short laugh, which sounded as if he was putting it on. Then he drew a couple of breaths and said, very nicely, 'I saw you here three days ago. You were with her then. I watched you.'

She said, 'What do you want with her?'

Then she understood, child though she was. She knew what men and women did together. She knew that when they wanted to have a baby they mated just like the animals did. She tried not to think about it, for it disturbed her.

This man wanted to do those things with Meggie. And Rosamund would have willingly gone into the chapel and sworn before God that Meggie didn't want him to.

She stood up straight, wishing her knees were not trembling so much. 'I don't know who you mean.'

He shook her hard. 'Oh, yes, you do,' he said, his voice cold and menacing, 'and you *will* tell me, even if I have to wring it out of you.'

Then a lot of things happened at once. Rosamund heard the sound of racing footsteps coming up behind her and, spinning round, she saw Ninian leap on Olivier's back and grasp him tightly, pinning his arms to his sides.

And in front of her, a cool voice said, 'You will not do that. I am here to stop you.'

Twisting back again, Rosamund saw Meggie standing before her. She had a sword in her hand.

Meggie and Ninian had left their horses on the forest fringe, tethered out of sight of the chapel. They had crept through the dense trees on tracks that Meggie knew as well as she knew the lines on her own hands, coming out behind the chapel. They watched as the two horses came to a halt out on the open ground, and they listened, as best they could, to what was being said.

Meggie had misinterpreted the threat. She believed, in the first horrified moments, that the lord in the russet tunic was hunting for the chapel's secret: for the Black Madonna that her own mother had sent back here from the goddess's former place of concealment in the cathedral at Chartres. She thought that the power surging through her came straight from Joanna, and that it was commanding her to defend the goddess and keep her safe from this man, whoever he was. Carefully, deliberately, she placed herself between him and the chapel.

Now she watched as he shook Rosamund. *He will make the poor child tell him what he wants to know*, she thought. She heard his furious words: 'You *will* tell me, even if I have to wring it out of you.'

Ninian had gone around behind the other man. Meggie did not even stop to think whether he was still a threat, or whether Ninian would succeed in holding him off. Drawing her sword, she stepped out from her hiding place in the underbrush and walked across the clearing.

Even as Meggie made her calm announcement, Rosamund was already pulling herself out of the lord's grasp and running over to her, calling out her name. Meggie put out her left arm and drew the girl fiercely to her side. 'Are you all right?' she whispered.

'Yes!' Rosamund breathed. Then: 'He wants you, Meggie. He wants to bed you.'

Meggie opened her mouth in amazement. For an absurd moment she wanted to laugh. He was not after the Black Madonna. He was after *her*. Then she saw that the younger man had wrestled himself out of Ninian's arms. Even as she watched, he pushed Ninian away and drew his sword.

Slowly, the man in the russet tunic stood up. He was looking right at her. 'It's you,' he said. It felt to Meggie as if the fire in his blue eyes was searing against her bare skin. He took a step towards her and instinctively, still clutching Rosamund, she moved back. Slowly, he shook his head in wonder. 'Against all expectation, this fool's plan –' he nodded in direction of the man – 'has achieved the right result.'

She stared at him. She could sense his fierce lust; she could smell it in the beads of sweat on his flushed face. He extended his hands to her. 'My lady, will you not approach and—'

She did not wait to hear any more. She raised her sword and brought it down in a wide, sweeping curve . . .

. . . only to have it blocked by his. He had reached down and drawn it from its scabbard with a speed she would not have thought possible.

She did not know what would have happened next had a sudden, piercing cry not rung out across the clearing. Rosamund shrieked, the lord spun round and, with the strong pressure his sword had been exerting on hers suddenly gone, Meggie stumbled and fell.

Ninian's opponent had a long cut on his left forearm and the blood was pouring down his hand. The cut was no mortal blow, however, and Meggie watched in horror as, with a howl of rage, the young man raised his sword and lunged at Ninian. Ninian, sword in his right hand and knife in his left, waited, poised on his toes, and Meggie could see the tension in him. The lord was already hurrying up behind him; Ninian was surrounded.

She pushed Rosamund away from her and launched herself after the lord. He spun round and snarled at her and, just for an instant, both Ninian and the young man were staring at her too. The blood pounded through her body, and she saw a red mist before her eyes; through it came the sudden, sharp aware-ness that all three men had bright blue eyes.

They all turned inward to face each other. Three swords were held high, and then, as the young man closed on Ninian and the lord launched himself on them both, the long weapons became useless and the knives were drawn.

For the blink of an eye she watched the struggle, then she ran over to join in.

She did not see exactly how it happened, but all at once the young man lay still on the ground, the lord was kneeling down clutching both hands to his shoulder and Ninian stood alone, a bloody knife in his hand.

She met his eyes. There was triumph in his face. But he was wrong to feel jubilant, for now the danger was even greater. '*Run!*' she yelled.

He looked at her, wiping blood from his lip with his left hand.

'*Go!*' She ran across to him, pushing at him. Still wild from the fight, he felt as hard as iron. She put her hands on his shoulders, pulling him close. 'Ninian, if he's dead they'll make sure you hang!' she cried urgently. 'He's a great lord, and you've felled one of his men! Even if you and I swear it was two against one and they attacked you, who will be believed?'

Still he did not move.

Desperate now, Meggie went in for the kill. 'What would it do to Josse if you were hanged?' she demanded, sobbing. 'He loves you like a son, and he's already lost our mother. Would you break his heart again?'

She had reached him. She knew it. He sheathed his knife, bent to pick up his sword and, straightening, gave her a hard hug. Then he turned and ran.

NINE

Meggie waited until she could no longer hear him. Rosamund had come to stand beside her, pressing herself close against Meggie's body. Absently, she smoothed the girl's fine hair. 'The danger is past now,' she murmured. 'You're safe with me.'

The desire to take to her heels and, grabbing Rosamund's hand, run as fast as she could to the hut in the forest was all but overwhelming. The hut was where she had lived as a child with her mother. It was the most secure place that she knew, for very few people were aware of its existence. Meggie knew how to make it all but invisible. She had seen her mother work that particular piece of magic when she needed to hide from the world, although Meggie did not think that her mother had known her little girl was watching and memorizing the chant and the actions.

Meggie wished with all her heart that her mother was there in the wildwood waiting for her. She wasn't; she had gone, and she would not come back.

Meggie knew she couldn't go where her heart desired. For one thing, if she ran away with Rosamund now, the girl's poor parents would have to wait even longer to know she was safe. Meggie could barely imagine what they had been enduring. She had briefly explored a little way towards Paradisa's mind, but it had hurt very much and she had stopped.

The other reason – two reasons, really – were in the clearing with her. One was lying on the ground and not moving; the other had sat down on the grass and, one hand clamped to his shoulder, was staring at the blood welling up between his fingers.

Meggie disengaged herself from Rosamund. Her hands on the girl's shoulders, she stared into the wide eyes. 'I want you to go over to the edge of the clearing and keep an eye on the abbey gates,' she said. 'If you see one of the nuns or monks, yell as hard as you can to catch their attention.'

Rosamund's trembling stopped as soon as Meggie finished

issuing her simple command. Watching her hurry away across the grass, Meggie smiled. She was a plucky girl and, given a task, she had put her fear and her horror aside and got on with doing what she was told.

Meggie spun round and went over to the man lying on the ground. She glanced at the man in the russet tunic and saw that his eyes were on her. 'I will come to you in a moment,' she said calmly. 'Your companion here appears to be the more gravely wounded, so I must tend to him first.'

She knelt beside the young man, her hand out to touch his face. His skin was cool and clammy. She put her fingers to his throat, feeling for the pulse of life. She was not sure if it was there. She bent over him, her cheek against his mouth, and felt the faintest in and out of his breath.

Then, when she knew he was alive, she began examining him. He had a wound in his side, under his right arm. It was quite deep and bleeding a great deal. She reached under her skirt and grabbed her linen underskirt, biting the cloth with her teeth and ripping a length of fabric. She balled it up and pressed it against the wound, undoing the man's belt and fastening it up again over the pad of cloth. She noticed bruising across his ribs and wondered if he had winded himself. He needed more help than she could provide, for she had no medicaments and no proper bandages, and the day was cold. She got up and hurried over to the older man.

'Let me see,' she commanded. He took his hand away from his shoulder. His wound was less deep, but still bad enough. She tore another length off her underskirt, again folding a pad and putting it against the cut. 'Press that, very hard,' she said.

He obeyed. She sat back on her heels watching as the blood stained the white linen. It seemed to her that the flow was already lessening.

She felt his eyes on her. Turning, she saw that he was smiling. 'I have had many wounds,' he remarked, 'but never such an exotic bandage. May I be permitted to keep this piece of your delectable underskirt, lady?'

Against all expectations, she laughed.

His smile widened, and he chuckled. 'I thought you might be offended,' he said. 'I thought you might get angry again, like you did just now, and stab my other shoulder.'

She was still smiling. Whatever sort of a predator he was, he had charm. 'That was then,' she said. 'Now, you are wounded. You are in my care, and I am not in the habit of sticking my sword into my patients.'

'That's lucky,' he observed. 'You swing a sword like a man, although your technique could be refined.' The blue eyes blazed up at her, full of a seductive heat that required the swift assembly of her defences. 'I'll give you some lessons, if you like.'

'Yes, I will accept,' she said calmly. 'Once you are healed, that is.'

She got to her feet. As she did so she heard him say her name, just once, so softly that she only just picked it up. She stared down at him. 'I am going to Hawkenlye Abbey for help,' she said. 'I will be quick. Your companion there is, I think, unconscious. He has a bad wound in his side, and he should stay still. I have stemmed the bleeding as best I can—'

'That wonderfully accommodating petticoat,' the man murmured.

'—but if he tries to sit up, it will get much worse.'

The man looked across at the still figure on the grass. 'I will try to make sure he does not,' he said. He met her eyes again. Serious now, he added, 'You have my word.'

She nodded. She had done her best. She turned and ran across the clearing, where she caught Rosamund by the hand. The two of them flew as fast as they could down the slope to the abbey.

No matter how strong the urge was to go back immediately with helpers and medicaments to aid the two men up by the chapel, Meggie's first duty was to Rosamund. She took the girl straight to Abbess Caliste's room where, much to Meggie's relief, the abbess was working at her table.

On seeing who Meggie had with her, the abbess's face broke into a brilliant smile. She leapt up from her chair and flew across the small room, swooping down and taking Rosamund in her arms in a quick, intense hug.

'You are unharmed?' She broke away, holding Rosamund at arm's length and running anxious eyes over her.

'I am perfectly well, thank you, my lady,' Rosamund replied politely.

Abbess Caliste looked up at Meggie. 'Where did you fid her? Did you—?'

'My lady, I am sorry but I cannot stay to explain,' Meggie said. 'Two men lie wounded by St Edmund's Chapel and, with your permission, I will take a party to help them and bring them back to the infirmary.'

Abbess Caliste stood up, put the emotion of the moment aside and said briskly, 'Of course. Tell Sister Liese that you have my authority to take whoever she thinks.' Her eyes slipped back to Rosamund, and a trace of her beatific smile returned. 'Meanwhile, you and I, young lady, will send word to your parents, so that they may come to rejoice with us and give thanks for your safe return.'

Meggie had to admire Sister Liese's efficiency. Within a very short time, she had assembled four sturdy monks to carry the two stretchers and a nursing nun to accompany her to tend the wounded. Meggie had briefly described the wounds, and Sister Liese and her companion each carried satchels containing all that they would need. Sister Liese nodded to Meggie and said, 'Lead the way, please.'

Meggie set a fast pace back up the slope to the chapel. To her great relief, the younger man was still lying just as she had left him. Pointing across the clearing, she said to Sister Liese, 'He has the worse wound. There is a bad cut under his right arm, a long slash to the left forearm and there may be other injuries too.' The fight had been so devastatingly swift that she had no idea what had happened.

Sister Liese nodded. 'What about him?' She looked at the older man, who was lying back with his eyes closed. 'Where's his wound?'

'In the right shoulder and not as bad. He has lost much blood, however, and is probably feeling faint.'

Sister Liese issued some brief commands, and immediately the nursing nun bent to attend to the man in the russet tunic. The infirmarer went over to the younger man, gently loosening the belt and removing the makeshift bandage. She looked up at Meggie, who had hurried to stand anxiously behind her.

'The bleeding is slowing,' she said. 'You did well.' For an instant she eyed Meggie with undisguised curiosity, and then went back to her patient.

Very soon, the infirmarer deemed both men ready to be moved. With gentle hands, the monks got them on to the stretchers, and they set off back to the abbey, the nuns in attendance. Meggie watched them as they carefully descended the slope. She was about to follow when abruptly her legs gave way and she found herself sitting on the grass.

Shock, she told herself firmly. Shock, and too much running around. She raised her knees and folded her arms on top of them, dropping her head and giving in to her fatigue. But as soon as she relaxed, an image of Ninian flew into her mind.

Her head shot up. Where was he? Oh, she did not even know if he had taken his horse! Leaping up, she ran to where they had left the two animals, on the fringe of the forest. Both horses were still there. She put her arms around Daisy's neck and leaned against her. The mare gave a soft whicker and nudged her nose against Meggie's shoulder.

'I don't know where he's gone,' Meggie whispered to her. 'He's fled on foot, so I guess he is within the forest.' In the most secret ways of the wildwood, progress on horseback was all but impossible. She put a hand out to Ninian's horse, unwinding the reins. 'You'd better come with us, my friend Garnet,' she said to him. 'Ninian may well have need of you, before long.'

Slowly, she led both horses along the track that curved around the bulge of the forest and back to the clearing before the chapel. She was about to head on down to the abbey, but all at once she knew what she needed. Tethering the horses once more, she crossed the grass and went into the chapel.

She knew straight away that something was wrong. The chapel was small and very simple, and one glance sufficed to take in the stone flags of the floor, the pale oak rood screen and the unadorned altar with its plain cross. Her heart beating hard, Meggie crossed to the flagstone that, although few knew it, was also a trapdoor concealing the steps down to the crypt. She had seen as soon as she entered that it was not quite closed.

Many possibilities raced through her head, each worse than the one before and all pointing to the terrible suspicion that somebody had slipped into the chapel, opened the trapdoor and descended to the place that held the chapel's secret. Would the Black Madonna still be there? Or had she vanished?

She pushed back the trapdoor, and it crashed against the floor. She flew down the narrow little steps and, ducking her head beneath the low arch, burst into the crypt.

In front of the niche where the Black Goddess sat, somebody

stood guard. She had a heavy stick in her hand. As Meggie sprang out before her, she swung it up over her head.

'Keep away! You cannot have her!' she shouted.

Meggie fell against her, enveloping her in her arms. 'It's me!' she cried. 'It's all right, it's me!'

The stick fell with a thud to the floor and Helewise said, 'Meggie! Oh, *Meggie*!'

The two women hugged. Meggie could hear Helewise's heart thumping in her chest. 'What were you *doing*?' Meggie asked.

'I heard voices, shouting,' Helewise replied, with a slightly shaky laugh. 'I was up in the chapel praying that Rosamund would be found today, and suddenly there were people outside and the sounds of a scuffle. I was quite sure they had come for the goddess. I had to save her.'

Meggie looked at her lovingly. 'Where did you get your weapon?'

Helewise laughed again. 'There's a little bench in the corner there, for when people want to sit in vigil down here. I pulled one of its legs off.'

'Strong as well as resourceful,' Meggie murmured. Then something struck her. 'Did you not feel similarly compelled to protect the wooden cross on the altar?'

Helewise gave her a serene smile. 'I did not feel that was in any danger.'

Meggie reached for her hand. 'Your prayers have been answered,' she said gently.

Helewise's expression went from confusion to doubt to a tentative hope. 'You mean they've found her?'

'Yes. She's down at the abbey.'

Helewise closed her eyes, and her lips moved silently. Then, looking at Meggie, she said, 'Go and find your father. Abbess Caliste will have sent someone to notify Rosamund's parents, and Josse should be told too, as soon as possible.'

'There's—' Meggie had been about to say that there was something else she had to tell Josse: about Ninian and what had happened outside the chapel. But she stopped herself. Let Helewise enjoy this moment of joy for a while. 'I will,' she said instead.

Back at the abbey, Meggie learned that riders had already been sent to New Winnowlands to find Dominic and Paradisa, and

out to the north and west of the abbey, to where Josse and
Gervase were searching. Josse and the sheriff, however, had
been on their way back to the abbey when the messenger
found them and, as he gave them the news, Gervase had very
gladly given the order that all search parties could now stand
down. Then he had headed down to Tonbridge to spread the
word there, and Josse had ridden as hard as he could back to
Hawkenlye, where Meggie had been waiting.

She took her father aside to speak to him privately. 'Father,
there was a fight up by the chapel,' she said quickly. 'Ninian
and I were trailing the men who had Rosamund. He struggled
with two of them and both were wounded, one badly.'

Josse's face had paled. 'Will he live?'

'I do not know. Both are in the infirmary.'

'And Ninian?'

'He was unhurt, at least I believe so. But, Father, these men
are important lords, men of wealth and power! They are richly
clad – at least, one of them is – and they ride fine horses.
They were hunting on the Ashdown Forest, and only men of
high position are allowed to do that. If Ninian has killed one
of them – even if the man lives, Ninian inflicted a grave wound
– then they won't rest till he's caught and hanged.'

Josse watched her, pain darkening his eyes. 'He has fled?'
he asked.

She nodded. 'I told him to. It seemed the only thing he could
do.'

Josse did not speak for some time. Then he put his arm
around her shoulder and hugged her to him. 'I don't know,
my love, if what you did was sensible,' he said. 'It could be
argued that Ninian would have been wiser to stand his ground
and defend his actions – you say there were two of them, so
he could surely have been forgiven for defending himself when
they attacked.'

'But—' she began.

He stopped her. 'Dearest, I said your action might not have
been sensible,' he murmured. 'What I was going to say was
that, sensible or not, it's what I would have done too.' He bent
to put a kiss on her forehead. 'Better to have fled than take
the terrible risk of a trial going against him.'

They stood together for some moments and, as she had
always done, she took strength from him and from the great

love she knew he had for her. Then he took her hand and, with a brave attempt at a smile, said, 'Come on. We had better visit these two important lords of yours.'

The men had been installed at the far end of the infirmary, a little away from the other patients. Josse, still holding his daughter's hand, walked the length of the ward, aware of many pairs of curious eyes on them. He smiled to himself. The average humble peasant coming to Hawkenlye with a broken wrist or a chesty cough was not normally treated to the spectacle of two of the lordly class borne in on stretchers, and the story would no doubt soon be spreading far and wide.

Josse glanced at Meggie. She was biting her lip, a sign that she was feeling anxious. She loved her half-brother dearly, Josse reflected. If she sensed that she had advised him ill, she would not forgive herself.

We shall have to make sure he is safe, Josse thought.

They had reached the far end of the infirmary. Sister Liese stood waiting for them. Greeting Josse, she drew back the curtain to the recess on her right. 'This is the more seriously injured man,' she said, standing back to allow Josse and Meggie into the cubicle. 'Your daughter did well,' the infirmarer added. 'The care she gave him immediately after he received his wound probably saved his life.'

Josse gave Meggie's hand a squeeze, which she returned. There would be time later to tell her how proud he was of her.

'How is he?' Josse asked. He studied the young man. He was around twenty, with a square face and brown hair, although the stubble of beard on his jaw was closer to red than brown. He recalled that the man who had taken Rosamund had been mistaken for Ninian, but under the present circumstances, with this man lying in bed and unconscious, it was hard to tell how strong the resemblance was. 'Do we know his name? Has anyone asked his companion?'

'I do not believe so,' the infirmarer replied. 'As yet, Sir Josse, we have been fully occupied with tending the two men, and there has not been time for such matters.'

'No, I understand,' Josse said. He took another look at the still figure. This man had a great deal to answer for. 'Sister, please will you inform me when he can speak to me?'

She bowed her head. 'I will.'

'Now, if you please, I would like to see the other man.'

Sister Liese led the way out of the recess, across the infirmary and into the cubicle on the opposite side. Here there was another narrow bed and, in it, a man dressed only in his undershirt, a clean sheet drawn up to his waist. The blood had been washed away from his shoulder, and now the wound was covered in a neat bandage that wove across his broad chest and around his arm.

Josse stopped dead and stared at him.

As the shock receded a little and he began to think he might be able to breathe again after all, the one thought that filled his head, loud and insistent as a war cry, was: *Thank God Meggie persuaded Ninian to flee!*

For the man in the bed was no ordinary lord . . .

Josse dropped on one knee, dragging Meggie down beside him. He waited.

'Josse d'Acquin,' the man said. 'It must be near twenty years since I have set eyes on you.'

Josse looked up to meet the intense blue stare. 'Eighteen years, if I may say so, sire.'

'I wondered if I would be seeing something of you,' the man went on conversationally, 'when the child mentioned that she lived at New Winnowlands. Your place, I believe.'

'Indeed it – er, that's so, lord.'

The man nodded slowly. 'I do not forget, you see, Josse,' he murmured. 'The little girl is kin to you?'

'Not to me. She is the granddaughter of Helewise Warin, once abbess here.'

'Ah, yes.' His eyes strayed to Meggie. Watching intently, Josse could have sworn his lips twisted into a quick smile. 'And who is this?'

Josse took a deep breath. There was a correct way of doing this, but he had quite forgotten what it was. Well, since memory had failed, common courtesy would have to do. He stood up, pulling Meggie with him. 'My lord, may I present my daughter Meggie?' He took her hand and put it into that of the man in the bed. 'Meggie, make your curtsey to King John.'

TEN

Meggie rose from her deep bow and found the bright blue eyes studying her intently. 'So that is who you are,' he said softly. He glanced at Josse. 'Who is her mother?'

Meggie did not know if it was against etiquette to address a king when he had not first spoken to you, but she did not let it stop her. 'My mother was Joanna de Courtenay,' she said.

His blue gaze had returned to her. 'De Courtenay,' he repeated. 'I believe I have heard the name before. Did she have connections at court?'

Meggie opened her mouth to speak, but even as she did so, Josse trod on her foot, quite hard. 'A distant cousin, I believe, my lord,' he said easily. 'That is probably why the name is familiar to you.'

The king studied Josse. Meggie could see that he was not entirely convinced. A warning sounded in her head. *This is a man to watch,* she thought. *He is intelligent and cunning, and he will not easily be deceived.*

She wondered why her father did not want her to reveal Joanna's connection with the court . . .

Josse had edged forward so that now he stood between Meggie and the king. 'My lord, I regret greatly the mischance that has brought you here, but might I be permitted to ask if you can help us with another grave matter?'

The king waved a hand in assent. 'You may.'

'You have been in the area for a few days, sire?'

'Yes. My agents came here to the abbey, and I took the chance to visit the chapel which my revered and lamented mother built in remembrance of my brother, the late king. From there I went on to the hunting lodge on the Ashdown Forest.' A smile quirked the side of his mouth. 'The sport was excellent.'

'I am glad to hear it, my lord,' Josse muttered. 'Did you – may I ask you if a man by the name of Hugh de Brionne was of your company?'

The languid air vanished as the king heard the name. 'Hugh de Brionne was with me when we reached the abbey,' he confirmed. 'I know him well. He is a sound man.' Narrowing his eyes, he stared at Josse as if he were trying to read his mind. 'You have news of Hugh; I see it in your face. Tell me.'

'He is dead, sire,' Josse said simply. 'His body was discovered early yesterday, by a bend in the river between here and Hartfield.'

'How did he die?' The words rapped out like a stabbing knife.

'It appears he was in a fight. There were the marks of fists on his face, and his hands were bruised and swollen. There was a wound to the back of his head, presumably where he fell, and this is probably what killed him.'

The king did not speak for some time. Meggie crept closer to Josse, in need of his stolid strength. She was afraid, and she did not yet understand why.

Eventually, the king closed his eyes and, with a wince of pain, leaned back on his pillows. 'Be careful how you break the news to my companion,' he said quietly. 'He is Olivier de Brionne, and he is Hugh's brother.'

Josse and Meggie were outside the infirmary. Sister Liese, coming to check on her patients, had observed the king's pallor, and his obvious fatigue, and sent them away. The other man – Olivier de Brionne, they now knew – was still unconscious.

Josse took hold of Meggie's hands. 'This is very grave,' he muttered, frowning deeply. 'We must find Ninian and help him get right away. No accusations have yet been made against him, but two men lie wounded and one of them is the king.' He looked down at his daughter. 'I am sorry that I crushed your foot,' he said with a faint smile.

'You did no lasting damage,' she replied. 'But, Father, why did you not wish me to speak of my mother's court connections?'

He frowned thoughtfully, trying to find the right words. 'Daughter, your mother had no reason to treasure the memory of what happened to her; far from it. A cousin of hers, considerably older than she was, took her to King Henry's Christmas court one year, because she was young, innocent and very lovely and the cousin wished to impress the king and his lascivious friends with new blood. Then—' He stopped. This was not his story to tell. If Joanna had not revealed to Meggie the truth of what had happened to her, then it was not up to Josse to do so. 'My love, it may be that one day you will be told,' he said. 'There is a connection between our family and the king, but, if he has forgotten it or did not know of it, then I do not want to bring it to his mind.' He studied her face. 'Is that enough?'

Slowly, she nodded. She was thinking hard, he could tell. 'It is,' she said presently. 'I trust you, Father.'

But Josse hardly heard. His mind had gone back to a day more than eighteen years ago when Joanna had first told him about herself. They had lain together beside the fire, in the house where Josse now lived with his extended family. The memory was so vivid, bringing both overwhelming joy and sudden sharp pain, that for a moment he felt faint.

Meggie was looking at him anxiously. 'What is it, Father?' she asked. 'Are you unwell?'

'No, no!' He hastened to reassure her. The day he was remembering was around the time of her conception. Such things were not for a daughter to hear, although he yearned to tell her. They all said she was so like him, this beloved child of his, and such remarks always made his heart glow with pride. But, sometimes, he wished she looked more like her mother . . .

He was aware of Meggie beside him, concerned for him and gently rubbing her fingers across the back of his hand. 'It's cold out here, Father,' she said. 'You are shivering. Won't you go inside?'

He turned to her, shaking himself out of his reverie and trying to summon a smile. There was enough to worry about in the here and now without mourning over things he could not control. 'Dearest, I must think what to do,' he said briskly. 'I sense some dreadful threat hanging over me – hanging over all of us – and I am fearful.' He attempted a laugh but it was a miserable failure. 'You will think I am being foolish, no doubt, and—'

But she took his hand and tightened her fingers around it. 'No, I don't,' she said. 'For one thing, I hardly ever think you're foolish, and for another, I feel exactly the same.'

He met her eyes. He did not know if to be relieved that she so readily gave him her support or even more worried because she shared his fears. On balance, the latter won.

'We should—' he began.

Just then one of the nursing nuns appeared in the infirmary doorway, looked around and caught sight of them. Hurrying over, she said, 'I am glad to find you still here, Sir Josse! Sister Liese sent me to fetch you. The second man brought in earlier has recovered consciousness. Sister Liese says you must come.'

With the sense that he was going to some fateful encounter, Josse squared his shoulders and, with Meggie beside him, went back into the infirmary.

The young man had awakened to fear so intense that his first instinct was to leap out of the strange bed with the worn but clean sheets and run. The smallest movement, however, caused such a fire of agony in his right side and his left forearm that he quickly changed his mind. Paralysed by his pain and his terror, he quickly closed his eyes again, taking refuge in the pretence of continuing unconsciousness.

He wondered where he was. Risking a quick look, he saw curtains and, in the narrow gap between them, a glimpse of more beds and a well-scrubbed stone-flagged floor. He saw a woman in black, then another. He closed his eyes once more. He must be in the infirmary at Hawkenlye Abbey. It was the obvious place to bring a wounded man.

He thought about the fight. He saw again the blue-eyed man with the knife and the long sword. He recalled the ferocity of the attack and the terrible moment when he had believed he was about to die. Then there had been three of them, grappling together in a painful knot of fists, elbows, knives . . . Somehow he had defended himself and, as the hot blood rush had coursed through him, he knew he had made a strike. Against who, he was not so sure.

He heard voices. His lord's, speaking to a woman who sounded calm and composed as she answered the questions. He listened. They did not seem to be discussing anything of great note.

Then his lord spoke a name, and suddenly the young man was fully alert. 'Hugh de Brionne is dead, they tell me,' the lord was saying, 'and his body lies here at the abbey.'

Hugh was dead. *Dead.* The young man began to shake.

'—must break the news as soon as he wakes up,' the lord went on. 'He will take it hard.'

A tear rolled out of the young man's eye.

After a moment, he called out in a weak voice for water, and almost immediately a black-clad nun appeared in the recess to tend him.

Josse watched as Olivier de Brionne's bed was carefully lifted by a quartet of lay brothers and carried across to where the king lay reclining against his pillows, in the opposite recess. There were matters to discuss, matters that could not be yelled out loud over the width of the large room. Turning to Meggie, gently Josse told her to wait outside. Then he went into the recess and drew the curtains.

The king said, 'Josse, this is Olivier de Brionne. Tell him, if you will, about Hugh.'

Josse turned to look at the young man. He saw straight away the resemblance to Ninian that Meggie had seen. The blue eyes were unmistakable. 'I am very sorry to inform you that your brother Hugh is dead,' he said gently.

Olivier opened and closed his mouth a couple of times, licked his dry lips and said, 'I heard them say so. How did he die?'

'From the bruises and abrasions to his face and his knuckles, it appears he was in a fight,' Josse replied. His heart ached with pity for the young man's evident anguish. 'His opponent drove him backwards, or perhaps pushed him, and he fell, crushing his skull against a stone.'

'Crushing his skull,' Olivier repeated in a whisper. Then he screwed his eyes up tightly, as if trying to shut out the dreadful image.

Josse wished there were some comfort that he could offer. He had been informed – by Hugh and Olivier's own mother – of the relationship between her sons. *The brothers are not close*, she had said. Yet, observing Olivier's evident grief and distress, he wondered if she had misread her sons.

'I do not think that he suffered,' Josse said, looking down at the pale, strained face. 'The blow would have knocked him out instantly.'

Olivier said nothing for some time. Then his eyes opened

and he stared at Josse. 'Who killed him?' he whispered. 'Have you any idea?'

'No,' Josse admitted. 'Gervase de Gifford, who is sheriff of Tonbridge, is on his way here.' A messenger had been sent urgently to find him as soon as the identity of Olivier's companion had been revealed. 'He is an efficient and resourceful man, and he does not give up. He will bring your brother's murderer to justice, have no fear.'

Momentarily, Olivier closed his eyes again, and Josse, respecting his grief, bowed his head.

But then Olivier spoke. 'I have a suggestion,' he said.

Josse glanced at the king, who nodded. 'We would hear it, if you please,' Josse said.

Olivier was silent for some time, as if collecting his thoughts. Then he said, 'I must first apologize most sincerely for my part in the business regarding the young girl.'

Josse, who had almost forgotten about Rosamund, mentally kicked himself. Dear Lord, but there was so much to this! 'And what was your part, exactly?' he asked.

Olivier looked shamefaced. 'I hate to speak ill of my dear brother, but the idea was his. I – we observed that our lord the king was much taken with her when he saw her up by the chapel and—'

'Most assuredly I was not,' the king's hard, cold voice interrupted. 'You and Hugh were gravely mistaken, Olivier.'

'Yes, my lord, and I must humbly beg your pardon,' Olivier said hastily. 'Believing we were acting in a way that would please you, Hugh sent me to find her and bring her to you. I was to go to join you at the hunting lodge and present the girl to you there so that you—'

'*Enough!*' roared the king.

Olivier flinched as if he had been struck. 'I did not know what had become of my brother,' he said in a whisper. 'I thought I had better proceed with the plan alone, which is what I did.' He hesitated.

'You said you had a suggestion,' Josse prompted him gently. 'May we hear it?'

Olivier shot him a quick look, almost instantly dropping his head. 'I am reluctant to speak it,' he muttered.

The king made an explosive sound of impatience. 'For God's sake, Olivier, pull yourself together!' Perhaps feeling he had spoken too harshly to a man who had so recently learned of a bereavement, he added, slightly more kindly, 'If you have information that has any bearing on Hugh's death, it is your duty to pass it on so that it can be acted upon.'

Olivier drew a shaking breath. 'Very well.' He looked up at Josse. 'What I have to say is this. Up in the clearing by the chapel, my lord and I were attacked by a madman wielding a sword and knife, and both of us were badly wounded.' He winced, as if speaking of his wound had made it throb with pain. 'The madman was acting, or so it would seem, in defence of the two women, the girl and her older companion.'

Josse realized that he meant Meggie. He felt very cold suddenly.

'I believe,' Olivier went on slowly, 'that it may have happened this way: the madman somehow learned of Hugh's plan and, while I was engaged with taking the girl to the hunting lodge, he sought out Hugh and challenged him, demanding to know where the girl was. Hugh, determined to carry out his scheme, would not tell him, and the two men fought. Perhaps the madman did not mean to kill him –' he turned earnest blue eyes first to the king and then to Josse – 'but, all the same, my brother died.'

Josse's heart was thumping very hard. *The madman.* Ninian. Dear Lord, this man was suggesting that Ninian had killed Hugh de Brionne!

He hadn't, he could not have done, Josse told himself over and over again.

But then, as if in a waking dream, he seemed to hear his own voice speaking.

I fear we must face the possibility that the man who fought the dead man is the one person who ought to be here and isn't. Whom none of us has seen since the evening we discovered that Rosamund was missing.

Ninian.

The king lay back and closed his eyes. He was alone; a state so rare in his life that he was tempted to simply relish the moment. It would not last, for the old knight Josse d'Acquin had just been informed that the sheriff had arrived and so had hurried away to inform him of the recent developments. Soon both of them would be there, and undoubtedly they would very quickly be joined by the gaggle of self-promoting lords and lordlings that habitually flocked in the king's wake like seagulls after a fishing boat. Not to mention his bodyguards . . .

The curtains that enclosed the recess had been left partly open, and he looked out at the infirmary. He usually had an instinctive reaction against all abbeys: the result of having spent the first years of his life a virtual prisoner in his mother's beloved Fontevrault. They had thought to make a monk of him, but even as a child he had summoned the means to demonstrate in no uncertain terms that, no matter what they did, *that* was never going to happen. He had escaped the cloister, yes, but those early experiences had left him with a deep-seated revulsion against the soft footfalls and the sombre robes of the avowed.

It was strange, then, he mused, that this Hawkenlye Abbey did not make his skin crawl. Quite the opposite, in fact; against all expectations, he was enjoying himself. The wound in his shoulder was not severe, and it was pleasant to be fussed over. In addition, that glorious woman was here and, whatever happened, he was determined to see her again, preferably alone.

Meggie. Her name was Meggie.

She had raised her sword to him, and normally that was a hanging offence. They would call it treason, in fact, and so the means of death would be longer drawn out and decidedly more painful. For a moment he thought of her suffering. Dying. It was not a good thought. He would spare her, he decided. He would make no accusation against her. She would be so very grateful, but he was sure he could come up with a way in which she could demonstrate that gratitude.

He thought about that, too.

Presently, his breathing slowing once more, he recalled that she had said her mother's name was Joanna de Courtenay. She'd had a distant cousin at court. He let his mind wander freely, and after a while a memory surfaced.

It had been one of those wild, rollicking Christmas celebrations when it seemed that almost all the rich and the powerful in the land gathered together, determined to have a good time. It had been at Windsor; he thought hard and tried to recall the year. It had been soon after his elder brother Henry, the Young King, had died, succumbing to a terrible attack of dysentery following his hare-brained looting of the holy shrine at

Rocamadour. The Young King died in 1183, so the Christmas in question must have been 1184. And a laughing, dashing, daredevil of a man called Denys de Courtenay had brought a young cousin to court, and the king had bedded her every night for almost a fortnight.

King John smiled at the memory. He'd had his fair share of women that Christmas, but he hadn't been invited to share any of his father's. He remembered Joanna de Courtney, though; she had been gorgeous, and they'd all envied King Henry and grumbled because a bandy, randy old man had won the best pickings of the season.

If she had borne a child following the rampant days of that Christmas, he had never heard tell of it. Meggie was too young to have been conceived so long ago and, besides, Josse d'Acquin had said she was his daughter and the resemblance between them supported the claim.

Yet there had been a child; a son. He was certain of it, for the evidence had been right before his eyes only a matter of hours ago. A young man had stood challenging him, a sword in one hand and a knife in the other, and for a weird, disorienting moment John had thought he was looking at his own father, as he had looked in John's earliest memories.

If he was right – and in his mind there was no shadow of a doubt – then his opponent in that short and ferocious struggle up by the chapel had been his half brother.

A slow smile spread across the king's face. He did not care to have stray half brothers loose in the land; you never know when some hothead might decide to make such a man a rallying point for insubordination. Well, this particular bastard brother had just attacked his king and gravely wounded one of his close companions, which had effectively signed his death warrant.

It was just a matter of catching him.

There was the sound of booted feet coming into the quiet infirmary; it appeared that Josse had located the sheriff. Swiftly, the king turned his mind to the orders he would issue, and then it would only be a matter of time before his blue-eyed half brother was screaming out his death agony.

The king's smile broadened, and he gave a soft laugh.

ELEVEN

J osse and Gervase stood outside the recess where the king
lay. The king had just finished issuing his orders to Gervase.
The sheriff was to gather together as many men as he
needed and send them out searching for the man who had
attacked the king and Olivier de Brionne in the clearing by
the chapel. The man was accused of gravely wounding
Olivier, of causing the death of Hugh de Brionne and, most
serious of all, of raising arms against the king. The king had
given a detailed description of the wanted man and curtly
commanded Gervase to circulate it among his men.

Several favourites from the king's inner circle had gradually
insinuated themselves into the recess, and they were joined
by a quartet of bodyguards and a couple of servants. As soon
as the king announced he was ready, they would organize a
litter or a cart and take him back to one of his London residences, where he could be nursed and fussed back to health
by his own team of physicians. Josse, Gervase and everyone
at Hawkenlye were redundant.

Gervase looked at Josse and silently jerked his head towards
the infirmary door. They walked quickly away, only stopping
when they were out of earshot of the building and the many
men loitering outside it.

Josse waited. He was all but certain Gervase had recognized
Ninian from the king's description. If so, he appreciated that
the sheriff was in an impossible position. His duty to his
monarch was indisputable, for he had been given a direct order
to find the wanted man and bring him to justice. But this wanted
man was the adopted son of his oldest friend, and Josse was
well aware that Gervase himself had grown to like, trust and
admire Ninian.

After a moment, Gervase sighed and said, 'Josse, I have to
go. There are things I must do . . .' He raised his head and
stared into the distance, his expression deeply grave and his
eyes narrowed, as if the tasks awaiting him were too awful to
bear contemplation. Then he turned back to Josse. 'I am going

to Tonbridge to organize my search parties, and to begin with I intend to concentrate on the main roads to London and the coast. Only when we have explored the most obvious escape routes will I start on the tracks and the byways.'

Just for an instant, Josse wondered why Gervase was explaining in such detail. Then he realized. He could have embraced his friend, but that would have been unwise for there were far too many pairs of suspicious and unfriendly eyes watching.

'Very well, my lord sheriff,' Josse replied stiffly and in a voice audible to the king's men by the infirmary. 'I will detail whatever men I can summon to begin searching in the vicinity of the abbey.'

Gervase hurried away towards the stables, calling for his horse as he ran. Very quickly he and his men were clattering across the courtyard and out through the gates. The king's men were watching and, taking advantage of their distraction, Josse slipped away, out through the small rear gate, around the side of the abbey and up the slope to where the trees began. He had had to leave Alfred in the Hawkenlye stables for a lay brother to take home later – he could not have fetched him without being seen – but he would do as well on foot, for he was going into the forest.

As he made his way along the tracks under the trees he wondered where Meggie was. He had hoped she would be waiting when he was finally dismissed from the king's presence, but there had been no sign of her down at the abbey. He told himself she would have gone to the hut, or perhaps on ahead of him to the House in the Woods. He prayed he was right.

He turned off the track along the path that led to the hut. The clearing around the hut was empty, but he could hear voices from within and there were wisps of smoke floating up from the roof. He tapped on the door, and Helewise's voice called out, 'Come in!'

As he entered she turned a joyful face to him and said, 'Josse, dear Josse, Meggie told me the wonderful news! Tiphaine and I have been giving thanks.'

His mind was so preoccupied with Ninian's peril that, again, he forgot for a moment. Then, quickly, he returned her radiant smile and said, 'Aye, Rosamund is safe and well, and by now

Dominic will no doubt be at the abbey and preparing to take her home to New Winnowlands and her mother's arms.'

He glanced at Tiphaine. The old herbalist's deep eyes met his and, just for an instant, he had the strange sensation that she already knew the news he was about to break to them. He shook his head, dispelling the thought. He had to be mistaken. His eyes went back to Helewise and he said, 'But I'm afraid there is more trouble.' Then he told them.

They left Tiphaine at the hut. She had volunteered to keep watch down at the abbey and come straight to Josse if there was any news concerning the hunt for Ninian.

Josse and Helewise went as quickly as they could through the wildwood to the House in the Woods. After a while he reached out and took her hand. He knew there was nothing she could do just then to help his terrible anxiety – there was nothing anyone could do – but all the same her touch was infinitely comforting.

Back at the house, Meggie was waiting. She ran to him, and he embraced her, holding her tight against him. She said softly, 'They will not catch him, Father. He has known the forest for the last ten years of his life. No king's man will find him.'

Josse stroked her hair. She was probably right, but there were two flaws in her argument. For one thing, it was not only the king's men who were hunting for Ninian, but also Gervase's men, who, being local, knew the area far better. For another, Ninian could not live out in the wildwood for the remainder of his life. One day he would have to emerge. The king's memory was long and phenomenally accurate, and he never forgot a grievance.

Josse did not mention either of these facts to Meggie. Instead, with his daughter on one side and Helewise on the other, holding both of their hands, he led them inside.

The household was assembled to greet him, and Geoffroi rushed over to stand close by his father. 'They all know what's happened,' Meggie said. 'I told them Rosamund's safe, and I also described what happened by the chapel.'

Josse nodded. Turning to address his loyal people, he said, 'You should all know that Ninian is a wanted man. He will be tried and probably put to death if he is caught. Anyone found helping him in any way will also be arrested, for he is a fugitive hunted by the king.' His eyes fell on Gus. 'If any of you with responsibilities for wives and children wish to slip away now, go with my blessing.'

Nobody moved, except that Tilly leaned closer to Gus and whispered something. Gus nodded. 'We'll take our chance, Sir Josse,' he said. 'This is our home and we're a family. We want to help, if we can.'

Josse was deeply moved. He looked at Will, and his servant's deep eyes in the lined old face looked steadily back.

'Me and Ella are staying too,' Will said briefly.

Josse cleared his throat a couple of times then, with an attempt at a smile, said, 'Well, then, we'd better decide what we're going to do.'

As if she had been waiting for the chance, Meggie said, 'I've been thinking. He's got to get away, but there are two reasons why he won't go immediately. The first is that he'll know he's going to have to go a long way and be absent a long time, and I'm quite sure he wouldn't go without saying goodbye to the people he loves. That's us, obviously –' she glanced around – 'but there's someone else, isn't there? Someone who doesn't live here.'

Helewise gasped. 'Of course,' she breathed.

Josse, too, knew instantly who Meggie referred to. Ninian was in love with Leofgar Warin's daughter, Little Helewise. She adored him too, and were it not for the interdict, they undoubtedly would have been wed a year or more ago. Little Helewise lived with her family at the Old Manor, the ancestral home of the Warins, which her father, being the elder of the two brothers, had inherited.

Josse felt his heart clench with fear. The Old Manor lay to the north of Tonbridge, and one of the roads to London passed close by. And Gervase was sending his search parties out along the main routes to London and the coast . . .

'We must stop him,' he said, faintly surprised at how calm and authoritative he sounded. 'Roads to London are going to be searched.'

Meggie's cool hand touched his wrist. 'Yes, all right, Father. We'll stop him, or at least warn him, for I do not think he will be stopped.'

'But we have to—' Josse began.

Meggie turned to smile at him. 'I said there were two reasons why he couldn't leave instantly, remember?'

'Aye,' he said cautiously.

'The second one,' she said, her smile widening, 'is that he's on foot. He'd be a fool to walk all the way to the Old Manor, and I know perfectly well that Garnet's munching hay out in our stables because I brought him back with me and I've just been out to him.'

Josse closed his eyes and said a quick but heartfelt prayer of thanks. As the image of Ninian apprehended on the road north out of Tonbridge and taken in irons to some dirty cell receded, he opened his eyes and whispered to Meggie, 'Thank you, clever girl.'

He waited for a moment and then said, 'We have to think where he's gone. Meggie has already pointed out that he knows the forest extremely well, and it's likely he'll be hiding somewhere nearby, since he's got to acquire a horse and the obvious place to get one is from here.' He paused. There was something nagging at him, something he knew he ought to remember, but it remained vague and would not come into focus.

Geoffroi was tugging at his sleeve. 'Father?' he asked tentatively.

Josse looked down at him. 'What is it, son?'

'Why doesn't Ninian just come here? He knows we all care about him and that none of us would betray him, no matter what they did to us.'

It was a sensible question and deserved, Josse thought, a proper answer. 'Remember what I said just now to everyone?' he asked, crouching down so that he and Geoffroi were eye to eye. 'That if anyone wishes to avoid the risk of being accused of helping a wanted man, they must leave straight away?'

'Yes, of course.' Geoffroi's worried frown cleared. 'I understand now. Ninian knows about that too, and he doesn't want to get us into trouble.'

'That's right,' Josse said.

'It's really quite simple, isn't it?' Helewise said. 'Ninian won't come to us for the help he so desperately needs, so we shall have to take it to him.'

'Aye,' Josse agreed heavily, 'and first we'll have to find him.'

Josse gathered his household together for the evening meal and, before they sat down to eat food for which nobody appeared to have much appetite, Helewise stood up and rather shyly asked if she might say a prayer.

He looked at her, studying her face in the candlelight. She was pale and drawn, and he wished he could take her in his arms so that each could take comfort in the other. Not yet, he thought. 'Of course,' he said with a smile.

'I know we are faced with a grave problem,' she said hesitantly, 'but we should not forget that, because of Meggie and Ninian, who refused to give up, Rosamund has been restored to her family. We should give thanks to God that she was unharmed.' Closing her eyes, she made a brief, eloquent and clearly heartfelt prayer. Then, with barely a pause, her tone changed. 'Dear Lord, we beg you to look after Ninian, wherever he is,' she said earnestly. 'Keep him safe and warm this night and, in the clear light of tomorrow's dawn, let him find a way through his difficulties.' She paused. 'Let him know that we who love him will not condemn him without cause, and remind him that we believe every man has a right to defend both himself and those he cares for.' She added some more, but Josse could not make out the words. Then she began the paternoster, and most of the household joined in.

Josse sat in his chair by the hearth. One by one everyone else had gone to bed, but he was restless, his mind too full to allow him to sleep. He had to do something positive to help Ninian, but unless – and until – the young man came home, there was little he could do. He wondered if Meggie had been right when she said with such conviction that Ninian would not flee without saying goodbye to his loved ones. He hoped so.

His thoughts were going round in circles. It was now very late, and he was exhausted; worn out with the exertions and the stress of that long day. Finally, he got up and, trying to move quietly, he set about preparing a pack containing everything a fugitive might want. He raided the battered old chest where Ninian kept his belongings, rolling up a woollen tunic, a close-fitting felt cap, a spare undershirt and two pairs of hose inside a warm cloak. He folded Ninian's heavy leather tunic around the bundle, fastening it with a belt. He went out to the kitchen, tiptoeing so as not to disturb Gus and Tilly and their children, asleep in the room beyond, and fetched a small, sharp knife suitable for food preparation. From his own experiences, he

knew how tricky it was to skin a hare or cut a cabbage
when you had nothing smaller than your sword and your
dagger. He inspected the family's food supplies – being largely
self-sufficient, they had plenty – and cut off generous slices
from the cured shoulder of a pig that Gus had recently slaught-
ered. He found some apples and half a loaf, then filled a
leather skin with fresh water. He packed everything up in his
own old campaign bag and set it by the door with the bundle
of clothes.

Meggie had reported that Ninian's horse was in the stable.
By morning, he would be well rested, well watered and stuffed
with food. Josse thought he might just go out and check that
Garnet's saddle and bridle were to hand, and before he slipped
outside he fetched a thick wool blanket from his own bed
and rolled it up neatly, tying it with a generous length of fine
rope. He took the packed bag with him, to leave ready out
in the stable.

He was on his way back across the courtyard when he heard
a tiny sound. He stopped instantly, standing utterly still, barely
breathing, all his attention concentrated into his hearing. The
sound came again. It was a very faint clink of harness; as if
someone had hastily bound the metal pieces of their horse's
bridle and not done quite thorough enough a job.

In an old soldier's reflex, Josse reached down for his sword.
It was not there. It was, as he instantly recalled, in its usual
place, in the far corner of his hall, stuck into a barrel of sawdust
to keep away the rust. He had his hunting knife in its scabbard
on his belt, but it was some days since he had honed it.
Nevertheless, he drew it and felt a little more confident for
the familiar shape of its horn handle in his hand.

He waited. Despite the chill night air, sweat broke out on
his back.

Somebody else had been wakeful that night.

Up at the Old Manor, where Rohaise and the servants had
been busy for days preparing for a lightning visit from the
king and his party, the mood between Leofgar and his wife
was delicate. One of Gervase de Gifford's senior deputies had
arrived late in the evening with the news that Rosamund was
safe and on her way home. He had also reported that the king
had been injured in an attack and now lay in the Hawkenlye

infirmary with one of his companions, whose wound had been more serious.

'Are we still to expect the king?' Leofgar had demanded. 'My wife has made everything ready, as you see.'

The deputy shrugged. 'I don't know.' He grinned briefly. 'They don't tell the likes of me about the doings of kings, sir.'

'Where did this attack take place?' Leofgar asked.

'Close by St Edmund's Chapel,' the deputy said. He leaned closer, eyes bright with the thrill of spreading a juicy tale. 'They say it was a madman with a mighty sword and a knife, and he's also wanted for the murder of some other lord. He had a woman with him, and the pair of them vanished into the wildwood like a pair of spirits!' Mastering his excitement, he added in a more sombre tone, 'Seems this madman was trying to defend the little lass.'

'He escaped?' Leofgar said.

'He did,' the deputy replied grimly. 'The sheriff's organizing a manhunt, and tomorrow my lads and I will be searching the road from Tonbridge up northwards over the downs. Keep your eyes open, sir, and make sure to lock and bar your doors. If you hear or see anything suspicious, we'll be back in the morning and you can report it then. Your family and your household are all safe indoors, I assume?'

'Yes. My son and my daughter are in bed, and the servants are in their quarters. What does the man look like?' Leofgar asked.

The deputy shrugged. 'We don't have much of a description. He's in his twenties, quite tall, lightly built, but strong. Bareheaded, brown hair down to his shoulders.' He let out a gusty sigh. 'Could apply to a hundred men.' He turned to go. 'Don't forget to lock up, now.'

Left alone, Leofgar and Rohaise had rejoiced for Rosamund and her family. They discussed the attack on the king, reluctant to come to the conclusion that both of them suspected.

'You told me that Ninian and Meggie were missing,' Rohaise said slowly. 'Then Rosamund turns up, in the company of the king and this other man who was also wounded, and the two men are attacked by a man who has a woman with him.'

'So you're saying this madman, as the deputy called him, must therefore be Ninian?' Leofgar made an impatient sound. 'It's quite a conclusion to draw on slim evidence, Rohaise.'

Rohaise was pacing up and down. 'Yes, I know,' she snapped. 'But you must admit that the description could be him.'

'It could be a hundred men, as the deputy pointed out!' Leofgar flashed back. Then, seeing his wife's distraught face, he went over to her and took her in his arms.

'I'm probably wrong,' she whispered, 'but what if I'm not? If it is Ninian, and if he's on the run because he attacked the king and his companion, then there's one place he might come . . . and that's right here.'

Leofgar nodded. 'Because he wouldn't leave without seeing Little Helewise.'

'They love each other, Leofgar!' Rohaise said passionately. 'She lives and breathes for him, and I pray he *does* come to see her! It would break her heart if he went without a word.'

Leofgar knew she was right. He had watched the love grow between his daughter and Josse's adopted son and, until this day, he had welcomed and encouraged it. Ninian was a fine man and, as Rohaise had just said, Little Helewise, mature for her sixteen years, adored him.

Yes, Ninian – if the fugitive was in fact Ninian – would almost certainly come to the Old Manor. Oh, dear Lord, and tomorrow the deputy and his men would be searching the very route a man travelling from Hawkenlye to the Old Manor would follow!

Another thought struck him and he groaned aloud.

'What is it?'

He stared down into his wife's anxious face. 'The king,' he said simply. 'If he does decide to make the planned visit here on his way back to London, he may well arrive to find the man he is searching right on our doorstep.'

Rohaise wrested herself out of his arms and resumed her pacing. 'I don't want him here!' she said, very softly but with surprising venom. 'They tell such tales of him, Leofgar, and now there's been this frightful business with Rosamund, and she's a *child*, God help us, and he likes them young and—'

Gently, Leofgar caught her in his arms again, stopping the wild words with a kiss. It was dangerous to speak in such a way of the king, even in your own house. You never knew who might be listening. 'Sweetheart, I know full well what they say,' he whispered in her ear.

Gradually, she calmed, her breathing slowing down and the

rapid beating of her heart, which he could feel as he pressed her against him, returning to normal.

'What would you have me do?' he asked her gently.

She looked up into his eyes. The ghost of a smile touched her mouth. 'You already know, don't you?'

He smiled back. 'I do have an idea,' he said. 'It may well be the same as yours, for it seems to me it would solve both our problems.'

'*I* think we must get Little Helewise away from here,' she said. 'Take her to stay with Dominic and Paradisa, over at New Winnowlands. If anyone asks where she is, we can say she's gone to see her cousin Rosamund to comfort her after her ordeal.'

'Which will not only get her out of this house if the king should honour us with his presence, but in addition—'

'In addition, if it *is* Ninian who is being hunted, and if he tries to see her before he leaves the area, he won't come looking for her in the very place where the deputy and his men are hunting for him!' she finished triumphantly.

He thought it through. There was only one problem, which was how they would let Ninian know that Little Helewise was no longer at the Old Manor. He would, he decided, deal with that once his daughter was safe.

Leofgar watched as, with quiet efficiency, his wife set about preparing a pack for Little Helewise of the things she would need for an indefinite stay away from home. It was late now, and he saw, with a stab of compassion, how tired she was. It seemed that it was only nervous energy that kept her going. She is not strong, he thought, looking at her with love. She hides it well, but she is too easily thrown when bad things happen.

Rohaise announced she was ready. Leofgar crept along to the small room where Little Helewise lay sleeping and, with a gentle touch, shook her awake. Putting his finger to his lips, he whispered, 'Something has happened. Get dressed and come along to the hall, where your mother and I will be waiting. Put on your warmest clothes and your heavy boots.'

True child of the Warins that she was, his daughter absorbed the shock with a brief nod and instantly set about doing what he had said. Shortly afterwards, she came softly along the passage to join her parents in the hall. Leofgar studied her. She was willowy and tall – all the Warins were tall – and, although she had her mother's beautiful creamy skin, she was not as pale as Rohaise. Also inherited from her mother was her hair: rich, dark brown, thick and heavy. Now, for convenience, she had bundled it up under a soft felt hat that belonged to her brother.

Leofgar put his hands on her shoulders and told her everything. Her first response, on hearing what Ninian was accused of, was to shake her head. 'He is not a killer,' she said with calm conviction. 'He would raise his weapon to protect someone he loved, or who was defenceless, and, naturally, if anyone attacked him he would fight back. But that is his right.'

Leofgar nodded. 'Yes, I know.'

She looked up at him. Her clear grey eyes, so like those of the grandmother she had been named for, were huge in the candlelight. 'You will not try to make me give him up, Father?'

He hesitated. 'I do not—' he began.

'It depends what happens!' Rohaise interrupted passionately. 'If he's arrested and tried, you may have to! The king is powerful and vengeful, and if we are known to support a man who attacked him and two of his lords, leaving one dead, then it would be the end of us, too!'

She was weeping. Leofgar made a move towards her, but she fended him off. Beside him he sensed his daughter straighten her back and raise her chin.

'I will not abandon Ninian,' Little Helewise said quietly. 'Father, if we are to make our journey under cover of night, we had better be on our way.'

He watched as she went to her mother, taking Rohaise in a hug and whispering something in her ear. Rohaise suppressed a sob, and then Little Helewise gently disengaged herself. 'Don't worry,' she said, smiling. 'Dominic and Paradisa will take good care of me.'

She caught Leofgar's eye, and together they left the hall. Leofgar had prepared their horses, and very soon they were cantering across the dark, silent countryside.

Josse stood in his courtyard, every muscle tense.

A large bay horse materialized out of the shadows under the trees. It was being led by a tall man with a girl walking beside him, and the girl led a grey mare. With joy, Josse recognized both the man and the girl, sheathing his knife and running to greet them. 'We'll put your horses in the stables,' he said to Leofgar, leading the way, 'then the two of you must both come inside and get warm.' Leofgar began to speak, but Josse hushed him. 'Not here,' he said quietly. 'Wait till we're in the house.'

A short time later, having prepared hot, spiced wine for his guests and poked up the fire, Josse sat back and digested what Leofgar had told him. 'I understand why you have brought her away from the Old Manor,' he began, 'but I don't—'

Leofgar, who had briefly relaxed, suddenly sat upright again. 'I have to go!' he exclaimed. 'It must by now be very late, and I have to be back home by early morning.' He leaned closer to Josse. 'It would be better if nobody knows of this mission,' he added. 'With any luck, Little Helewise's absence won't be noticed straight away, and we can be vague about when she left.'

'Aye, I appreciate the need for secrecy,' Josse said. 'But what's puzzling me is why, having planned to go to New Winnowlands, you've turned up here.' He turned to Little Helewise. 'Am I to take you on to Dominic and Paradisa in the morning, sweetheart?' He was very fond of Helewise's elder granddaughter.

Little Helewise exchanged a slightly guilty look with her father. Then, turning to Josse, she said, 'No, Josse. I'll stay here, if you'll have me.' She took a breath, and it seemed to him that her face flushed slightly. 'It's just that we told Mother I would be at New Winnowlands, and it's better if she thinks that's where I am. That way, only Father, you, your household and I know where I really am.'

Then he understood. Rohaise's husband and daughter, knowing that, under provocation, she might inadvertently give away too much, were quietly making sure she couldn't. And, for all that he could appreciate that the subterfuge was necessary, he could also see that it hurt.

He got up, went across to Little Helewise and took her hand. 'Of course we'll have you. As soon as we've seen your father on his way, I'll take you along to your grandmother's quarters and she'll make up a bed for you.' He turned to Leofgar. 'Don't worry. We'll look after her.'

He thought, as, hand in hand with Little Helewise, he watched

Leofgar ride off, how thrilled her grandmother was going to be to see her.

Josse walked along the short corridor to the chamber he had made his own. He sank down on his bed, took off his boots and tunic and slipped beneath the covers. As at last he closed his eyes and relaxed into sleep, his last thought was the fervent hope that Ninian was warm enough . . .

TWELVE

In his hiding place, Ninian stirred in his sleep and woke. Still groggy, he focused his mind on the message he had to send, concentrating on the image he was trying to impart. He brought Josse to mind, visualizing him lying deeply asleep, and gently attempted to introduce the vivid image into his dreams.

He and Meggie could sometimes communicate in that way, although it was haphazard and only worked intermittently. They practised regularly, and Meggie was sure they were improving. Would it work with someone who was not of Joanna's extraordinary blood? Would it work with Josse?

Ninian fervently hoped so.

When Ninian had obeyed Meggie's fierce command and run away from the fight up by the chapel, he'd had no idea of where he would go, other than that it was undoubtedly best to stay within the great forest. He had first encountered it when he was a child, a fugitive with his mother and on the run from a cousin of hers whose plans for Joanna and her son were not at all to Joanna's taste. There had been several years when he had lived a very different life, but a decade ago he had come back. Since Josse had adopted him and they had all gone to live in the House in the Woods, Ninian's knowledge of the wildwood and everything that lived within it had grown until it was almost as great as his half sister's.

Without even thinking about it, he knew as he'd fled that it was the obvious place for a man like him to hide.

To begin with, the overriding necessity had been to get away. As soon as he was some distance from the chapel he had deliberately slowed right down. A running man could not help but leave tracks because, for one thing, his headlong flight tended to break branches and flatten undergrowth and, for another, if you were racing along you could not see where you were putting your feet, and it was all too easy to leave footprints in muddy patches.

In the depths of the dense woodland, Ninian had moved silent and light-footed as a shadow. The immediate danger was past, and so he had turned his mind to what he was going to do. He had wounded a great lord and in all likelihood killed another. He heard Meggie's words in his head: *if he's dead they'll make sure you hang.*

He did not want to die. Life was sweet, and he was not ready yet to leave it.

Having decided that, he began to make plans. Get far away, preferably across the Channel. Yes, that was good. He would need his horse, some good, weatherproof garments, some food supplies. Some money. None of those could he acquire except from his home, so he would have to make contact with the household. Well, he would have to do that anyway, for to leave England without saying goodbye was impossible. He pictured Josse and Meggie, and then an image of Little Helewise's lovely face gently took their place.

Before he could be undermined by his emotions, he deliberately closed them away in a corner of his mind and returned to the practicalities.

He wondered how grave the accusations against him were. Was he exaggerating the danger? Would they listen if he said that both lords had advanced on him, each bearing arms, and his actions had been purely in self defence? They might. But what if they did not? He shook his head fiercely. Oh, but it was hard, not knowing the outcome of the fight.

He had drawn close to the little hut where his mother and Meggie had lived. He had not been aware of heading that way, and he wondered if perhaps his mother's spirit had tugged at him. He stopped under the trees at the edge of the clearing and, trying to empty his mind as Meggie had taught him, he waited. There was a faint whisper, as if a soft breeze had swirled up from the ground around him, and he found that he was smiling. Then it – she – was gone.

Meggie was not at the hut, but he had not expected her to be. Some time had passed since the fight, but he guessed she was still involved with the wounded men, probably down at the abbey by now. But somebody was there.

As he approached, the door opened and Tiphaine said, 'You'd better come in and tell me what's happened.'

She made him sit down by the fire, and swiftly she made

a hot drink for him. It was some herbal concoction that had the effect of swiftly soothing him, so that he was able to tell his tale calmly.

When he had finished, she nodded and said, 'I knew something was amiss. Josse has been here, and he told us, but I'd already felt it in the air.' She paused. He wondered if she would go on to explain, but he ought to have known better. Turning to face him, her eyes seemed to snap back to the present moment, and she said, 'You didn't kill either of the men you fought.'

He was about to shout with relief, but he knew from her expression that his joy was premature. 'Go on.'

'Two things,' she said. 'One: there's a third man at Hawkenlye and he *is* dead, and they're saying you killed him.'

'I did not,' he said quietly.

She nodded impatiently, as if to say *of course you didn't.* 'Two: out of the two you fought up by the chapel, one's the dead man's brother and the other's the king.'

Ninian felt as if somebody had punched him very hard in the stomach. Of all the men in the land, he'd had to go and inflict a wound on the king. He recalled the older of the pair. He hadn't recognized him, but then there was no reason why he should have done. He had never met him in his life.

He looked up to find Tiphaine watching him. He almost told her: *the king is my half brother.* But it was his mother's secret, and not his to tell. As if she heard his thought and understood, Tiphaine reached out and briefly clasped his hand.

Then she said, 'You need help, but you can't go to the House in the Woods.'

'I know,' he agreed. 'If they find out my family sheltered a wanted man, Josse will be in trouble too.'

'Not much future in staying here either,' she went on, as if she had not heard. 'Much as this place would welcome you, and much as I reckon you'd be safe here indefinitely, you can't spend the rest of your life in a hut in the forest.' She fixed stern eyes on him. 'Your mother saw great things for you, my lad. She thought she was doing the right thing by you when she placed you in that knight's household where you went as a boy, but it turns out that wasn't your path after all. Now you spend your days dreaming under the trees and tending the wild creatures.'

'I *like* the forest!' Ninian protested sharply. 'I'm happy with my life.'

She studied him, quite unmoved by his outburst. 'So you might be, young Ninian, but I reckon what occurred today happened for a reason.'

He thought about it. 'You mean it was all predestined, just to shake me out of my comfortable ways and force me to do something different?' He spoke with heavy sarcasm, intending to make his suggestion so preposterous as to be laughable.

Tiphaine wasn't laughing. And, as he listened to the echoes of his bitter words ringing in his head, he realized he wasn't either.

In this place, in the depths of the wildwood and with the distillation of his mother's strange legacy strong around him, it all sounded horribly plausible.

He had stayed with Tiphaine until dusk. Then he got up to go. She came out into the clearing with him, looking up into the night sky and sniffing the air. 'Mars is rising,' she observed. 'He'll give you courage if you set out with your head high.' Then, to his surprise – for he had never thought her a demonstrative woman – she stepped up to him and put her arms round him in a quick, tight hug. She muttered something in a tongue he did not know, but he guessed it was a blessing. Then, without another word, she went back inside and closed the door.

He had already made up his mind where he would go. Keeping off the main tracks, he followed the faint animal trails that only he – and probably his half sister – knew. Even there, he was careful only to walk where the ground was firm and the leaf mound lay deep. As the light faded and he could no longer see clearly where he was putting his feet, he took to feeling his way with his toes. Progress was slow, but he was all but sure he was leaving no traces of his passing. Besides, he was not in a hurry. He had all night.

He was not sure he could find the place. When he knew he was near, he stopped, leaned his back against a birch tree and made himself relax. Memories returned: they were bitter-sweet, for his mother was wound up in them and, as always, bringing her to mind was both a pleasure and a deep, unhealed pain. For a moment he thought he heard her voice – *you are too far to the east and should turn towards the North Star* – but it was probably just his imagination.

He decided to follow the suggestion in any case. Presently, he spotted the landmark he had been searching for and a wide smile broke across his face. 'Thank you,' he said aloud.

Dawn was breaking now, and Ninian awoke in his secret sanctuary. The fire had died down, but its embers still glowed faintly, and it did not take him long to build it up again. Last night he had arranged the stones in a circle for his hearth, and there was plenty of dead wood around. He had cut sheaves of dead and dying bracken for his bed, and he had been warm enough. He was, however, very hungry. Tiphaine had fed him and given him what food she had, but he had not eaten a proper meal in days.

He crept out of his hiding place and located the stream that ran nearby, bending to wash his face, neck and hands, and scooping up draughts of the clean, bitingly cold water. Standing up, he made his way slowly back again, staring intently to make quite sure there was no sign of his presence. The fire was placed so that what little smoke it made was concealed, but, now that it was day, he decided to let it die down. If Josse came looking, he would need no pointer to tell him where Ninian was. Or so he hoped . . .

Josse woke in the thin light of the pre-dawn from a dream he could not recall. Vivid in his mind, however, was the elusive memory that he had tried to pin down the night before.

There was no time to waste. He got out of bed and swiftly dressed, drawing on his boots and reaching for his cloak. The place he was going to was secret, and he must on no account give its location away by leaving tracks or inadvertently leading someone else there. He felt reasonably safe. None of his own household was awake yet – not that they posed any threat – and he did not think any search parties would be about so early. It was, after all, only just getting light.

He hurried out to the yard and, greeting Alfred, put bridle and saddle on him and led him out of the stable. Mounting, he urged him forward and set off. He briefly wondered if he should take Ninian's horse with him, and the pack he had prepared, but he decided against it. He might be wrong – although he didn't think so – and, besides, he knew Ninian would not leave without saying goodbye.

Josse thought he would remember the way without difficulty, but he was wrong. It was not far short of twenty years since he had first been taken there, and at the time he had been suffering from the after-effects of a blow to the head. He had been tended by a small boy, and the two of them had forged a deep bond which existed to this day. Now, his desperate need both driving him on and making him too tense to calm down and concentrate, he reined in and swore softly under his breath with frustration.

He would not find it standing still, he thought. Nudging Alfred, keeping to the side of the narrow, winding path so as not to leave hoof prints, he rode slowly on. The trail climbed up a slight rise, and he heard the sound of running water.

He stopped, dismounted and, leading Alfred, went for some way along the top of the ridge, looking intently down to the left. He came to a place where the stream he had heard ran through a shallow valley. There was no track down there now, although he thought he remembered that once there had been. He tethered Alfred and climbed carefully down into the valley. He was looking for a spot where a large ledge of sandstone stuck out from the side of the valley, its base concealed by a tangle of thorn bushes.

He smelt wood smoke. Only very faintly, and had he not been expecting it, he would probably have missed it. He looked around, but there was no wisp of smoke on the cold air.

He spotted an outcrop of rock. It was not precisely as he remembered, but it was worth investigating. As he drew nearer, he realized that the tangle of thorn that had once been knee high now reached up to his chest. It was the right rock, and the hiding place he sought lay beneath it.

He edged forward. Should he call out? If Ninian was within, asleep perhaps, and Josse took him by surprise, the consequences might be grave. He went right up to the sandstone and, with the hilt of his dagger, tapped lightly on the rock.

A voice behind him said, 'I'm over here.'

Josse spun round. Ninian was emerging from beneath the down-sweeping branches of a yew. 'I had to be careful,' he began. 'I don't think anyone else knows about my old camp, but you can't be too careful. I—'

He didn't get any further. With a soft cry, Josse bounded over to him and took him in his arms. After a moment Ninian eased himself away and stood smiling up at Josse. 'You found me,' he said. 'I thought you would. Come inside.' He pushed aside the stiff and viciously-barbed branches of thorn and revealed the hidden entrance.

Crouching down, Josse went in, Ninian right behind. Josse straightened up and looked around him. The small space was just as he had remembered, although the withies woven between the posts that formed the walls were sagging and there were large gaps. But Ninian had made the place neat, and there was a fire dying in the hearth.

Josse turned to him, slowly nodding. 'I lay there, beside the fire, which was exactly where it is now,' he said.

Ninian grinned. 'I used the same stones. Although several of them had become dislodged by the wild animals, they were still pretty much where I left them. I don't believe anyone's been here since you and I last visited. Nobody will find me here.'

The last comment jerked Josse back to the present. It was all very well indulging a fond memory, but Ninian was in danger. 'You can't stay here,' he said, rather too brusquely. 'They *will* find you, Ninian, for the crimes of which you stand accused are very serious.'

'I am no murderer, Josse,' Ninian said.

Josse regarded him steadily. 'A man died as the result of a fight, Ninian. It seems somehow he was involved in the plot to abduct Rosamund, and we all know you would defend those you care for to the death, if necessary.' And your whereabouts were not known at the time the man died, he could have added.

'Josse, I give you my word. I have murdered nobody. The wounds I inflicted in the fight by the chapel were as much to defend myself as attack the others.'

'Aye, I appreciate that,' Josse replied. 'But one of the men you wounded—'

'Was the king,' Ninian interrupted gently. 'Yes, Josse, I know. I went to see Tiphaine, and she told me everything.'

'Your horse stands ready for you back at the House in the Woods,' Josse plunged on, 'and I've prepared a pack for you, and a blanket.' He had not expected this moment to hurt so much. Ninian had to go, and it was Josse's task to make sure he left as quickly as he could.

Ninian put out his hand, but then let it drop. 'I have to say goodbye,' he muttered. 'I won't leave without seeing Meggie, and there's Little Helewise. She – she—'

Josse saw tears in his son's eyes. 'She is at the house,' he said. 'Leofgar brought her over in the night.'

Ninian's face lit up. 'Why?' he demanded. 'Oh, you can't know how relieved I am, but I don't understand.' He frowned. 'Unless—'

'Ninian, we all know you. We've been working it out, and we realized that, while you would never come to the House in the Woods – or, indeed, go to the homes of any of the people you care about – because you would not bring trouble to our doors, yet you are incapable of fleeing without a word of farewell.'

'Am I so transparent?' A bitter smile twisted his mouth. 'If that's the case, I might as well give myself up right now.'

Josse grabbed him by the shoulders and shook him, quite hard. 'You are *not*; only to we who know and love you,' he said harshly. 'And don't you ever, *ever*, speak of giving yourself up!'

Ninian wriggled free, wincing. 'I was only joking,' he muttered.

'Then don't,' Josse replied shortly. 'It isn't funny.'

There was a pause. 'I'm going abroad,' Ninian said.

'Aye, I know,' Josse said heavily. Then, for he was finding this unendurable, he made for the entrance and crouched down, preparing to crawl out. 'Wait here,' he said. 'Don't leave your hiding place. There will be search parties, although they're going to concentrate on the main roads to begin with. We ought to have today, at least.' He looked back at Ninian. 'I'll be back as soon as I can.' Then he hurried away.

Back at the House in the Woods, Tilly had food on the table and the household were sitting down to eat. Meggie rushed to Josse as he came into the hall, Little Helewise hard on her heels. 'Have you found him?' Meggie cried, at the same moment as Little Helewise said, 'Is he all right?'

'I have, and he is.' He smiled at them. 'You guessed, then, where I'd gone.'

'It wasn't difficult,' Meggie replied.

Helewise got up and came to take his hand. 'He is not hurt?'

Josse looked round at the circle of anxious faces. Little Helewise was pale, biting her lip. Geoffroi was frowning, as he often did when his emotions threatened to overwhelm him.

'He is unharmed and safe,' Josse said. 'Safe for now, anyway, although there is no time to waste. If we are quick, there is time, for those who wish to do so, to go and see him and see him on his way.'

Helewise squeezed his hand. He glanced at her and saw there were tears in her eyes. 'He'll be all right!' Josse said heartily, with a confidence he was far from feeling. 'He's resourceful and brave. If anyone can get away to safety, it's Ninian.'

'Where will he go?' Little Helewise asked in a whisper. She caught his eye and twisted her mouth in a brave smile.

Josse looked at her, compassion filling his heart. 'He'll have to get out of England,' he said gently. 'The king's reach is long.' He had a plan, which presently he would suggest to Ninian, but for now he thought he should keep it to himself.

'When – how long will he have to stay away?' Little Helewise said.

Josse sighed. 'I don't know.' Then, overcome with helpless fury, he added bitterly, 'Until the king either forgets him or dies, I expect.'

There came the sound he had been unconsciously listening out for and dreading to hear: a horse's hooves clattering into the yard and Will's voice raised in greeting. 'Sit down, all of you,' he hissed, pushing Meggie and Helewise before him and flinging himself down into his chair. 'We're an ordinary family having breakfast. We're very worried about one of our loved ones, but we have no idea where he is or what he plans to do!' He looked round at them all. They were too pale, too anxious. 'Eat!' he said in an urgent whisper. 'Go on, *eat*, curse you all!'

He regretted his furious words as soon as they were out of his mouth. It was too late to apologize – he could hear Will's heavy tread outside as he ushered their visitor up the steps to the hall – but hurriedly he glanced at everyone round the table, begging their forgiveness with his eyes.

The door opened.

Will said, 'Sir Josse, the sheriff's here.'

Josse turned to see Gervase de Gifford walking towards him.

Gervase studied them all. Turning to Josse, he said, 'A word in private, if I may.'

Josse got to his feet and hurried over to him, taking his arm and walking with him out of the hall and back down the steps, crossing the open ground in front of the house until they were on the edge of the surrounding trees. Stopping, he turned to Gervase. 'Nobody will hear us out here.' He studied the sheriff's grave face. 'What is it?'

'Josse, I should not be here. Certainly, I should not have come on the mission that has brought me to you.' He paused.

'You have a conflict of duty,' Josse said quietly. 'I understand.'

'Do you?' Gervase's light eyes were intent. 'I'm not sure you do. Ninian attacked the king and Olivier de Brionne, and they are saying he killed Olivier's brother. The king has given me a direct order – find the madman who fought him by the chapel and bring him to justice – and the penalty for disobedience will be terrible and swiftly demanded.' He passed a hand over his face. 'My family – Sabin and the children – may suffer too, I cannot say.'

'You don't have to—' Josse began.

'I don't have to help you?' Gervase snapped. 'Oh, Josse, but I do. You are my oldest friend, we have endured much together and each has put his trust in the other. You saved my life, and I told you then that you had made a lifelong friend. Such things make bonds that do not fade away when trouble comes. Besides, I—' Whatever he had been about to add, he bit back.

Josse bowed his head. 'Nobody here will say a word concerning this visit,' he muttered.

'I know,' Gervase replied. He paused, cleared his throat and then said, 'Josse, Ninian must leave England today. I can postpone a search of the forest, for we are first going to concentrate on the main roads and tracks where a fleeing man can move swiftly, but only until tomorrow. Wherever Ninian is – *and I don't want to know*,' he added quickly as Josse opened his mouth, 'get him right away from here.'

'Aye, I will, and I thank you from the bottom of my heart for a day's grace,' Josse said. 'Everything is prepared. His horse stands fed and watered and loaded in the stable, and the bag I have packed lies ready on the floor. As soon as we've said our goodbyes, Ninian will be off.'

Gervase nodded. 'Excellent.' He hesitated, eyeing Josse and

then quickly looking away. 'I – er, have a suggestion,' he said tentatively, 'if you would hear it?'

'I would,' Josse answered.

In that moment of desperate urgency, it struck Josse that Gervase was strangely reluctant to speak. He was about to press him – this was no time to be so sensitive and tactful! – when Gervase seemed to jerk himself out of his reverie.

To Josse's surprise, for there was nobody near, Gervase leaned close and, speaking right in his ear, whispered to him. He spoke for some moments, and Josse's eyes widened as he listened.

'I had forgotten,' Josse said when Gervase had finished. 'You did tell me, years ago, but it had slipped my mind.' Then, his eyes on Gervase, he said anxiously, 'I pray it will not come to that!'

Gervase shrugged. 'The king's reach is long,' he murmured. 'Tell Ninian he must—' He stopped. 'Tell him to bear it in mind.'

'Aye, that I will, and thank you.'

Gervase looked hurriedly away. Then, glancing up at the sun, he muttered, 'I must go.'

He had turned aside, but Josse caught his arm and held him back. He fumbled for Gervase's hand and they clasped, palm to wrist. Then Gervase hurried off back towards the house, and very soon Josse saw him emerge from the stable yard. Putting spurs to his horse, Gervase raced away.

In the end, only Little Helewise and Meggie went with Josse to say farewell. Geoffroi begged to be allowed to go, but Josse, knowing how painful it was going to be, gently forbad it. 'Stay here with me,' Helewise said softly to the boy. 'I need someone to cheer me up, and there's nobody like you for doing that.'

Catching Josse's eye, she said, 'Give Ninian my love. Tell him I shall keep him in my prayers and my heart until we meet again.'

They went on foot, leading Garnet. The various bundles that Josse had prepared were all now securely fastened, and Tilly had added a linen square in which she had tied some of her freshly-baked honey cakes. If love could protect Ninian, Josse reflected as they walked in silence beneath the trees, then he would leave his homeland in the best armour in the world.

Ninian was waiting for them in the little valley. The hiding place was once more concealed behind the thorn bush; Josse wondered absently how long it would be before it was used again. If it ever was . . .

He could barely cope with his sorrow. Taking refuge in being brisk and efficient, he showed Ninian what had been prepared for him and, waving aside the young man's thanks, said, 'Now, once you're safely across the narrow seas, remember that you have kin there and go—'

He had not expected Ninian's reaction. His face mottled with fury, he said, 'They are not my kin! My mother *hated* that terrible old man they made her marry, and I would not seek them out even if they were all that stood between me and the gallows!'

There was a gasp of horror, from Meggie or Little Helewise; Josse did not know. He realized his mistake. 'Ninian,' he said quietly, 'I do not refer to the family of Thorald de Lehon. I would never make such a suggestion to you, knowing even better than you how your mother loathed the lot of them.'

Only slightly mollified, Ninian said, 'Who, then?'

'I meant the d'Acquins,' Josse said. 'My brothers Yves, Patrice, Honoré and Acelin, and their families. They are all at Acquin, and it is not very far from the coast. They will take you in and care for you.' He paused, collecting his thoughts. It was a long time since he had seen his family – he did not even know if all his brothers were still alive – and now, in that moment full of painful emotions, he felt another one: regret that he had not made the time to visit them. With an effort, he brushed the thought aside. Yves and the others would help Ninian; that was all that mattered now.

He realized Ninian was watching him closely. 'What is it?'

Ninian smiled. 'They are not really my kin, Josse,' he said gently. 'I'm only your adopted son, remember?'

Josse waved a hand, momentarily unable to speak. He had quite forgotten. He drew Ninian to him, taking him in his arms. Very quietly, he said, 'There is somewhere else, too.' And he told Ninian what Gervase had said.

He hugged the young man once more, then let him go. He strode away to the edge of the valley and turned his back. He heard Meggie's soft voice, speaking some urgent reminder to her half brother. Then she came to stand beside him.

For rather longer, he listened to the quiet sobbing of Little Helewise and the gentle tones of Ninian as he tried to comfort her.

Finally, she, too, came to join them.

They all turned and saw Ninian, already mounted on Garnet, one hand raised in farewell. He put his heels to Garnet's sides, and the horse went up the slope out of the valley. For a few moments they heard the thud of his hooves as Ninian kicked him first to a canter and then, as the trees thinned, to a gallop. Then the sounds faded and they heard no more.

Speed him on his way and let him find a safe haven, Josse prayed. He thought he was praying to God, but suddenly an image of Joanna flashed before his eyes. *He's your boy*, he reminded her, as if she needed reminding. *You make sure he's all right.*

There was no answer.

On either side of him, Meggie and Little Helewise each took one of his hands. Together, not speaking, they went home.

THIRTEEN

Helewise had been praying. She wished she could go through the forest to St Edmund's Chapel, for it was a place very dear to her heart and she felt that God's presence was very close there. Something to do with its simplicity, she often thought, and also with its air of slight detachment, situated as it was above and apart from the hectic bustle of the abbey. It ought to have been locked up, of course. That was what the interdict meant to the ordinary people. They had few comforts in their hard lives, and now, just because two great men of power had squabbled like a couple of small boys each determined to have their own way, even the solace of the church's services had been taken away.

Somehow, the chapel seemed to have been overlooked. And, besides, there was no lock on its door.

She could not go there now. She had seen Josse's face as he left to say goodbye to Ninian. He would have to support Meggie and Little Helewise all the way home, and he would need some support himself by the time he got back. So she went out into the woods, following one of her favourite tracks deep beneath the trees to a private place she had discovered. An ancient oak had fallen a year or so back, and the sudden absence of its huge crown had allowed the sun into a place of darkness. The glade always appeared full of light, even on a dim day, because of the contrast to the surrounding shadowy gloom.

She knelt on the mossy ground and prayed, for Ninian and for those left behind who would miss him so much. She stayed there on her knees for some time and, when eventually she got up and returned to the house, she felt as if she had a strong, silent ally to help her face the difficult times ahead.

As she walked back along the path, something occurred to her. She stopped in surprise – why on earth hadn't they thought of it before? – and then carefully studied the idea. Was it right? Was it practicable? She thought it was.

Hurrying, eager now to speak to Josse, she picked up her pace and strode home.

They were back. She could hear someone sobbing: it was her granddaughter. Of all of them, this was perhaps hardest for Little Helewise, she reflected, for the child was young still, deeply in love and, until this dreadful business, had happily expected to marry the man she loved as soon as the church was permitted to perform the service. Now Ninian had gone, out of her loving arms for an indefinite time.

We must keep her occupied, Helewise thought. Misery was far worse if not distracted. Suddenly, she heard Meggie's voice, quite close. 'Come with me, young lady,' she was saying firmly. 'I have been absent from my work for far too long, and I must go over to the hut and prepare more cough syrup, for my supplies are all used up. I need another pair of hands, and yours will do admirably.'

Helewise smiled. Meggie, clearly, had had the same thought.

She stood in the doorway and watched the two young women walk across the yard and off on the path through the woods. Then she went to find Josse.

He was out in the stables. He had been grooming Alfred – Will had passed her in the yard, muttering under his breath about the master doing the man's work – but now he was just standing there, a curry comb in one hand and strands of Alfred's luxuriant tail in the other. Alfred stood half asleep, languidly munching on a mouthful of hay.

She went up to Josse and, as he heard her footsteps, he turned to see who it was. The misery in his face briefly lifted. Then he said, 'He's gone,' and she thought he might break down.

'It was the only thing to do,' she said fervently. 'We have no guarantee that he would receive any trial at all, never mind a fair one, for the king is capricious and surrounded by ruthless men elbowing each other out of the way as they strive for the king's favour. Even if King John wished to act in accordance with the law, who can say that one of his close circle might not take matters into his own hands?'

'Like the king's father and Archbishop Becket,' Josse murmured.

'Exactly! This way, we are robbed of Ninian for a time, but not for ever.'

He looked down at his hands, twisting a strand of Alfred's tail this way and that. 'How can you be sure it's not for ever?' he asked.

She hesitated, mentally arranging her words. She had to convince him. Then she said, 'Josse, you said earlier that Ninian couldn't come back till the king either forgot or died. There is another alternative: find out the truth about how Hugh de Brionne died, and try to prove that, up by the chapel, Ninian acted in self-defence, having no idea that one of the men he was fighting was the king.'

Apart from the grinding of Alfred's big teeth, there was silence in the stable. She thought she had failed. She fully expected him to give a scathing reply, such as: *and just how am I to work this miracle?*

He didn't. He reached for her hand and raised it to his lips, kissing it. Then, his voice gruff with emotion, he said, 'We have worked our way through such insurmountable obstacles before, you and I, have we not? Shall we do so once more?'

She smiled, blinking back her tears. 'I was hoping you would say that.' They stood for a moment, not speaking, and she imagined he was taking strength from her just as she was from him.

Finally, she stepped away. 'If you've quite finished with that horse's tail,' she said, making her tone brisk, 'then let us go into the hall and work out exactly what we are going to do.'

They sat opposite each other at the big table in the hall. At some time Tilly must have brought food and drink, but Helewise only noticed when she found herself absently reaching out for bread and cheese. She was concentrating deeply, and she knew Josse was too.

'So, let us go through how we see the sequence of events,' Josse finally said.

Helewise had stylus, ink and scraps of parchment; she had been making notes, but they were in random order, and now she prepared to make a fair copy. 'Rosamund was taken by Olivier de Brionne,' she said, writing as she spoke, 'acting according to a plan devised by his brother, Hugh, that was designed to please the king by presenting him with a young woman.' Josse made an explosive noise. 'Don't say it,' she said. 'I know. Olivier takes Rosamund with him on his horse, and they set out westwards, making for the hunting lodge on the Ashdown Forest, where Ninian and Meggie tracked them. According to Olivier, Hugh was meant to be there too, but for some reason he did not turn up. We now know that he died during the time that Olivier and Rosamund were travelling between this house and the hunting lodge.'

Josse was gazing into the distance. 'Mm.'

When he did not continue, she prompted him. 'Well?'

'I was thinking. I believed Ninian could have been involved in Hugh's death because we all knew how desperately he wanted to find Rosamund and bring her back, and he was not with any of us at the time Hugh disappeared. He had not even joined up with Meggie then.' He fell silent.

'And now? What do you believe now?'

He buried his face in his hands. 'In truth, I do not know. Ninian gave me his word that he is no murderer, and I have no doubt that he spoke the truth. However, what I fear is that he was careful in his choice of words. We know that Hugh de Brionne was in a fight, for he had bruises on his face and knuckles, indicating that he fought back. Supposing Ninian caught him, found out somehow that he was involved in the abduction of Rosamund, and demanded that Hugh tell him where she was? It seems quite logical that a fight would break out, and possible that Hugh's death was in fact an accident, caused by his falling over backwards.'

Slowly, she nodded. 'If that's how it happened, then Ninian would indeed have spoken true when he said he was no murderer,' she muttered. 'But Josse, would he not have told you if that was how it was?'

Josse removed his hands, and she saw his haggard face. 'That's the question I can't answer,' he admitted.

'Did he have marks similar to Hugh's on his knuckles?' she asked. 'I know he had no bruising to his face, or at least none that I saw.'

'I saw none either,' he agreed. 'But Ninian is very useful in a scrap. Those years he spent as a squire in Sir Walter Asham's household served him well, and I don't reckon many men could easily land a punch on his face. I did not, however, think to look at his hands.'

It was too late now. She did not say so. Josse's mood had

lifted marginally since they had set to work on the challenge of finding out the truth, and she did not want to remind him of Ninian's absence.

He was watching her. 'What now?'

She was ready for the question. She completed the note she was making and then folded her hands and said, 'I have two suggestions. We know that Hugh died while Rosamund was being taken by Olivier to the hunting lodge. I appreciate that it's unlikely, but I think we should ask her if she noticed anyone else on the road or lurking around. If Ninian is not responsible for Hugh's death, then someone else is.'

'Aye, that's sound,' he said. 'Your other suggestion?'

'I am concerned that we only have Olivier de Brionne's word for it that this scheme was his dead brother's idea,' she said. 'It is easy, if not very honourable, to lay the blame for a plan that goes awry on someone who can no longer speak up in his own defence. Perhaps Olivier was the instigator and Hugh the second in command?'

'Would that make a difference?' Josse asked.

'I don't know,' she admitted. 'I just feel strongly that for Olivier to say, as you tell me he did, that Hugh was the instigator is too easy. I am suspicious,' she concluded.

'Your suspicions have in the past often led to the posing of the right questions,' he said. 'How should we proceed in this?'

'Would you return to the abbey and speak to Olivier again?' she asked.

He considered it. 'Aye,' he said. 'In addition, it would do no harm to let the king know, if and when anyone comes right out with it and says Ninian killed Hugh de Brionne, that we do not accept it.'

'You would dare do that, when for all we know he may already have made up his mind?' She was instantly very worried for him. 'Oh, Josse, you would be walking on very delicate ground!'

He grinned. 'I have done so before,' he replied. 'The king is far from being a mindless fool who cannot think for himself. He will know by now of my connection with Ninian, and I believe he will not be surprised that I am trying to clear the lad's name.'

'Be careful,' she warned.

'I will. And you; what have you planned for yourself?'

'We all must do our best to take Little Helewise's mind off her heartbreak, and as soon as she and Meggie return from the hut, I plan to take her over to New Winnowlands to see her cousin. While we're there, I will find the opportunity to ask Rosamund to tell me all that she remembers of her time with Olivier.'

'Good!' Abruptly, he stood up, and she sensed the impatient need for action that flowed through him. 'I'm off to the abbey. Make sure you are back here by tonight, won't you? I don't know why, but I have the feeling that we have no time to waste.'

She might have queried that, except that she felt it too.

Helewise and her granddaughter set off in the early afternoon. Helewise rode Daisy, and Little Helewise, subdued and with red-rimmed eyes, was mounted on her grey mare. Helewise did not try to make her talk. The loss was very raw, and everything about the girl seemed to be quietly saying: *leave me alone*.

The ride to New Winnowlands took them around the wide eastwards bulge of the great forest. The track was well used, and the going was firm, for of late the weather had been dry and quite cold. As they neared the small manor house that had once been Josse's and was now the home of Helewise's younger son and his family, both of them kicked on their horses and they reached the house at a smart canter.

The family came out to greet them. Rosamund, Helewise noticed, kept very close to her mother. Dominic came to help her down from her horse, and she said quietly, 'Ninian has had to leave England.' Briefly, she explained.

Dominic's eyes widened. 'You cannot believe he is guilty of murder?'

'No, none of us thinks that. Josse and I are going to try to find out who really killed Hugh de Brionne, and thus clear Ninian's name.'

Little Helewise had also dismounted and was embracing her young cousin. Dominic watched the two girls. 'She is taking this hard,' he observed, indicating Little Helewise. 'She is pale and it's obvious she's been weeping.'

'We are trying to keep her busy to distract her from her sorrow,' Helewise replied. 'Hence the visit here.'

Dominic nodded. 'She is welcome to stay. She and Rosamund get along well, and New Winnowlands has fewer associations with Ninian.'

'Thank you for the thought. We'll suggest it to her. There is one other thing.'

'Yes?'

'I would like to speak to Rosamund concerning the time she spent in Olivier's company. Is she, do you think, ready to talk about it?'

'Why do you want to question her?' Then, before she could respond, he provided the answer. 'Of course. To prove Ninian's innocence, you have to discover the identity of the murderer. And you are hoping Rosamund can help.'

'Have I your permission to speak to her?' Helewise tried to keep the urgency out of her voice. She did not want to put pressure on Dominic to give his consent, but, on the other hand, there were more people than just Rosamund to consider.

'You have,' Dominic said. 'It would be better, I think, not to question her in front of Little Helewise; you said you're trying to distract her from thinking about Ninian, and she would quickly realize the purpose of your questions. But go carefully with Rosamund, won't you?' His sombre face broke into a quick smile. 'As if you wouldn't,' he muttered.

She embraced him. 'Thank you.' Then she hurried after the two girls.

Dominic must have explained to Paradisa that Helewise wished to speak to Rosamund, for she came in, took the elder girl's hand and said, 'The stable cat has just had kittens. One of them has a little black moustache – come and see!'

Helewise caught her daughter-in-law's eye and mouthed, 'Thank you.'

Left alone with Rosamund, Helewise went to sit beside her and explained why she had come to see her. 'If there is anything you can recall that might be relevant, please tell me,' she said. 'You can see how Little Helewise suffers, and it will not be safe for Ninian to return until we can prove he was not involved in Hugh de Brionne's death.'

'I don't know this man,' Rosamund said, frowning. 'He is Olivier's brother, you say?'

'Yes.' Helewise, appreciating that it was distressing Rosamund not to be able to help, decided to change her approach. 'Tell me about Olivier,' she invited.

Predictably, Rosamund's expression lifted with relief at being able to supply an answer. 'He looks like Ninian,' she said. 'When I saw him on the path close to the House in the Woods, I truly thought he was Ninian. After I'd realized my mistake, I wasn't really afraid of him, because he was nice and he said we were going to a surprise party. He was kind to me and he looked after me, always asking if I was warm enough and making sure I was comfortable when we slept out in the open.'

Her frown was back. Helewise wondered what she was remembering. She was about to prompt her when she spoke again. 'He – I don't know how to explain, but quite often he seemed to be talking to someone, and at first I thought there must be another person with us, somehow keeping just out of sight, but then, of course, lots of the time we were out in the open and there was nowhere for anyone to hide, and in the end I thought he must be talking to himself.' She looked at Helewise. 'That was quite frightening,' she admitted.

'I'm sure it was,' Helewise said. Dear Lord, the poor child must have been terrified. 'Could you make out what he was saying?'

'Not really. He muttered quite quietly, although often he seemed to be arguing about something. It was almost as if whoever was talking to him was giving him orders, and he didn't want to obey them.'

Helewise stored that away. She was beginning to develop a picture of Olivier de Brionne, and she did not much like what she saw. 'You slept out in the open,' she said.

'Yes. He took me for a ride on his horse – he's a lovely horse, black with a star on his brow and he goes like the wind – but we got lost. He – Olivier – was very good at making a camp, and we had a fire and some food, and I wasn't really scared. I thought we'd just go home in the morning. Or, at least, that's what I told myself.'

The child had courage, Helewise thought. Many girls of her age would have been out of their wits with fear, sobbing and screaming uncontrollably. And what would this Olivier de Brionne, who heard voices and believed it was appropriate to present an eleven-year-old child to a king, have done if

Rosamund hadn't been so calm and level-headed? She did not want to think about it. 'But next day he didn't bring you back,' she said. 'What happened?'

'He had packed up our blankets and stamped out the fire and we were about to set off,' Rosamund said. 'We'd camped in the middle of a stand of trees, up on a slight rise above a bend in the river. There were lots of bracken and bramble bushes, and you could hide in there among the trees. We heard a horse in the distance and quite soon I saw a rider approaching, although he was too far away for me to see his face. He had a dark cloak with a hood. He was riding really hard, spurring on his horse. When he saw us, he starting yelling something and waving his arm.'

'What did you do?' Helewise asked gently. 'Did you think he'd come to rescue you?'

Rosamund looked ashamed. 'No. It was silly, but I felt really frightened of him, I don't know why. Perhaps it was just that he was shouting so much, and I was worried because, although his horse was clearly very tired and doing its best, he was spurring it really hard. It had foam all round its mouth and blood on its sides,' she added in a whisper.

'Could this horseman have been Ninian?' Helewise hardly dared ask the question.

Rosamund stared at her in amazement. 'Ninian? No, no, of course not! Ninian loves all animals and he would *never* treat a horse like that!'

Helewise began to feel a warm glow of relief. But the story wasn't told yet. 'You said you weren't afraid of Olivier,' Helewise said. 'It sounds to me as if your instinctive fear of this horseman was because you had no idea what he wanted, and he could have been more dangerous than Olivier.'

'Yes, perhaps,' Rosamund said. 'He – Olivier – quickly told me to hide under the trees where we'd left Star. I ran and nestled down in the bracken. It was all dry and prickly, but I felt safe in there. I heard the horseman come galloping up the slope, and he must have drawn his horse up really harshly, because it gave a sort of yelp of pain, and I heard Olivier's voice and another man's. They were arguing. Then there was a thump, and then some sounds as if somebody was doing something strenuous, and some talking, then Olivier yelled something, and there was lots more angry shouting as the other man rode away.'

Helewise felt the harsh disappointment run right through her. As Rosamund told her tale, she had really started to believe that she had been given proof of Ninian's innocence. Just for a moment, she had wondered if the unidentified horseman could have been Hugh de Brionne, hurrying to check on how his brother was progressing with the scheme to take the gift of Rosamund to the king. She had imagined the two brothers arguing, falling out, fighting. In her mind's eye she had seen Olivier land the blow that knocked Hugh backwards, so that he fell and struck his head.

For one precious moment she had believed she knew what had happened. But she was wrong. The horseman could not possibly have been Hugh, for Hugh died there on the rise above the river and, as Rosamund had just so clearly stated, the horseman had ridden away, still arguing with Olivier as he did so.

If he was indeed Hugh, then it was perfectly possible that, soon after leaving his brother, he had encountered Ninian, desperate to find Rosamund and none too fussy how he went about getting information from anyone he thought might be able to help.

Proof of Ninian's innocence was as elusive as ever.

Helewise could have wept.

FOURTEEN

Josse reached Hawkenlye Abbey around the middle of the day. Meggie had come with him as far as the hut. Not seeming to mind repeating the journey she had earlier done with Little Helewise, she had asked if he'd like company and he said yes.

He guessed his daughter would stay in the hut for a while. She had wanted to go off with Ninian so very much. She had not said so, but he knew her well enough to read the yearning in her eyes as they parted from him. He wondered what he would have done had she simply fetched her horse and ridden after him. He was very glad he had not been put to that particular test.

At the abbey, he went into the infirmary to find a crowd of men around the recess where the king lay. Sister Liese came to greet him.

'He is impatient to be gone,' she said softly, with a subtle jerk of her head in the direction of the king's recess. 'He demands incessantly for transport, for even he admits he is not fit to ride, and those who attend him here are torn between obeying their lord and listening to we who have the care of him, who insist he is not yet ready to leave us.'

'The wound is severe, then?' Josse asked anxiously.

'No, it is quite shallow and it heals well,' the infirmarer replied. 'However, we fear the dreaded infection, which can make a man's blood burn like fire in the space of a day. He is more at risk if he sets out on a journey.'

Josse nodded. 'How long before he can go?'

Sister Liese considered. 'Perhaps tomorrow, all being well.'

'Thank you.' He stared at the curtains around the king's bed.

'He already has five men with him,' the infirmarer said. 'If you wished to speak to him you would have an audience, I fear.'

Josse made a grimace. He wanted to discuss the very delicate matter of Ninian's innocence, and that was not a conversation to have when a handful of the king's sycophants were listening avidly. 'May I see Olivier de Brionne?'

'You may,' she said. 'He is awake, although much disturbed.' She gave Josse a sweet smile, lightening her serious face. 'Perhaps you will do him good, Sir Josse. You usually appear to do that when you come visiting in here.'

Glowing from the unexpected compliment, Josse crossed the long ward towards the recess where Olivier lay. He heard voices as he approached, which, when he parted the curtains to look inside, resolved into a single voice. Olivier, his face screwed up with tension, was muttering agitatedly to himself.

He looked up and, in the first instant before he recognized Josse, there was abject terror in his eyes.

Josse walked up to the bed and said swiftly, 'It's me, Josse d'Acquin. I came to see you before, remember?' He smiled, opening his arms in a vaguely benevolent gesture, hoping to reassure the young man.

Olivier's lips were moving, but Josse could not hear what he was saying. 'What's the matter?' he asked kindly. 'Will you let me help you?'

A fleeting smile crossed Olivier's face. 'Are you strong?' he asked. 'Can you combat devils?'

Devils. What in God's name was wrong with him? Josse sat down on the end of the bed. 'I have fought many an enemy,' he said, 'although I must confess that they have all been resolutely human.' He grinned, and there was a faint response from Olivier. 'What ails you?' he asked.

Olivier twisted away from him, his face anguished. 'They will not leave me alone,' he muttered. 'They talk to me all the time, giving me orders, telling me I have made bad mistakes.' He shot Josse a sly look. 'They warn me, too. They tell me I must be on my guard, for my enemies surround me and all the time they close in on me.' He shot out a hand and grasped Josse's wrist, his fingers digging in painfully. 'Are you my enemy?' he hissed. 'The voices are unclear . . .' Violently, he shook his head.

Josse wanted very much to pull away. Olivier seemed to have lost his reason, and Josse felt the deep, atavistic fear of insanity flood his mind. Trying to keep his voice calm and friendly, he said, 'I am not here to harm you, Olivier. I merely wish to ask you if there is anything you can tell me about

your – er, your journey with the girl, Rosamund. You have
been told of the tragic death of your brother, Hugh, and I am
attempting to discover how he died.' He thought quickly. Was
there any harm in being more forthcoming with this poor
young man? He did not think so. Leaning closer, he lowered
his voice and said, 'You see, Olivier, someone very close to
me is suspected of having fought your brother and caused his
death, and I do not believe he is responsible.'

Olivier was watching him, the blue eyes wide. The resemblance to Ninian was quite marked, although this young man
was more heavily built. He withdrew his hand, slipping it
beneath the covers. He muttered something inaudible. 'What
did you say?' Josse asked.

More muttering. Then Olivier said, 'They tell me I must
not talk to you. They tell me that you will twist my words
and use them against me. That madman did it – they say he
killed Hugh, and they are right! I saw how he attacked my
lord the king and me – he is as wild as they say! Leave me
alone! I will speak no more to you.' He clamped his lips closed
and turned away.

'Olivier, you do not help yourself by this silence,' Josse
said. 'I give you my word that I will not do what you suggest.
I merely ask you to help me.'

There was no answer. After a moment, Olivier reached down
for the bed covers and drew them right up over his head.

Josse stood up and quietly left the recess.

He tried to see the king, but two large men stepped in front
of him and barred his way. 'Tell him that Josse was here,' he
snapped angrily. 'Tell him I do not believe his so-called
madman is guilty of any crime, and that I am setting out to
prove it.' Then he spun round and strode away.

Left alone, Olivier emerged from under the covers and peered
out. He had been very afraid when the big man had sat
down on his bed. The big man looked kindly and said he
wanted to help, and Olivier had wanted so much to believe
him. Could he call him back? Everything had gone wrong,
and Olivier very much needed to talk to someone. The big
man said he had fought many enemies. He would be a good
person to have on your side. Olivier took a deep breath, about
to call out.

With the speed of diving hawks, the voices joined together and shouted him down with such deafening volume that his head rang. He whimpered in pain. 'All right!' he whispered. 'All right!'

He lay back against the pillows. The voices were still nagging at him, although they were quieter now. They told him he was a fool, and they were right, because he had forgotten something very important. Something he had found out because he was skilful and cunning, adept at creeping around and listening to other people talking, so that he usually knew a great deal more than people thought he did.

They had all thought he was unconscious but he hadn't been, or at least not for long. They had discussed what had happened up by the chapel. They had called the madman by name or, at least, somebody must have done, for Olivier knew his identity. He had listened some more and, even before the big man had told him, he had discovered that the madman was somehow related to him. Not his son, but there was a bond of love between them, that was for sure. The big man would protect the young man. He had just said as much: *someone very close to me is suspected of having fought your brother and caused his death, and I do not believe he is responsible.* Oh, it was all very confusing, and Olivier found it hard to think about it. His head hurt.

The voices saw their chance and started on at him again. *They don't like you. They will try to harm you. You have to do something.* They told him what that something was.

He wondered if he could do it. Carefully, he inspected his wounds. The long cut on his left forearm and down across his wrist hurt quite a lot if he used the arm, but he was right-handed, and he could rest it. The nuns had bandaged it heavily, so it was well protected. The wound under his right arm ached constantly, and if he coughed or sneezed, a red-hot pain shot through it. He would have to be very careful.

He did not want to obey the voices. He wanted to lie there in the bed with the nice clean sheets, having the young nun with the pretty face bringing him dainty little meals and the older one who looked calm and dependable coming to check on him twice a day. He felt safe in the infirmary and, for the first time in as long as he could remember, people seemed to like him and spoke to him with a smile. But the voices said he couldn't stay. He thought the voices were probably right; they usually were. And even he could see that his lord would not be staying there much longer.

He was clad in his shift, which the nuns had laundered to get the blood out and then given back to him. He wondered where his outer clothes were, and then he remembered. Of course – the nuns had put them under the bed. Cautiously, he eased over and peered into the dim space. There were his boots, and there was his tunic and cloak.

You have no excuse, the voices said coldly.

He was all alone. He had nobody to turn to. Everything had gone wrong.

He knew he must do as they said.

Josse stood outside the infirmary, undecided as to what he should do next. He wanted above all to talk to Helewise and discuss with her this fresh evidence of Olivier's strange state of mind. In the past, his footsteps would have set off for the abbess's little room without his volition. It was not that he had no faith in her successor – far from it. Josse had the utmost admiration for Abbess Caliste, but just now only Helewise would do.

But Helewise was not there. In addition, Gervase, no doubt busy organizing his search parties out looking for Ninian, was also unavailable. Josse was on his own.

His thoughts returned to Olivier. The young man's father had known his son was not right. *There's something wrong with the other one*, old Felix had said. Lady Béatrice, too, had spoken of her sons. *They are not close*, she said. And, when Gervase had asked if Hugh might have gone to the place where his body had been found because he was looking for Olivier, she said she doubted it.

They are not close. Josse thought it over. Yet, when Hugh de Brionne had hatched his plan to abduct Rosamund, his choice of conspirator had been his brother. Had they deliberately maintained the semblance of distance between them, so as to set a smokescreen around their actions? Or was it simply that their mother did not know them as well as she thought she did?

The last time Josse had been to the de Brionne manor had been the day after the discovery of Hugh's body. The household had had a little while to get over the first shock; Josse decided it was time he went back.

He drove Alfred hard, riding into Felix de Brionne's courtyard in the early afternoon. He was ushered into the hall where, as before, Lady Béatrice sat alone.

'I have come from Hawkenlye Abbey,' he said when he had greeted her and accepted her offer of refreshments.

She studied him, her face unmoving. 'And how is my son? Word was sent,' she added, 'that he has been wounded. I would very much like to go to him, but my husband lies abed and I cannot leave him.'

'Of course, my lady,' Josse said. He pitied her, that she had had to make such a decision. 'Olivier's wound is not life-threatening and, indeed, I have just come from speaking to him.'

Now she looked wary. 'Speaking to him?'

He wondered what thoughts were running through her head. Disturbing ones, from her expression. 'My lady, he is deeply troubled,' he said. 'It may be that his mind has been affected by his injury. Such things do happen.'

'Troubled? In what way?' she asked cagily.

'He hears voices and he talks back to them,' Josse said bluntly. 'I am sorry if my words alarm you, lady. I know no other way of expressing what I have seen.'

She had bowed her head. 'Olivier is not like others,' she murmured. 'He – life has been hard for him. I told you before of the rivalry between him and Hugh. What I did not say is that my husband never made a secret of his preference for Hugh.'

Josse waited. He understood – or believed he did – Felix's reason. Leofgar had reluctantly mentioned the rumours concerning Olivier's parentage. Felix himself had referred to having forgiven his young wife. The world was cruel in many ways, he reflected, but it was particularly bitter that a man should be disliked for who had or had not fathered him. It was scarcely his own fault . . .

He wondered if Lady Béatrice would confide in him. He hoped she would. He thought he had already guessed her secret, but he did not know for certain if he was right. Perhaps, if he opened his heart to her, she might reciprocate. 'My lady,

I too have troubles,' he said. 'A young man whom I love as much as the son of my blood is accused of something that I know he did not do, and I am trying to find out the truth of the matter. I have—'

'This young man is your wife's but not yours?' she interrupted.

Josse realized that he had inadvertently provided the perfect prompt. 'He was born to the mother of my other two children, but at a time before I knew her,' he said. Joanna flowed easily into his mind, momentarily taking all his attention. She was smiling, her dark eyes full of laughter and love. He caught his breath. Then, forcing himself to continue, he said, 'She was taken to a court Christmas by a cousin and she was seduced by one of the lords there.' There was no need to name Ninian's father. 'They married her off to an old man she hated, and in time her son was born. He and I met when he was a child and a deep affection sprang up between us. Later, after his mother died, I adopted him.'

She studied him for some time. Then she said abruptly, 'Your son is more fortunate than Olivier.' He thought she would say no more, but she took a deep breath and, the words tumbling out as if she had longed to release them, she said, 'The first child that I bore my husband was a daughter. He was displeased and chose to punish me by – never mind. I was unhappy and, when temptation came, I readily surrendered.' Her dark eyes were misty. 'For a time I was ecstatically happy, for my lover was a wealthy and important man and, until he tired of me, there was nothing that he would not give me. When I told him I was carrying his child, he gave a wry laugh, totted up in his head the new total of his bastards and told me that he did not bed pregnant women.' She paused. 'I never saw him again,' she said quietly.

Josse ached for her. 'Your husband forgave you.' It was a statement, not a question, for Felix had implied as much when Josse went to see him.

'He did. He was also good enough to allow me to raise my son as his. Olivier was provided with a home, and he was brought up in much the same way as my other children. Quite soon I conceived again, this time in my own marital bed, and I gave birth to Hugh.' Her eyes returned to Josse. 'I do not expect you to understand or condone my actions, Sir Josse.'

'It is not for me to criticize or condone, lady,' he said quickly.
'I am not here to judge you. None of my children, natural or
adopted, was born in wedlock,' he added with a smile.

'I would judge that your own children were born in love,'
she replied.

'Aye, that they were,' he agreed. Again, he could see Joanna.
He smiled at her, and she blew him a kiss.

Lady Béatrice was watching him. 'I have come to the conclusion that knowing he or she is loved matters more to a child
than anything else,' she said slowly. 'I love Olivier and always
have done, even when—' She stopped. Then: 'But he has
always sought the love of the parent who withholds it. When
he was little and did not understand, he suffered greatly from
Felix's coldness. By the time he was old enough to know the
truth, it was too late.' She sighed. 'Sir Josse, Olivier seeks
constantly for approval. Never having been given any by Felix,
he seeks it elsewhere. Now that he has managed to gain
advancement and grow close to the king's private circle, it is
his one aim to make himself indispensable and gain the position
with the king that he has never enjoyed with Felix.'

Josse tried to imagine one of his own sons suffering in the
way Olivier had done. He compared the two of them, seeing
straight away that Lady Béatrice was speaking good sense.
Geoffroi, who had known since he first became aware that his
father loved him and was always there to support and protect
him, was typical of a child brought up in a secure, warm
household. He was confident, independent, outgoing and transparent. Ninian, on the other hand, had been forced to live the
early years of his life with a cold and vicious man who had
mistreated both his young wife and her son. Then, after Joanna
had run away and taken Ninian with her, the boy had only
just got used to life alone with his mother when she, too, had
disappeared from his life. He was, Josse had to admit, a young
man who believed he must prove his worth in order to be
loved.

Olivier de Brionne, his mother seemed to be implying, was,
in this crucial way, remarkably similar.

Josse wondered why he should feel quite so frightened by
that realization.

FIFTEEN

Ninian blotted the departure from everyone he loved out of his mind. It was just too painful. There was plenty to think about to distract him, and for the first few hours he concentrated on ensuring he kept off the road, making his way along little-known tracks and trails and keeping to the forest fringe wherever he could. He decided not to make for one of the big channel ports. Josse had said the search parties would explore the road to the coast, and it seemed reasonable that they would also hunt for him in places such as Hastings and Pevensey. It did not matter. Ninian knew of other ways of getting a man and a horse across to France.

He had dismissed the idea of going in disguise. If he tried to make himself look like a peasant, they'd spot him instantly because poor men didn't ride horses like Garnet and they'd arrest him as a horse thief. He wore his good boots and, under his old leather jerkin, good-quality but well-worn tunic and hose. His heavy travelling cloak went over the top, its hood drawn forward to throw a shadow on his face, and there was nothing to distinguish him from any other traveller.

He crossed the South Downs on paths that were little more than animal runs. Descending towards the sea, he kept a lookout for a small jetty that he knew of where the fishermen went out into the deep water for cod and whiting. Spotting it, he was relieved to see that two boats lay in the shallows. He haggled briefly with the skipper of one of them and arranged his passage across to Boulogne.

The boat was going to sail on the evening tide. With the skipper's help, Ninian got Garnet safely aboard. Then he found a sheltered spot on deck, wrapped himself in his cloak and, exhausted by fear and emotion, went to sleep.

He woke to find that the boat was in mid-Channel. The water was rough, but not enough to trouble him. He leaned his elbows up on the deck rail and stared out. Dawn was beginning to lighten the sky, and land was visible ahead. His belly gripped tight with apprehension. Soon he would have to disembark and head off into the unknown. Would he be able to find Acquin? Josse had given him directions, but Ninian had scarcely taken them in. Perhaps he would be able to ask . . . But then another anxiety rose up. Josse had been utterly confident that his brothers would take Ninian in, but what if he was wrong? On his own admission, it was years since Josse had seen them. Supposing they closed their doors against him and refused to have anything to do with him? Supposing they had gone away? Supposing they were all dead?

Very firmly, he told himself not to be so stupid. One of Josse's oft-repeated sayings was: *don't hunt troubles out; wait and deal with them if and when they come looking for you.* It was sound advice. Ninian was going to take it.

The skipper brought his craft to shore at a small port to the south of Boulogne. He helped Ninian ashore, wished him well and set off back to sea even before Ninian was out of sight. Ninian had never felt more alone in his life.

He pressed on all day, although his progress was slow. Unnerved by other travellers, frequently he slid off Garnet's back and led the horse off the road to hide until they had passed. When darkness fell, he had no idea how far there was still to go. He found a sheltered spot in an apple orchard, bedding down in the corner furthest from the road and making a small fire to keep him warm and to heat water for a comforting drink. On the boat he had shared the fishermen's supplies, so he had not yet touched the food Josse had given him. The bread was dry as bone now, but he was so hungry that he ate every last crumb. He was glad he had good teeth.

He woke at first light. There were people passing on the road, and the sound of their voices had disturbed him. He lay perfectly still, his heart hammering. Had they seen him? Had they come from the coast? Against all logic, he found himself almost certain they had been sent by the king and, with unbelievable speed and efficiency, had found him after less than a day . . .

The tramping footsteps went straight past, and the cheery voices faded in the thin air. Rebuking himself for his folly, Ninian got up, rolled up his blanket, saddled Garnet and rode on.

He found Acquin late that afternoon. He had taken several wrong turns, and the people he had asked for directions hadn't heard of it. He had envisaged a large village or even a small town, well known and much frequented, but the truth was different. There was little to the place but a church and the fortified manor itself. His first glimpse was of the tops of two high watchtowers and, as he rode closer, he made out the long, low roofs of the buildings within the strong outer walls. He passed a church and a few meagre dwellings sheltering beneath the high walls. Then, following the walls, he turned up to the left and soon found himself in front of imposing gates, firmly closed.

There was a small opening in one of the wooden gates, presumably to allow those within to see who had come calling. He peered through it. Storerooms, workrooms and stables lined the courtyard on two sides, and on the third was what must be the family's accommodation. The short day was already darkening, and lamps had been lit. Smoke rose up from the slate roof.

Ninian was cold and lonely. He reached out and rang the heavy rope that worked the clapper of a big bell, and its deep note rang out.

A young man with light-blond hair emerged from the stables, wiping his hands on a sacking apron. He stared out suspiciously at Ninian. 'Who are you?'

Ninian had forgotten they would speak French. It was Josse's native tongue. Ninian had been forced to learn and speak it when he had lived with the terrible man his mother had married. He thought briefly, bringing to mind the right words, and replied in the same tongue: 'My name is Ninian de Courtenay. I have come from the house of Sir Josse d'Acquin, in England. If you please, I would like to speak to Sir Yves d'Acquin.'

The lad looked at him in surprise. Then he nodded and hurried away. Quite soon afterwards he returned, accompanied by another man. He was shorter and less heavily built than Josse, but he had the same dark eyes and thick brown hair. He had a round, pleasant face and laughter lines around his eyes and mouth. He looked at Ninian and said, barely suppressing the excitement, 'I am Yves. Is it true? Have you come from Josse?'

'I have,' Ninian agreed. 'He sends his greetings to his brothers and their families –' quickly, he reeled off all the names of the brothers, the wives and the children – 'and he asks that you take me in, for I am his adopted son.'

Yves was already shooting back the bolts and opening one of the gates. 'Come in!' he cried. 'I felt sure that you were who you said you were, even before you proved it by your recital of every last one of my immediate kin. Stephan, take his horse –' Ninian slid down and handed the lad Garnet's reins – 'and tend him well, for he looks as if he has ridden all day.'

'I got lost,' Ninian admitted as Garnet was led away and Yves ushered him inside. 'I left in a hurry, and I didn't listen properly to Josse's instructions.'

Yves stopped, turning to look at him. 'You left in a hurry,' he repeated worriedly. 'There is trouble?'

'Josse is perfectly well, as is everyone else,' Ninian said quickly, cross with himself for causing this affectionate, friendly man anxiety. 'Something happened. They – er, some quite important people think I killed someone and injured two others. I was in a fight with the two men, but any injury I inflicted was in defence of myself and others. I swear to you that I have killed nobody.'

Yves was looking at him intently. 'It's not every man who can claim that, in these troubled times,' he observed. He went on staring at Ninian, who found himself steadily becoming uneasy under the scrutiny. Eventually, Yves spoke again. 'My brothers say I am too quick to trust my own instincts, but all the same I intend to do precisely that,' he said. 'I like you, Ninian de Courtenay. I know a little of who you are and how you come to be Josse's son, and I would judge that you are a man who tells the truth, at least to those he cares about. Finally –' he started to move on as he spoke, leading Ninian along a passage towards an arched doorway – 'I do not believe that my brother would have sent you to me unless your credentials were impeccable.' He waved a hand, inviting Ninian to go on into the room beyond the arch. 'Come and meet my family.'

Back at the House in the Woods, Josse and Helewise sat on by the fire after the rest of the household had gone to bed. Before she retired, Tilly had returned and quietly left a jug of spiced wine beside the hearth. Josse had just stuck a hot poker into it, and the fragrant steam was scenting the hall.

'I wish Meggie was here,' Josse said, breaking the companionable silence.

Helewise thought she knew why. She had observed how, when young Geoffroi had gone to sit beside his father after supper, Josse had at first clutched the boy convulsively to him, swiftly releasing him when he realized the grip was too tight. Having just been forced to wave goodbye to one of the people he most loved, Josse obviously wanted to keep the others close.

'She will be home soon, I expect.' She tried to make her tone calm and reassuring. 'We all mourn Ninian in our own way,' she added softly.

'Don't use that word!' he snapped.

She rose and went to sit beside him. Taking his hand, she bent to kiss it. 'I am sorry,' she said. 'I only meant we mourn his presence here with us. No more.'

With a tentative hand, he reached out and lightly touched her cheek. 'I know,' he said gruffly. 'I didn't mean to shout at you.'

She got up and poured wine for them both. She handed one of the pewter goblets to him and, raising her own, said, 'To Ninian, wherever he is. May God keep him safe until he can return to us.'

'Amen,' Josse muttered, instantly taking a gulp of the wine.

Helewise went back to her seat on the opposite side of the hearth. Earlier, she and Josse had shared what sparse information their day's enquiries had discovered. Something that he had told her concerning his visit to Lady Béatrice was puzzling her. She thought about it – years as a nun had taught her to think before she spoke, so as not to waste time on idle chatter – and then said, 'Josse, I have been worrying about this scheme of Hugh's to use our Rosamund as a gift with which to gain the king's favour.'

'Aye, it's shameful,' he agreed. 'I—'

She interrupted him. 'It is, of course, but that wasn't what I meant. You paint a picture of Olivier as the outcast, the son whom his mother's husband tolerated but did not love. Surely, if one of the brothers had such a burning desire to gain the favour of an older man, it would not be Hugh, who already had a father's love, but Olivier. Yet Olivier claims the whole idea was Hugh's.'

'Aye, and Hugh is dead and cannot tell us otherwise,' Josse replied.

'I was so sure, when I spoke to Rosamund, that I had guessed what happened,' she said bitterly. 'Yet I was wrong, for this horseman whom Rosamund heard but did not see rode away again.'

'Aye, and in any case, had it been Hugh, and had he died there at that time, then what happened to his horse? Olivier would have had to take it away with him, and Rosamund would have told us had that been the case. She loves horses, doesn't she?'

'Indeed she does,' Helewise replied. 'Besides, she said that she rode with Olivier on Star. She'd certainly have described in great detail any horse she'd been loaned to ride by herself, especially the sort of mount ridden by a wealthy man.'

Neither of them spoke for some time. Then Josse sighed heavily and said, 'We still have no proof that it wasn't Ninian who fought Hugh.' He drained his goblet and set it down beside the empty jug. He straightened up and looked at her, his expression so sad that she almost leapt up to take him in her arms.

Something in his eyes held her back. 'I'm going to bed,' he said shortly. 'Sleep well, my lady.'

She listened as his heavy tread faded to nothing. My lady, she thought. Perhaps it was unconscious, brought about by the stress of the moment, but he had called her by the formal name that had been her right when she was abbess of Hawkenlye.

Slowly, she got up and went through to her own quarters. She made her preparations for the night, then went into her small sleeping chamber, quickly removing headdress and outer tunic and lying down. The bed was soft – far softer than the hard plank bed she had slept on for so long in the Hawkenlye dormitory – and the blankets were thick, soft wool. She even had a fur bedcover for when the weather was very cold. It was so luxurious, and Josse had provided it all for her.

She wanted more than anything to go to him. She loved him, and she knew he loved her. Even though she had made the vast break away from the cloister and Caliste had succeeded her at Hawkenlye, she seemed somehow to have brought her former life with her. People still sought her out for help and advice – well, she didn't mind that at all, since in leaving the abbey she'd had no intention of ceasing to serve God, in whatever way he dictated – and apparently, in the minds of almost everyone around her, she was still a nun. Still an abbess.

And Josse had just called her by her old name.

She turned on her side, sad and hurt, and tried to still her thoughts so that she could get to sleep.

That same evening, Hawkenlye infirmary's most illustrious patient finally reached the limit of his tolerance. He was a restless man by nature, his quick and able mind ever flying on to the next thought or challenge and his body swiftly leaping to follow. For far too long these well meaning but stern women had made him lie in bed because of a wound that really was not very serious. He knew he should respect them, for they were nuns and he had always been taught that the brides of Christ were to be honoured. The trouble was that they made him feel like a child again. He found himself automatically obeying when the infirmarer said *do this, don't do that*, for no better reason than that the sister's smooth-skinned, handsome face within the close-fitting wimple and headbands was so like his mother's. As was her air of serene confidence that the person to whom she had just given a command would do just as she said, even if he was the king of England.

He was sick of the infirmary, sick of the abbey, sick of this tour of the religious foundations, watching the work of his agents as they milked everything they could from the monks and the nuns. Yes, he managed to slip away and go hunting at times, but those times were not nearly frequent enough. Anyway, there was no need for him to involve himself with the group inspecting the abbeys; he had able servants who were as enthusiastic for this work of legalized plunder as he was himself. Coming out into the field of operations to see for himself had been a mistake, in hindsight. The trouble was that he had been bored and more than ready for a distraction. His wife had borne him two children in quick succession and, for the time being, she was too tired, plump and slack to hold much allure. She had ways of making it quite clear she did not want him anywhere near her – not that that would have stopped him had he desired to bed her – and he had decided that life was more pleasant without her sharp tongue and her endless complaints. Let her amuse herself with that half brother of hers. There were plenty of prettier women to be had.

His boredom had stemmed from an additional cause: life had seemed strangely flat ever since he had returned from his triumphant expedition to Ireland. Whatever the rumours might say – and if he knew who had started the mutterings that he had left the country in a ferment, he would have them put lengthily and unpleasantly to death – he knew, in his own mind, that he had outplayed the lot of them and ought to have the undiluted praise that was his due.

Tomorrow he would return to London. He would ride his own horse – he would have no truck with this suggestion of a litter – and he would set a fast pace. He had a vague memory of having told his people to arrange overnight accommodation on the way, but he had changed his mind and now wanted nothing more than to be back in his own sumptuous surroundings.

This would be his last night at Hawkenlye. He would make it one to remember. Calling for his attendants, he told them to fetch his outer garments and help him dress.

King John let his men accompany him as far as the clearing, then told them curtly to remain on guard while he went into the chapel. Opening the door, he went inside. It was not yet fully dark, and the soft light reflecting off the white walls still held the glow of sunset. The curved east wall, over to his right beyond the simple altar, was brilliant with the sunlit colours of the stained glass in the west end of the small building. He stopped and looked up at the window.

St Edmund rode a richly-caparisoned horse and was depicted with his sword arm raised, ready to strike down the enemies of the Lord. He was tall, broad, auburn-haired and blue-eyed, and he resembled John's elder brother far too closely for it to be coincidence. Only Queen Eleanor, her son reflected, could have got away with it . . .

He stood quite still in the middle of the little chapel. She was not here, but he believed she would come. This place was clearly important to her. It was where he had first seen her and, when he had fought with the madman who had launched his ferocious attack, she had been here, defending not only the little girl but also – he saw her clearly in his mind's eye – the chapel.

He would wait for her. If he was wrong and she did not come, he would explore the surrounding woodland. It was dense and dark, and there were alarming rumours concerning the magical creatures that dwelt within its shadows, but he had no time for peasant superstition and he did not believe in magic.

She lived nearby: of that he was certain.

The sun sank down behind the trees, and the brilliant illumination that had lit up the west window slowly faded. Only then did he realize that a lamp burned on the altar. As the shadows grew, it shone relatively more brightly. Presently, it was the only source of light in the chapel. His eyes were drawn to it.

The door opened, and one of his guards looked in. He shouted at him and, with a bow, the man backed out again.

When the door opened a second time, it was to admit her.

Meggie did not know what drew her repeatedly back to the chapel. She knew full well why she wanted to stay at the hut for the time being: because she wished with all her heart that she had gone with Ninian, and, back at the House in the Woods, she knew she would find his absence a constant reproof. He needed her, she kept telling herself. Their mother would have wanted them to go together. But, against those two powerful facts, a third had been even more forceful. The look on her father's face when he realized she was on the point of hurrying off after her half brother had done something funny to her heart. She had known then she had to stay.

Being in the hut made her feel close to her mother. She sensed Joanna's vivid presence; she even saw her sometimes, or thought she did, although the image was faint, as if seen through mist. Her mother understood why she could not go with Ninian. Joanna had loved Josse too and knew what he meant to Meggie.

Perhaps it was Joanna who wanted her to keep vigil at the chapel. Meggie had been wrong in thinking that the great lords – one of whom, as she now knew, was the king – had been there because they were hunting for the Black Madonna. The king was after something far more earthly than a mysterious black goddess.

Still, Meggie could not relax. Repeatedly, she found herself returning to the chapel, simply, as she told herself, to make sure all was well. Late in the afternoon, just before sunset, she decided to pay a last visit. She was some way down the path when, with a soft exclamation, she turned and retraced her steps. Going back inside the hut, she took a small, hard object wrapped up in a leather bag out of a specially-crafted wooden box that was screwed to the underside of the sleeping platform. Obeying some indefinable impulse, she had brought it with her from its habitual hiding place at the House in the Woods. Holding it lightly in her right hand, once again she walked briskly out of the clearing.

As she emerged from beneath the trees, she saw a group of armed men lounging around outside the chapel. One of them said something to the others, making a vulgar gesture with his hand and jerking his head in the direction of the chapel. Meggie leapt back under cover. She knew, then, who was inside.

She feared him, for she knew what he wanted of her. Yet when he had spoken to her, against all logic she had found herself liking him. She had had no dealings with men such as him; Josse had once lived in those elevated circles, but now, on his own admission, he was an ordinary family man doing his best for those he loved. She did not really understand the power of sophisticated, intelligent, determined charm . . .

Her own feelings must in any case be put aside, for he was in the chapel, only a few feet above the place where it held its secret. She waited until the men were not looking – that was easy, for now another of them was telling a joke or a lewd story, and all their attention was on him – and, slipping out from the shadows, she ran round to the chapel door, opened it and went inside.

He turned to look at her. 'Meggie,' he said softly. 'I knew you would come.'

She made herself walk closer to him. Standing right before him, she made a low curtsey. 'We are honoured by your presence here, my lord,' she said.

He reached out for her hand and raised her up, putting his fingers under her chin so that she lifted her head and looked at him. They were roughly of a height; if anything, she was a little taller.

It was difficult to take in anything other than the bright eyes. He was in his forties now, the strong body getting fat around the middle, but she found that those factors weighed little against the compelling power of his gaze. *He is dangerous*, she told herself. *Do not forget it.*

'I shall leave the abbey in the morning,' he said softly, 'but I could not go without saying goodbye to you.'

'You flatter me, lord,' she replied.

'I have wanted you since I saw you outside with your little friend,' he went on. 'That mad fool Olivier must have seen me watching you both and mistaken the object of my attention.' Anger briefly contorted his face: there and gone in an instant. He moved closer to her, and she felt the heat of his body. 'What I want,' he murmured, 'I usually get.' He ran his fingers down her hair. 'Such beautiful curls,' he murmured. 'You smell clean, Meggie. I like clean people.'

'I smell of herbs,' she said. 'I work with them.'

He nodded. 'Very laudable.' His eyes seemed to bore into her. 'You have light in your face, and your eyes flash like sun on the water,' he murmured. Then he took her face gently in his hands and kissed her.

For a moment the temptation was strong to kiss him back. This man held Ninian's life in his hands. If Meggie were to give him, willingly and generously, what he so clearly and so badly wanted, perhaps he would grant her the one thing *she* really wanted and spare her half brother's life. Besides, man of broad experience that he was, the prospect of making love with him was not unappealing.

A voice like cold water spoke in Meggie's head. It was a voice which, other than in dreams and visions, she had not heard for more than a decade. Her mother said, firmly and clearly: *have no truck with kings, for they take what they want and do not give anything in return.*

Meggie pulled away. The moment of weakness was gone. She knew her mother was right. He would not give up the pursuit of Ninian, even if she slept with him until he grew tired of her. More than that – worse than that – if she allowed him close to her, she might inadvertently give away some small fact that would lead him to the very person she was so desperate to protect.

He moved his hands so that he gripped her shoulders. 'You

would give me the sport of forcing you, would you?' A cruel smile crossed his face. 'Oh, Meggie, and there I was believing you were about to yield to me right here in the sanctity of my late and much-mourned mother's chapel!' He gave her a shake. 'I will have you,' he said, his voice as soft and dangerous as a snake's hiss.

He released her briefly, dragging at the neck of her gown and at the lacings of his own tunic. She knew she had to act then or be lost. Grasping the leather bag, which hung from her belt, she loosed the drawstrings and took out the object within.

Then she held up the Eye of Jerusalem and, just as she had so desperately hoped, the light of the lamp burning on the altar shone on it, brought its incredible heart to life and flashed blue fire all around the chapel.

The jewel was her inheritance, coming to her from her father and her grandfather, accompanied by the prediction that she would be the first person in its incredibly long history to discover its full potential. She had worked with it as much as she dared, tentatively exploring its incredible power, nerving herself to push her experiments steadily further, even though she had frequently terrified herself and regularly caused herself at worst injury, at best a crushing headache that took days to dissipate. But magic was like that; she never complained.

One thing that she had discovered was that the great sapphire had the ability to send her into a trance. She had sat with it in the hut one night, idly swinging it to and fro so that the light of the fire burning in the heath caused it to flash intermittently. Transfixed by the sight, she had felt her eyes go unfocused and her mind empty itself of whatever she had been thinking about. She had only emerged from the Eye's spell when she had fallen over sideways on to the floor.

Few people knew about the jewel. Her father did; so did Helewise. So did one or two others. Josse and Helewise had reluctantly agreed to allow her to try out her discovery on them, and both had succumbed to the stone's trance-inducing power even more swiftly than she had done.

Now, when so much depended on it, she prayed to her guiding spirits that it would not let her down.

She swung it gently on its gold chain. He tried to grab it, but she flicked it up out of his reach. She went on swinging it, and the blue light flashed out so brightly that it was almost blinding. She remembered to look away; this was no time to entrance herself.

There was a change in him. His hands dropped to his sides, and the brilliant eyes followed the stone in its arc – left, right, left, right – their intense blue seemingly lit from within by the light radiating through the great sapphire.

She said, very softly, 'You do not want me. This place is hallowed, and to make love to a woman in it would violate its sanctity. There is a power here that you cannot comprehend, and it does not do to offend it.'

She went on swinging the Eye. He was deeply under its spell now, his face blank, his eyelids heavy. She knew she must stop soon. If he went right under, he would fall on to the hard stone floor and possibly injure himself. The noise of his falling might bring the guards running, and she would instantly be arrested and taken away in chains for assaulting him.

'Leave this place,' she intoned, almost singing the words. 'Go away from here. I am not for you, for my fate is connected with the secret of this place and I would not have you risk its vengeance by taking from me what I do not freely give you.'

The trance was deepening. Slowly, she lessened the Eye's swing until it hung still. Then she enclosed it inside her palm, and its light went out. Now they were just two people standing face-to-face in a small, simple chapel.

His eyes opened fully. He seemed totally bemused. He looked around him, apparently searching for something. Finally, he turned to her. 'Meggie?' he said. He sounded as if he doubted even that.

'I am here, my lord,' she said calmly. The jewel was back in its bag, hidden in the folds of her skirt. 'What do you wish of me?'

He shook his head violently. 'Nothing! You are – you are—' He frowned, clearly confused. Then, with the ghost of a smile, he said, 'You, my dear, are a vestal virgin. Keep your fire burning . . .' The frown deepened, and for a moment he spun round as if some memory stirred. 'There *was* a fire,' he muttered. 'A blue fire.'

'There is a lamp on the altar.' She pointed. 'I have observed myself how some trick of the light allows its flame to catch in the blue of the window there.' She indicated St Edmund on his horse, the sky blue above his head.

He did not look convinced. He was eyeing her suspiciously. 'I would believe there was magic here,' he murmured, 'and that you, my Meggie, were a witch, only I do not believe in magic and, whatever the ignorant peasantry may say, there are no such things as witches.'

She bowed her head. 'No, lord.'

His hand was under her chin. She raised her eyes and looked at him. 'I leave for London in the morning,' he said. He looked momentarily puzzled, as if half-recalling that he had already told her. 'I wish that I could take you with me.' He leaned forward and kissed her mouth, gently, affectionately. 'But you belong here, witch of the wildwood.'

He took one long, last look at her. Then he turned away and strode out of the chapel.

She made herself wait. She heard his voice, shouting out some command, and another man's raised in reply. There was the faint patter of conversation, quickly fading. When she was sure they had gone, she hurried over to the flagstone trapdoor and, raising it, flew down the steps into the crypt.

She did not bother with a light. She knew every inch of the place and, besides, the goddess's power drew her unerringly. She fell to her knees before the niche where she knew the Black Madonna sat, opening her heart and pouring out her gratitude.

A long time later, she rose to her feet, went back up the steps and left the chapel. She looked down at Hawkenlye, most of its lights darkened now. She sent King John a silent good night.

Then she hurried off through the woods towards the hut and her bed.

SIXTEEN

At Hawkenlye Abbey, the nun who had replaced Sister Martha in the stables was surprised one morning when a shabby-looking peasant brought in an extremely handsome horse. It was not in very good condition, for its coat was dull and matted, its ribs showed, and its expensive leather harness was dirty. The reins had broken, and the two ends had been clumsily knotted together. When Sister Judith asked the man what he was doing with such a horse, he shuffled his feet and said lamely, 'I found him.'

She guessed there was more to it than that. She suspected that the man had thought about keeping the animal, only to discover pretty soon that a fine riding horse is not very much use to a peasant. She knew she ought to report the man – the dear Lord alone knew how long the horse had been in his keeping – but something about his sad, defeated face and the dejected slump of his shoulders stopped her. If it were to be discovered that some time had elapsed between his finding the horse and bringing it to the abbey, they'd probably accuse him of trying to steal it, and horse thieves were invariably hanged.

Times were hard enough anyway without hanging a man. He might have dependants. Most men did. Sister Judith made up her mind. 'You did right to bring the horse here,' she said. Fixing the man with a hard stare, she added, 'I am not going to ask you to tell me how and when you found him. If there are sins on your conscience, I suggest you pray for forgiveness. Now, be off with you, before I change my mind.'

He grabbed her hand, squeezed it, muttered something and ran.

Sister Judith saw to the horse's immediate needs, removing the dirty saddle and bridle, giving him water and what she could spare of her meagre supplies of feed. Then she went to report to Abbess Caliste.

Abbess Caliste had had so many matters to occupy her mind since the drama of having a king in the infirmary that it was some time before she thought to connect the arrival of an unknown horse with recent events. It was a couple of days since the king had left, and she felt that the dust was still settling.

Abbess Caliste thoughtfully put down her stylus. She had been hard at work for hours, and a brief walk in the fresh air would do her good. She got up, put on her cloak and went outside, crossing the cloister and slipping out through the front gates. She hoped that one of the people she sought would be at the chapel; if not, she would have to send a messenger to the House in the Woods.

Helewise was on the point of leaving the chapel to go home. She would have left sooner, only a woman with a small child had appeared outside the tiny cell where Helewise had once lived, begging for food. The child, a little boy, had looked at Helewise with huge eyes in his dirty face. He was too weak to walk, and his mother had been carrying him.

Not for the first time, Helewise had raged silently against the men of power who cared not a scrap for the people. She hurried off to Meggie's hut, where she heated water and prepared a thin soup, putting it in a pot and wrapping it in her cloak so that it would keep hot while she returned to the clearing. She also cut up the last of her small supply of bread so that the woman could dip it in the warm gruel and let the boy suck in the nourishment. She told them they could stay in the cell that night.

It was so little, but the woman fell on her knees in gratitude.

Helewise had gone to pray, trying to find it within her to ask pardon for her inner fury against her king. The battle with herself was long and, ultimately, futile.

As she closed the door of the chapel, Abbess Caliste came up the rise and approached her. She made a reverence, but, as she always did, Caliste caught her up and gave her a hug. Then she told her about the horse.

Helewise thought hard all the way home, and her concentration was so intense that she was back sooner that she had thought possible. She could hear Josse's voice in the stable yard, and she hurried to find him.

'Josse, I think—' she began.

He took her hands and instantly exclaimed, 'You're freezing. Come inside. You can tell me whatever it is when you're sitting by the fire.'

She did as she was told, containing her impatience while he fussed around her, shouting to Tilly for hot food and tucking a blanket round her. She resisted the urge to scream at him to stop. It was, she had to admit, lovely to be looked after.

When finally he was seated beside her, she said, 'Josse, I want you to listen. I'm going to tell you a version of how Hugh de Brionne was killed, and I don't want you to interrupt. When I've finished,' she added as a concession, 'you can comment.'

He grinned. 'Very well, I'll do as you ask.' Putting a hand in front of his mouth to indicate that he would keep silent, he nodded for her to begin.

'We know that Olivier de Brionne took Rosamund from the track leading to this house,' she said, 'and carried her on his horse off towards the hunting lodge on the Ashdown Forest, spending the night on a rise above the river. As they were preparing to leave the next morning, they spotted a horseman approaching and Olivier ordered Rosamund to hide in the trees. He knew the horseman – it was his brother, Hugh, who had contrived the plot to seek favour with the king by taking Rosamund to him.'

She could tell from Josse's expression that he had something to say but, true to his word, he did not speak.

'I don't know what Hugh wanted with Olivier, but the matter was urgent, for Rosamund said that he was in a hurry and yelling out to Olivier even as he rode towards him. Perhaps Olivier should already have been at the hunting lodge, and Hugh was anxious in case something was wrong. Whatever it was, the brothers had angry words, and then, according to Rosamund, Hugh rode off again, with Olivier still shouting after him.'

She paused. This was where fact ended and conjecture began. There was nothing to be gained by waiting, so she plunged on. 'Josse, Olivier talks to people who aren't there. Rosamund told me; it frightened her. What if it happened like this? Hugh and Olivier fought, and it was Olivier who left the marks of his fists on Hugh's face. In the course of the fight, Hugh stumbled and fell over backwards, striking his head and receiving the blow that killed him. Olivier, horrified, realized what he had done, but couldn't accept it. Perhaps acting on instinct, for I don't suppose he was capable just then of thinking rationally, he slapped Hugh's horse hard on the rump, cried out really loudly and frightened it into bolting. To Rosamund, hiding under the trees and unable to see what was happening, it would have sounded as if Hugh had ridden away. I don't think it ever occurred to her that he never left the place, or that Olivier killed him only a matter of a few paces away from where she crouched. Then, once Olivier had hidden the body and made sure the horse was no longer in sight, he went to fetch her and together they rode off on his horse.'

She stopped. She tried to judge from Josse's expression whether or not he agreed with her version of events.

'If you're right,' he said slowly, 'then what became of Hugh's horse?'

'According to Abbess Caliste, a rather fine horse has just turned up at the abbey.'

After a moment he said, 'There's one way to find out if you're right.'

Her heart leapt. 'What is it?'

He stood up. 'I'll ride over and have a look at Olivier's hands.'

Josse made the return journey to Hawkenlye more swiftly than Helewise had walked it, choosing to take his horse and keep to the main tracks. The distance was longer, but the going faster. Leaving Alfred at the gates, he sent word to the abbess to tell her what he was doing and hurried to the infirmary.

On hearing his request, Sister Liese shook her head and said simply, 'But Olivier has gone.' She indicated the two recesses where Olivier and the king had been treated. 'They have all gone, back to one of the king's London residences. His apartments in the Tower, I believe they said.'

Josse felt bitterly disappointed. But there was still one slim chance of finding out what he needed to know: 'Did you treat him yourself, Sister?'

'Yes, to begin with,' she said, 'and then I was called away to more pressing cases and I handed his care to one of my nuns.' She gazed out along the infirmary. 'Sister Bridget took over.'

'Will you describe his wounds for us?' Josse asked.

Sister Liese looked doubtful.

'Please, Sister!' he urged. 'It is very important.'

'Very well. He had a deep cut over his ribs, beneath his right arm, and a long cut down his left forearm, extending on to the wrist and the back of the hand.'

'Aye, I recall now that his left hand was heavily bandaged,' Josse muttered. 'Did you notice anything else, Sister Liese?'

Her eyes narrowed. 'I am trying to visualize him . . . Yes, there was extensive bruising to one of his hands. I remember asking the herbalist for a burdock poultice, and I did fear that a bone might have been broken, although in fact he had use of the hand and so that was unlikely.'

'Do you remember which hand?' Josse asked.

'The right,' she said instantly. 'I could not have put a poultice on his left hand, for the cut in it had been bandaged.'

Josse visualized the dead man. 'The damage to Hugh's face was on the left side,' he said quietly. 'Where a right-handed man would have hit him.'

At Acquin, Ninian was beginning to relax and enjoy himself. He had settled very happily with the family. Josse's brothers and their wives were avid for every last little detail of life in the House in the Woods, and in the evenings, when work was done for the day and the family relaxed together, they all plied him with endless questions.

'How I should love to see him again,' Yves sighed one evening, wiping away tears of laughter after Ninian had excelled himself in describing Josse's attempts at herding the household's small flock of sheep off Meggie's herbs and back into the sheep fold. One ewe, which Josse claimed was unique among the creatures of the earth in having been born without a brain, had frustrated him so severely that he had tried to pick her up by the back legs and drag her, upon which she had kicked him soundly in the groin. 'England is not so far away,' Yves went on sadly, 'yet the years pass, the days are so full and it is easier to sit here and reminisce than to get up and set out on a visit.'

'Josse would say the same,' Ninian replied. He had warmed to Yves and did not think it was fair for him to take all the blame on himself. 'Besides, there are four brothers here, and Josse is only one. It's up to him, really, to come to you.'

Suddenly, he experienced one of the strange moments which happened occasionally, when he saw something that was going to happen. He had learned not to worry about them; it was, he had decided, probably a gift inherited from his mother. He had also learned to trust them.

What he saw, as he sat across the fire from Yves, was a perfectly clear image of Josse sitting beside his brother.

He decided not to tell Yves. If he was right – and he knew he was – then the visit would come as a lovely surprise.

Yves insisted that Ninian be shown all over the Acquin lands. On several successive mornings, they saddled up their horses and, sometimes accompanied by one of the other brothers, sometimes just the two of them, they would set off on a long morning ride.

On the fourth day of Ninian's stay, he was riding back towards the house with Yves and Patrice and looking forward to the meal which would be waiting for them. Patrice was pointing down to the little river that ran through the valley, telling him where the best spots to fish for a trout or a perch could be found, when they heard voices on the road ahead. They were not far from Acquin and, up a narrow path that led up to the right, a group of alders grew around a pond. The voices came from under the trees.

Somebody was weeping, loudly and uncontrollably.

Yves spurred on his horse, Ninian and Patrice in his wake. They dismounted at the end of the path, tethered their horses and ran up the gentle slope to the huddle of people.

They were all local people; Ninian recognized quite a few of the faces. Seeing Yves approach, most of them stood back and some bowed their heads to their lord. As a gap opened up and the pond became visible, Ninian, just behind Yves, saw what was causing the commotion.

A body lay on the edge of the water. It was that of a man, clad in down at heel boots, darned hose and a jerkin that seemed to be made out of sacking. His dirty hair was pale blond. A woman was crouched over him, patting at his face, weeping, crying out a name: 'Stephan! Oh, Stephan!'

It was Yves's stable lad.

Yves was already on his knees in the mud beside the young man's mother. He had his hand on the lad's throat and, as Ninian watched, he bent down to put his cheek beside the open mouth. He glanced up, and Ninian saw him catch his brother's eye and briefly shake his head. Then he stood up, ran his eyes over the gawping villagers and, selecting a couple, told them to escort the wailing, shocked woman back to her home. Two more were sent to fetch a stretcher for the body. There were still four or five people hanging about and, with a swift, impatient gesture, Yves said, 'Get back to your work. There is nothing anyone can do for him now.'

When everyone had gone, Yves beckoned to Patrice and Ninian, and they approached the body.

'How did he die?' Patrice asked. 'Did he drown?'

'I do not think so, for his hair is dry,' Yves said. He was running his hands over the body, searching for the fatal injury. With a soft exclamation, he pointed to the neck. On the left side – the side on which the body lay – there was a short, deep cut beneath the ear. The young man's life blood lay in a great pool beneath it. 'See,' Yves said softly. 'A stab to the neck.' He touched the dead cheek with a gentle hand. 'Such a small wound, to bring about a man's death.'

Ninian had seen something else. The lad's right hand was tightly clenched, but the edge of a small leather bag was visible, sticking out between the thumb and the forefinger. He reached down and opened the fist, extracting the bag. Opening it, he saw that it was full of coins. Silently, he handed it to Yves, who quickly counted the coins, his eyes widening.

'There's several months' income here!' Yves whispered. 'However did Stephan come by so much money?'

'Perhaps he stole it,' Patrice suggested.

Yves frowned. 'I would have said Stephan was an honest man, but recently he has changed. He wishes to marry,' he went on, looking at Ninian, 'and he has not the means.'

'Someone desperate for money may turn from his former honest ways,' Ninian said.

Still Yves looked doubtful. 'Who could he have stolen *from*, though? We see few strangers here, and nobody local carries this sort of sum around with them.'

Patrice stood up. 'I will go and ask among the villagers,' he said. 'I'll take Ninian with me, unless you wish him to stay with you until they come for the body?' Yves shook his head. 'Then I would be grateful for your company,' Patrice went on, turning to Ninian with a smile. 'Your eyes are a lot younger than mine, and you may well spot something that I miss.'

Not many of the villagers had obeyed Yves's order to return to work. Stephan's mother had disappeared, presumably now pouring out her grief inside her house, and a group of the men who had stood around the body were gathered close to the church. They had been joined by several more. A man stood in the middle of the group, speaking urgently. Seeing Patrice, he fell silent. As one, the men turned to look at Patrice and Ninian.

'Stephan was murdered,' Patrice said. There was a low rumble of comment, although Ninian was almost sure the men had already known. 'He was clutching a bag of money. We don't know how he came by it. If any of you has anything to say that might help us find out what happened, you must tell us immediately.' One or two of the men exchanged glances. 'If you prefer to speak privately, come to the manor house.'

He waited. Ninian looked around the group. Nobody made any move to speak. 'Very well,' Patrice said. 'We will return to the manor.' He paused. 'Remember, all of you, that a young man who was one of the Acquin community has been brutally slain. He leaves a widowed mother, who depended on him. He leaves a pretty young girl who was expecting to marry him. Both women will be heartbroken.' He turned his horse, nudged it and moved off, Ninian behind him.

'Do you think anyone will respond?' Ninian asked once they were out of earshot.

Patrice smiled grimly. 'I fully expect it,' he replied. 'The man who was addressing the crowd – his name is Pierre – makes it his business to know everything that goes on among the Acquin peasantry. He might have spoken just now, but he likes to make himself important by adopting the role of spokesman for the village.' They were back at the house, and Patrice reined in to let Ninian ride ahead into the yard. 'Besides,' he added, 'Pierre knows there's always a mug of ale and a sweet cake to be had when he comes here with useful information.'

They had not been back long when Yves arrived home. He assembled the household and briefly told them all what had happened. There was a cry from one of the kitchen women, quickly stifled, and several of the younger servants looked pale and shocked.

The family sat down to eat and had almost finished when a servant came into the hall and spoke quietly to Yves. He nodded, stood up and then glanced at Patrice and Ninian and jerked his head in the direction of the passage that led along to the kitchens. Both got up and followed him out.

'Pierre?' Patrice asked.

'Aye.'

Pierre was waiting for them in the small covered area between the main house and the kitchens. He was a wiry, thin-faced man with restless eyes set close together. He doffed his cap when they approached, twisting it in his hands.

'You have something to tell us, Pierre,' Yves said.

'I have, sir.' He glanced at Ninian.

'You may speak in front of him,' Yves reassured him.

'Er – thank you, sir. It's not that, not exactly.'

Yves frowned. 'What, then?' he demanded.

Pierre gave a faint shrug, as if of resignation. Then he said, 'There's been strangers in the village. One man in particular, asking questions. He knew the name d'Acquin, and he was looking for a young man who had come to stay with the family here.' He waved a hand, indicating the spreading manor house.

Ninian felt as if a cold fist were closing around his heart. He made as if to speak, but Yves put a hand on his arm, restraining him. 'This man was offering to pay for information, I imagine?' he said coldly.

'That he was, sir, and I hope I need not say that, almost to a man, we were having none of it.' Pierre managed to form an expression with his sharp features that was a perfect mix of indignation and hurt loyalty.

'No, Pierre, you do not,' Yves said. 'You are decent people, I know that.'

Pierre acknowledged the comment. 'Well, Stephan, he was the exception,' he went on, 'but then, as we all know, Stephan is in love and that can turn a man's head, and when he was offered more money than he sees in half a year, just for passing on what was no deep secret anyway, he thought to himself: *where's the harm?*'

'He has been reporting to this stranger concerning the movements of my nephew?' Yves demanded.

'That he has, sir,' Pierre answered.

'You did not think to come and tell me?' Yves sounded angry. 'Had you done so, Stephan's death might have been averted.'

A crafty look came over Pierre's face. 'Well, now, it might and it might not,' he said. 'Trouble was, sir, if you don't mind me saying so, that, according to what I heard, this stranger told young Stephan that your – er, your nephew here was a wanted man back in England. Killed a man, they say.' His eyes shifted to Ninian, then back to Yves. 'Now, I don't necessarily believe it, but it wasn't my place to come here repeating such accusations to you, now, was it, sir?'

'I—' Yves bit back whatever he had been about to say. Instead, he fixed Pierre with a steely stare. 'What my nephew may or may not be accused of is no business of anybody here,' he stated firmly. 'The full story is known to me already, and there is to be no speculation. Do you understand?' Pierre nodded. 'Now, tell me everything you can about the man who paid Stephan for information.'

Pierre shrugged. 'There's not much I can say, sir, for I never met him. Nobody did – only Stephan.'

'Was the man who paid him for information alone?'

'I can't say, sir. Stephan seemed to think there was a group of them in the area, fanning out on their manhunt, but he only dealt with the one.'

Yves was silent for some moments, evidently thinking hard. Then he said, 'Thank you for coming to speak to us.' He handed a coin to Pierre, who grasped it and tucked it away with a conjurer's speed. 'Tell Stephan's mother that we will do what we can for her. As for the rest of the village, it would do no harm to point out that, whatever happiness Stephan hoped to buy for himself by his betrayal, it has come to naught.' He stared at Pierre. 'Men who are willing to pay other men so well to spy for them are not in the habit of leaving them alive to tell the tale.'

Pierre bowed. 'No, sir.'

'You may go,' Yves said. Pierre looked up hopefully. 'Via the kitchens,' Yves added.

With a muttered, 'Thank you, sir,' Pierre turned and scurried away.

Ninian went straight to the sleeping space that he had been allocated and, kneeling on the floor, began to pack his belongings.

Yves watched him for a while and then said, 'You know who this man was, don't you?'

'Not exactly,' Ninian replied. 'It's obvious who has sent him, though.' He sat back on his heels, looking up at Yves. 'I did not think the king would act so swiftly. I even wondered if he would think that it was not worth hunting for me this side of the Channel.' He sighed. 'Perhaps Hugh de Brionne was very close to him. I don't know.'

'The man you are accused of killing?'

Ninian nodded.

'Hm. They say King John is quick to anger and slow to forgive.'

'They say right,' Ninian replied grimly. 'Now it seems he's sent a search party to comb northern France till they find me and take me back.'

Slowly, Yves shook his head. 'It is the act of a vengeful man.'

'Yes, and unfortunately one with many men at his disposal.' Ninian rolled up his spare garments and tied the bundle with a sharp jerk of the string.

Yves frowned. 'There must be somewhere we can hide you. There's an old disused mill on the road out of the valley to the east, and we could—'

Ninian stood up and faced him. 'I appreciate the offer, more than I can say, but I cannot accept it.' He met Yves's eyes. 'I bring danger, Yves. One man is already dead because of me, and, as Patrice said, two women are heartbroken. That is hard enough to live with. I cannot take the risk that my continuing presence here would bring about similar tragedy in your household.'

'But if you were to hide in the old mill—'

Ninian did not let him continue. '*No*, Yves.' He grasped the older man by the shoulders. 'I have a place to go.'

'Where is it?'

Ninian shook his head. 'I cannot tell you. It is better for all of us that you do not know.'

'Let me at least provision you!' Yves's voice was anguished. Glancing down at Ninian's belongings, he said, 'Winter approaches, and you have not packed near enough warm clothes!'

'I have, truly I have. There's so much in my pack that I haven't even reached the bottom yet!' Ninian protested.

But with a muttered, 'Wait here,' Yves hurried off.

He returned quite soon with a heavy, deeply-hooded cloak, lined with fur. He also brought gauntlets, two warm wool tunics, thick hose and two more blankets, and a capacious leather bag for the spare garments. 'I've got food for you for several days,' he said, holding up another bag, 'with wine, bread and a good supply of dried meat. That'll keep you going. Now, have you money?'

'I have, Yves,' Ninian said with a smile. He was overcome by Yves's kindness. He finished his packing, then straightened up. 'I will leave immediately,' he announced. 'There are several hours of daylight, and I can be well away from here by night-fall.' He took one last look around the room, then stepped out into the passage. He stared along it to the great hall. 'Say goodbye to your family for me,' he said softly.

'I will.'

They walked quickly across the courtyard, and Ninian put the bridle and saddle on Garnet, fastening his packs and his bag. The he turned to Yves.

'Thank you for all you have done for me,' he said. 'I wish I could stay. I like it here.'

Yves smiled. 'We liked having you.' He hesitated. Then, speaking in a low voice, he said, 'You will not tell me where you are bound, and I appreciate that you have good reason, but, Ninian, consider this. You have kin in England who love you. Do you not think that, one day, they might come here looking for you? They know you were heading for Acquin, so it is naturally the place they would come seeking you. I could not face my brother, Ninian, when he asks where you have gone, if all I have by way of answer is to say *I do not know*.'

Ninian dropped his head. Yves was right; his position would be intolerable. But every instinct was telling him to keep his destination a secret, even from Yves. He thought hard and finally came up with a compromise. Looking up, he met Yves's anxious face and smiled. 'Tell Josse, if ever he asks, that I'm going to the place he suggested. He will know what I mean.'

Yves walked slowly back towards the house. He had tears in his eyes, and he paused to compose himself before going inside to face his family. He knew Ninian was right to leave, although he hated to admit it. He could not help but feel that he had failed the young man. But, as Ninian had said, where one man had come to seek him out, others would probably follow. Even now, the man who had paid Stephan to spy for him and then callously killed him was probably reporting back to the rest of the search party. They would be making plans to approach Acquin, go through every chamber, every barn and every storeroom until they found the man they were hunting for.

Yves had done all he could for Ninian. Now the young man was out of his reach. With a sigh, he turned his mind to how best to lay the smokescreen that would both throw the pursuers off the scent and protect his family.

SEVENTEEN

The day was drawing to a close, but Josse could not bear to wait until morning. He curbed his impatience for long enough to visit Abbess Caliste, explaining briefly what he had just discovered and asking if she would send someone over to the House in the Woods to take the news to Helewise. Then he ran back to where Alfred was tethered, mounted up and rode as hard as he could down the hill to Tonbridge.

Gervase was home, and Josse found him about to sit down to eat with Sabin and his three children. Sabin invited him to join them but, apologizing, he explained that he had come on a matter of urgency and must speak privately to Gervase.

'What is so important that you must drag me from my food?' Gervase asked lightly as they retreated to the far end of the hall.

'I am sorry, Gervase, I—'

'No need to explain, old friend,' Gervase interrupted with a smile. 'I know you would not be here, out of breath and mud-spattered, if it were not vital. What has happened?' Abruptly, his expression changed, his face growing tense. 'Is there news of the lad?'

'No,' Josse said shortly. Gervase's relief was evident.

He explained, as succinctly as he could, everything that had led him to conclude that Olivier de Brionne had been responsible for Hugh's death. Gervase listened, occasionally asking Josse to elucidate some point, and, when Josse stopped speaking, stood deep in thought.

'Well?' Josse demanded. 'What do you think? Am I right?'

Gervase turned to him. 'It would appear so, yes, although the evidence is far from conclusive. But,' he added firmly as Josse opened his mouth to speak, 'I do believe the case against Olivier is stronger than against Ninian, who was only suspected of the murder because Olivier suggested it. As, indeed, he would, if it was in truth he who killed Hugh.'

'What are you going to do?' Josse could hardly bear to ask.

Gervase punched him lightly on the shoulder. 'Josse, for the past few days I have gone on sending my men out on a manhunt for someone they have no chance of finding, for, as you and I both know, the man in question is by now safely across the Channel.' He hesitated, frowning. 'There's nothing I'd like more than to tell them tomorrow morning that the search parties may stand down, with the explanation that another suspect has turned up. However, there is still the matter of the wounding of the king and Olivier, for which Ninian stands accused.'

'It was a fight at close quarters!' Josse protested. 'Who can say who wounded whom?'

'I know, Josse, but we still have to convince the king of that,' Gervase replied. 'In the meantime, the pretence that we are still looking for Ninian here in England must, I am afraid, continue.' He grinned at Josse. 'If you will now accept my wife's invitation to come and eat, we will offer you a bed for the night, and tomorrow you and I will go and present this tale of yours to the king. If he reacts as I fully expect him to, he will no doubt command us to arrest Olivier de Brionne, inspect his right hand and accuse him of killing his brother.'

Late that night, leaving his wife asleep, Gervase crept out of their bed and fell on his knees beside it, burying his face in his hands. Had he been a more fervent believer, he might have said he was praying. He was used to deception – in his role as sheriff, he often spoke blatant untruths in pursuit of a greater good – and normally his conscience did not bother him.

But, as he was so painfully discovering, apparently it all depended on who was being deceived . . .

Gervase was looking his usual elegant self as he and Josse set out early the next morning, and Sabin had done her best to spruce up Josse, even to the extent of trimming his ragged hair. Gervase's groom had prepared their horses, and the coats of both shone in the autumn sunshine. It was not every day, Josse reflected, that a man rode off to seek audience with his king, and it was worth a bit of effort.

They crossed the Thames around noon, via the newly-completed stone bridge that, the previous year, had finally replaced the successive wooden versions which had spanned the river there for a thousand years. Trying not to look like an overawed country bumpkin, Josse stared at the impressive structure. Its many pointed arches slowed the flow of the river, so that white water constantly boiled and splashed against the piers. In the middle of the bridge stood a chapel dedicated to St Thomas Becket. Josse would have liked to stop and look, but he was not there for his own entertainment.

The White Tower loomed higher and higher above them as they steadily approached. As a symbol of the king's power, Josse reflected, it was hard to beat. Regular coats of whitewash kept it shining bright and impossible to ignore, and its forbidding appearance was like a constant, unspoken threat.

Josse and Gervase were stopped by several sets of guards before finally, having left their horses, they were permitted to climb the external staircase that soared up to the entrance, high above the ground. There were further challenges, and then at last two heavily-armed guards led them up to the king's apartments on the top floors. They were led through a great hall, the roof of which soared high overhead, then into the chamber where, they were told, they must wait for the king.

He did not keep them long. He came into the chamber alone, dressed in a scarlet tunic with extravagant, fur-lined sleeves and edged with panels of embroidery worked in real gold thread and sparkling with jewels. He wore a heavy gold chain around his neck, and on each of his fingers and one of his thumbs there sparkled a precious stone set in more gold. He looked, as he always did, so clean that he appeared to shine.

He stopped before his visitors and extended his hands. Josse and Gervase approached and made their reverences. Then, as if suddenly impatient, the king waved away their attentions and, fixing Gervase with a hard blue stare, said, 'You are here, I hope, to tell me that you have made an arrest.'

Josse winced on his friend's behalf. Had it not been for Gervase's first loyalty, to Josse and his kin, then his answer would undoubtedly have been *yes*. However, Gervase was a man of authority in his own right, and it soon became apparent that he was not going to be cowed, even by a king. With admirable brevity, he outlined his reasons for believing that Hugh de Brionne's killer was not the madman from the clearing by the chapel – whom he now named as Ninian de Courtenay – but Olivier. 'With your permission, my lord king,' he concluded, 'I will see Olivier de Brionne to verify what the Hawkenlye infirmarer has stated concerning the bruises on his right hand

and, once I am convinced, I will charge him with being responsible for his brother's death.'

The king, congenitally unable to stand still for longer than half a minute, had begun slowly pacing to and fro as Gervase spoke. Now, coming to a halt in front of the two men, he turned and fixed his eyes on the sheriff. 'Admirably deduced and utterly reasonable,' he declared. He glanced at Josse, stabbing a finger in his direction. 'Of course, this conviction that Olivier is guilty has nothing at all to do with the fact that, if he is, then *your* lad will no longer be wanted for murder.' Josse made to speak, but the king had not finished. 'Oh, Josse, Josse! I have known for some time exactly who this man is.'

'My adopted son is no murderer, sire,' Josse said steadily.

'So you do keep saying,' the king murmured. His eyes hardened. 'Nevertheless, he attacked Olivier and me. I have the scar on my shoulder to prove it, although already it is fading.'

Josse steeled himself to speak. He knew the risks – so much depended on the king's mood, for he could switch from genial host to furious tyrant in the blink of an eye – but, for Ninian's sake, he had to speak up. 'Sire, I would speak concerning that fight in front of the chapel,' he said, wishing his voice sounded more authoritative.

'Yes?' The one cold syllable seemed to hang in the air. Josse sensed Gervase go tense, and he could all but hear the sheriff's warning: *take care!*

'Sire, Ninian was deeply concerned for the little girl, Rosamund Warin, who Olivier had brought to you. He had followed your party from the hunting lodge to Hawkenlye, and when he saw two of the group break away and take the child up towards the woods, he was very afraid for her safety.' *Steady*, he told himself. He wanted to put it into the king's mind that Ninian's anxiety had been justified but, if he went too far and hinted that the king had been about to seduce an eleven-year-old child, then the king would lose his temper and he and Gervase would probably end up in the grim dungeons all those floors below.

He eyed the king, trying to gauge his reaction, but John was giving nothing away. 'I do not know the details of what occurred,' he plunged on, 'but, from Ninian's point of view, he believed Rosamund was in danger, and he launched himself against the two men who were with her. He did not know your identities,' he said, 'and had no idea that one of the men in the clearing was his king.'

John watched him intently. 'Do you think,' he said silkily, 'it would have made any difference if he had?'

That, Josse realized, was the point on which his whole defence of Ninian really hung, and it was typical of the king to have pinpointed it. He made himself meet the king's eyes. 'I do not know, sire,' he said. Then – for it was not wise to treat the king like a fool – 'Probably not.'

There was a long silence, broken only by the swish of thick, costly silk as the king resumed his pacing. Finally, he stopped, turned and faced Josse once more. 'I am of a mind to be generous,' he said. 'You speak with passion and eloquence for your son, Josse – yes, very well, your *adopted* son – and, indeed, your picture of a man rushing in to take on two armed men because he fears for the safety of a young woman has echoes of the deeds of the chivalrous knights in the tales so beloved by my late mother.' He paused, clearly thinking hard. Then he said quietly, 'Rosamund was as safe in my company as in that of her mother, whoever she is. But I will not pretend that I am unaware of the wagging tongues; indeed, one of my close circle believed he would greatly please me by his gift of this pretty child.' His expression hardened, and he said icily, 'I will not add fuel to this particular fire; I want this matter to remain between those few people who are already aware of it.'

It was a direct order. Josse and Gervase both bowed their heads in acknowledgement.

'Revenge would have been singularly sweet,' the king murmured, 'but, perhaps, unjustified. Besides,' he added after a moment, 'my wound is, as I said, all but healed, and, in the melee before the chapel, I cannot put my hand to my heart and swear it was Ninian who inflicted it. It seems, Josse –' some change in the king's voice made Josse look up and meet his eyes – 'that your son is safe.'

Gervase said, 'Sire, have I your permission to send for Olivier? There is no reason to delay the resolution of this sad business, and faced with our suggestion of what really happened, he may realize that there is no point in protesting his innocence.'

'Well he might,' the king replied, 'and I would not prevent

your summoning him, except that it would serve no purpose. He is not here.'

'Not here!' Josse exclaimed. 'But he left Hawkenlye when you did, sire, and we thought he had ridden here to London with you.'

'He may have left with us, although I do not recall seeing him,' the king said. 'He certainly did not arrive with us.'

'Then where is he?' Josse was looking wildly around.

'Stop that, Josse, he's not hiding behind the wall hangings,' the king said sharply. 'I do not know where he is. I will send word that I wish to see him and, when he arrives, I will let you know. Is that good enough for you?' The irony was unmistakable.

'Aye, my lord king, of course,' Josse muttered.

There was an awkward pause. Then Gervase cleared his throat nervously and said, 'Hugh de Brionne paid a high price for his insolent scheme, and—'

'You think the plan was Hugh's?' the king interrupted.

'Well, Olivier claims it was,' Gervase said. Josse nodded his agreement.

The king sighed. 'Hugh would never have come up with anything as dangerous and misguided as abducting a child as a present for his king,' he said softly. 'Everything about this matter smacks of Olivier. He is unbalanced, you see.' He sighed. 'We should have taken better care of him, but he was tucked away down there in the house on the downs and it was all too easy to forget his existence. By the time I invited him to come and join the circle of my close companions, it was already too late.'

Josse did not understand. 'Sire?'

'Hugh de Brionne was already of my company,' the king said. 'His father, as you will know, Josse, was a friend of my brother's, and, indeed, of my father's as well, and it followed, as these things do, that Hugh in turn would be one of my companions. Then, later, Olivier came too.'

'But Olivier is not Felix's son,' Josse whispered. Despite everything, it was still hard to speak Lady Béatrice's secret out loud.'

'No,' the king said softly. 'He is mine.'

Ninian wondered how far he would have to ride before he felt safe. The exhilaration of escaping from Acquin kept his spirits

high for many miles but, as the hours went on, he began to
be haunted by the feeling that someone was following him.

He decided that, reluctant as he was, it was time to put his
fears to the test. In a stretch of wooded, hilly country, he kept
an eye out for a suitable location and soon found one. He
dismounted, led Garnet under the cover of the trees and then
took up the position he had picked out. It was on top of the
steep side of a long stretch of the road that ran almost straight
– Ninian had heard it said that such roads had been left by
the Romans – and thus afforded a good view back the way
he had come. The road was enclosed on the east by the high
stone cliff on the top of which Ninian now stood. On the
opposite side, the ground fell away to a valley where a river
ran, its water glinting silver in the thin light.

He waited.

Some time later, he saw what he had dreaded: a horseman
was approaching. He was still a long way off, but it was clear
even from a distance that he was following a trail. He would
ride a few paces, then draw in his horse and bend over towards
the ground. Ninian guessed he was checking for the marks of
Garnet's hooves.

They have followed me all the way from Acquin, Ninian
thought. He was surprised at how calm he felt. He could
understand how the king's men had tracked him to Yves's
manor, for anyone who knew of Ninian's relationship to Josse
would have guessed that he might well flee to seek refuge
with Josse's family. However, it seemed an extraordinary piece
of ill fortune that the pursuers had unknowingly guessed
correctly as to the direction that Ninian had taken when he
left Yves.

But, of course, they hadn't. He smiled grimly as the realization dawned. The king had many men at his disposal. There
would be a group hunting for Ninian along roads leading away
from Acquin in each direction.

He wondered if he should try to overpower the man. He
baulked at any stronger word, even in his own mind; he could
not contemplate killing someone purely because that person
was following orders. Could he somehow imprison the man,
but in such a way that he would be found and released once
Ninian was far enough away?

No, no! He was angry with himself. There would be no

point in such an action, for this man would be expected to report back to the rest of his group and, when he didn't, they would instantly become suspicious and the whole lot of them would come swooping down on Ninian like crows on a corpse.

There was only one thing to be done: Ninian would have to disappear. So far, for the sake of speed he had been travelling on the roads and the better-maintained tracks. At night, tired, dirty, hungry and with money in his purse, he would lodge at small, out-of-the-way inns. Well, now all that would have to change. He would set out across country, checking his direction by the sun and the stars, and at night, when he and Garnet could go no further, he would sleep out in the open.

The weather was very cold, especially at night. Silently, Ninian blessed Yves, for providing him with extra clothes and wrappings.

Down on the road, the man had stopped. He sat leaning forward over the pommel of his saddle, one arm up to his head as if he were wiping sweat off his face. That was odd, for the day was chilly. Perhaps he had been riding hard.

It did not matter. What was important was that, for the moment, he had come to a halt. Ninian crept backwards, away from the cliff top, and moved quickly and quietly back through the undergrowth to where he had tethered Garnet. He mounted, checked the sun and then, branching away from the road, set off.

The man on the horse was in agony. He did not think he could ride any further, and he did not know what inner strength had kept him going this far. Fire raced through his body. It hurt abominably to move, but the pain barely lessened when he stayed still.

He was trying so hard to follow orders. *Find him.*

He had done what the voices had commanded. He had found his man, tracking him to the place where he had guessed he would go, then paying that fool of a groom for information. He had paid lavishly but, even so, the greedy young man had demanded more, whining about having an elderly mother and a prospective wife to please. It had been so easy to stop him, although the man wished now that he had removed the bag of coins from the dead hand. The voices were *really* cross with him about that.

It was sheer luck that had enabled him to pick up his quarry after leaving the little village. He had stood at a place where four roads came together and, shutting his eyes, spun round a few times. When the dizziness forced him to stop, he happened to be facing in the right direction.

The orders had gone on echoing in his head. *Catch him. Silence him.* He had tried; God knew how hard he had tried, riding on, ignoring his increasing pain, ignoring the demands of common sense that told him to stop, find help, creep away somewhere and rest until he felt well again.

Every time he thought about giving up, they began again with their nagging and their haranguing, warning him, shouting at him, until he barely knew what he was doing.

He must be stopped, they insisted. *He carries the blame for your crime. If ever he is permitted to speak in his own defence, the truth will come out.*

Do not let him get away.

He had come to a halt. He wondered vaguely how long he had been standing there, with his lathered horse growing cold beneath him. He must go on. Feebly, he tried to kick his heels into his horse's sides, but the gesture had no effect. He put his hand down to his side. Then, alarmed, he slid his fingers inside his tunic and under his shirt. He felt wetness. When he withdrew his hand, his fingertips were stained with blood and pus.

His head ached so much that he could barely see.

He closed his eyes. Presently, he slid off his horse and fell with a thump down on to the road. His horse ambled away, put down its head and began to tear at the thin grass on the verge.

Some time later, a miller returning home from market with an empty cart came across him. He caught the horse, which had wandered some way along the road, and then went to the huddled shape lying motionless right in his path.

The man was dead. The miller crossed himself, muttered a few words and then raised the body with powerful arms and laid it in the cart.

Olivier de Brionne, son of Lady Béatrice and bastard of the king of England, was taken away to be laid out by an elderly village midwife and, when she was done, buried in a small churchyard somewhere in the middle of France.

EIGHTEEN

Josse and Gervase got back to the sheriff's house late in the evening. Josse, who was exhausted by the long day and beginning to think he was getting too old for such exertions, gratefully accepted when Sabin asked if he would like to stay again. He slept deeply and dreamlessly, and when at last he woke, it was to be told by Sabin that Gervase was already out giving orders to his men that the hunt for Ninian had been called off.

The long sleep and a large plate of breakfast did much to restore Josse. Impatient to get home and tell them all the news, he left as soon as he decently could and set off up the hill towards the forest. Arriving back at the House in the Woods, he assembled the household and told them what had happened up in London. Meggie, back from her stay out in the hut, came up to him and quietly hugged him.

Later, sitting by the hearth with Helewise, he finally gave voice to the thought that had been gradually firming in his mind since the previous day. 'Now that it is safe, we – you and I – could go and fetch him home,' he said.

She did not answer at first. He wondered what she was thinking. There were many reasons why she would not want to go with him. Autumn was rapidly turning into winter, and the weather was unremittingly cold. Crossing the Channel was a gruelling experience that, in November, most people avoided if they could. If it turned wet or snowy, the roads would soon become impassable. He shied away from what he thought was probably her real reason for refusing: that such a journey would mean many days alone with him, and she was not ready – might never be ready – for that.

Eventually, she smiled and said, 'I have always wanted to see your home. I will go and ask Tilly to prepare food for us. How soon shall we leave?'

They crossed to Boulogne the next day, finding an adequate inn at the port where they spent the night. The inn was full, and the only accommodation was in the big communal sleeping area. Helewise, wrapped up warmly in her robe and her cloak, tried not to think about the hundreds of people who had slept on the bed before her. Meggie had given her some lavender bags against the busy insects and, as far as she could tell, they appeared to work.

They made an early start and reached Acquin as the sun was setting. Josse, as excited as a boy, pointed out to her the tall watchtowers and the strong wall that surrounded the house and the outbuildings. There was a note of pride in his voice. Even though he had left his ancestral property in the care of his brothers many years ago, she reflected, still the homecoming clearly meant a great deal to him.

She reined in her horse and let him ride ahead of her into the courtyard. He called out, 'Halloa, the house!' and a round-faced, brown-haired man emerged from a door at the top of a short flight of steps.

Helewise recognized Yves, for he had once come to Hawkenlye to seek out his elder brother. She watched as Josse leapt off his horse and the two men embraced. But then, almost immediately, Josse broke away and, his hands on his brother's shoulders, said, 'Where's Ninian?'

She knew, even before Yves spoke. She saw his face fall as he shook his head. He said something she did not catch.

'How long?' Josse demanded and, when Yves muttered his answer, Josse spun away from him and violently punched his fist into his opposite palm.

He came to stand by her horse. 'He's gone,' he said. 'We missed him by just a few days.'

She felt his crushing disappointment as if it were a fever in him. She put out her hand and gently touched his face. 'Josse, dearest Josse, we will go after him,' she said. 'We will not give up. Not yet.'

Yves came over to them, greeting her with a low bow. Straightening up, he frowned in puzzlement. 'My lady?' he said.

'No longer an abbess, as you rightly surmise, I think.' She smiled down at him, and he held out his hand, helping her to dismount.

Yves was far too polite to question her, although she saw the interest and curiosity in his face. 'Whatever your condition, lady, it is a pleasure to welcome you here,' he said.

Josse, clearly impatient with his brother's good manners, could contain himself no longer. 'He was here, then? Ninian reached Acquin safely?'

Yves turned to him. 'He did. He was here for a couple of days, and then something happened.' Briefly, he told them the stark details of how his own stable lad had sold information concerning Ninian to the man who had come looking for him. 'We fully believed more men would follow, for if one knew to look for him at Acquin, others would surely do so too. I took steps to protect my family, for we had seen one death already. But nobody else came!' He raised his shoulders and spread his hands in a gesture of amazement. 'We could not understand it.'

'I believe I can,' Josse said grimly. He looked at Helewise. 'We know that Olivier de Brionne is missing. Whoever it was who came here hunting for Ninian appears to have been alone. It is likely, I would suggest, that the man was Olivier.'

'Why would he be hunting Ninian?' Helewise asked, very aware of Yves watching, his face screwed up in incomprehension.

'He tried as hard as he could to make everyone believe that Ninian was responsible for Hugh's death,' Josse replied. 'He must have realized that Ninian would protest his innocence and, all the time he was alive, there was always the chance that he would succeed. Then, as indeed has happened, we would look round to try to see who else might have killed Hugh.'

Helewise, horrified, whispered, 'You think he has come here to kill Ninian?'

'What better way is there of silencing a man?' Josse said bitterly. 'We know why Ninian had to flee but, for someone trying to implicate him in a crime he did not commit, the fact of his flight could be used to argue his guilt. We must go—'

'You will go nowhere this evening but into the great hall of Acquin, where we will do all we can to refresh and restore you,' Yves said firmly. 'Yes, I know you want to turn round and set off right this instant, Josse, but it's getting dark and it will be a cold night.' He looked at Helewise, smiling. 'You will persuade him, my lady, to be sensible?'

Despite everything, she laughed. 'I have rarely been able to do that,' she said. 'But I do think you are right, Yves. Josse?'

To her relief, he grunted his agreement.

Helewise was very impressed by the speed with which Josse's family made arrangements for a feast. Only a short time after their arrival, she and Josse found themselves the guests of honour in the great hall at Acquin, seated on sturdy chairs padded with cushions and set either side of Yves and his wife Marie at the top of the table. Dish after dish appeared, borne along the passage from the kitchens by a line of servants. The wine was French and a great improvement on anything that was available to all but the very wealthy back in England. It was a shame that neither she nor Josse felt much like eating. For the sake of these kind and generous people who were clearly so delighted to have the head of the family back with them, they accepted everything they were offered, but Helewise could see Josse did not really want to be there. He wanted to be off on the road, following Ninian.

Josse waited until the rest of the household had retired for the night and only Yves remained. The brothers were finishing the last of the wine. Josse turned to Yves and said, 'Helewise and I will leave early in the morning. We will—'

But it became apparent that Yves was not going to pass up this chance of a private conversation. 'When did she leave Hawkenlye?' he demanded. 'And where does she live now?'

Josse sighed. He did not want to discuss the thorny question of Helewise but, on the other hand, his brother had a right to ask. 'She has her own quarters in my household,' he said. 'She left the abbey in the summer, although she was allowed to stand down as abbess some years before that. For her final years as a nun, she lived in a little cell and tended a chapel close to the abbey. And, before you ask, I'm not going to discuss exactly why she left, for I am not entirely sure I understand.'

'She loves you,' Yves murmured. 'And I know you love her, too.'

'Aye,' Josse said heavily.

Yves, ever sensitive and tactful, thankfully did not press him further.

After a while Josse said, 'Where has Ninian gone, Yves? We'll go to him, wherever he is, and take him home.'

Yves looked down at his hands, slowly turning the empty wine goblet. 'He would not tell me. He said it was better for all of us if nobody here knew where he was heading.'

Josse nodded. 'Aye, I can imagine why. But, Yves, surely he gave some hint?'

Now Yves looked slightly happier. 'As a matter of fact, I was able to extract a clue from him. I asked him what I was to do if ever you came looking for him, and I pointed out that I should feel wretched if I could offer you no help in finding him.'

'And he saw the sense of that?'

'He did. He told me to tell you that he's going to the place you suggested. He said you'd know what he meant.'

'The place I suggested,' Josse repeated. He thought hard. 'But I suggested that he came here. I didn't—'

Then he remembered. It had not originally been his suggestion; it had come from Gervase. Relief flooded him, accompanied by a sinking of the heart. The place that Gervase had mentioned was a very long way away.

'I think I do know,' he said softly. He gave his brother a rueful grin and told him.

He had not expected such a reaction. Yves's face paled, his eyes expressed his shock and he breathed, 'But he can't go *there*!'

And he told Josse why.

Josse leapt to his feet. 'I must go and get him back! I must leave now – there's no time to waste!'

Yves grabbed his sleeve and pulled him down again. 'You can't go after him, Josse! You won't find him – it's just impossible. Go home. Take Helewise and return to England. Only God can protect him now.'

Josse barely heard. He was filled with just one desire: he had to talk to Helewise, and it would not wait. As soon as he decently could, he detached himself from his brother's anxious presence and went to find her.

In the morning, Josse found he simply could not set out for the coast before at least trying to find a trace of Ninian. Helewise, looking at him out of anxious, loving eyes, agreed that they would follow the road south for just one day. As she pointed out, if they failed to pick up his trail very soon, then there was little hope they would stumble across it later.

They said their goodbyes to the family. Yves, who had a little knowledge of the south-east of England, promised that he would come to find them back at the House in the Woods. In a bleak leave-taking, it was the one consolation.

They rode south all day. They stopped soon after dark in a small town, and Josse found lodgings for them in the house of the priest. He was happy to offer them hospitality in exchange for news of the outside world and, when he discovered they came from England, he was overjoyed.

It was late in the evening, and the priest was more than a little drunk when he revealed the one item out of the ordinary run of small town life that had recently happened. A body had been found on the road leading south out of the town, stone dead. The body bore grave wounds, one of them swollen with suppuration. A fine horse had been grazing nearby.

Josse's fuddled brain instantly cleared. 'Who was this person? Man or woman?'

The priest, clearly gratified at having such an interested response, elaborated. 'A man, in his twenties, with brown hair and a square-jawed face. He was well dressed, and his horse was most handsome: black, with a star-shaped mark on his brow.'

There seemed nothing else to do but turn for home, although it took half a day of Helewise's most eloquent reasoning to persuade Josse of that painful fact. 'Ninian is gone, Josse,' she said, aching for the pain she saw in his eyes, 'and although we know where he is heading, it is far away. Yves has told us what is happening there and—'

'There's danger there!' he interrupted. 'We must stop him, catch him before he gets there and—'

'Josse, he has many days' start on us!' she interrupted in her turn. 'How are we to find him in all of the vast heart of this land? By some wonderful chance we found this place, and we can return with the huge blessing of knowing that, with Olivier de Brionne's death, the greatest danger to Ninian no longer exists.'

'There's no need for him to be a fugitive now!' Josse cried. 'He can come home!'

Home. The word undermined her, and for a moment she could not speak. Then, reaching for his hand and folding it between both of her own, she said softly, 'He *will* come home, Josse. But not through any action of ours.'

He pulled his hand away. 'You go back if you like,' he said coldly. 'I'll go after him on my own.'

His words cut right into her heart. Tears filled her eyes, and surreptitiously she wiped them away. When she could trust her voice she said, 'Your daughter, your son and all who love you have already borne the pain of seeing Ninian ride away. Will you put on them the further burden of knowing you have hared off after him because that action, risky and futile though it is, is easier for you than gathering your courage and your resolve and going home?'

There was silence for a long time. She heard the echoes of her own words and noticed absently that she had addressed him in exactly the same tone as when she had been abbess of Hawkenlye. It was agonizing but no surprise, then, when eventually he gave a deep sigh and said, 'You are right, my lady, as usually you are. We will go back.'

That night they stayed in a dirty, run-down inn where the fleas jumping on the soiled mattresses forced them both to sleep on the floor.

Lying awake, closely wrapped in her cloak and both her blankets, Helewise tried to get comfortable. She knew Josse was awake, not more than an arm's length away, but there was a distance between them that had nothing to do with their physical presence. She wept, the tears silently running down her face and into the high collar of her gown. *I love him*, she thought, *and I believe that I have lost him.*

Would it have made any difference if she had behaved differently since going to live in the House in the Woods? *Of course it would*, the sensible part of her answered. They would still have had today's devastating argument, and she would still have persuaded him, for she knew she had employed unfair tactics by reminding him of his family and, once she had done so, there had only been one possible outcome. But oh, if they had already taken that great step that she knew they both wanted, and become man and wife in law and in body as they already were in heart and spirit, then she knew in her very bones that, argue as they might, this night they would have lain in each other's arms and made it up.

She heard his voice again in her mind. *You are right, my lady, as you usually are.* Dear God, if he had added *abbess* after *my lady*, the two of them could have been back in her little room at the abbey, disputing hotly from their accustomed positions either side of the large oak table that had always divided them.

Was she still abbess, then? In her soul, was she still a nun? She turned over, trying to pad her cloak under her hip bone. Deliberately, she made herself go back over the long and painful months and years between her first doubts and her final decision. It was not that she no longer loved God and wished with all her heart to serve him; it was that she had lost her faith in the church which men had built in his name.

She thought now of what Yves had told them of the horrors in the south. It was the ultimate persuasion, had she needed it, that she had been right.

She felt drowsy at last. She stretched out a hand to Josse's broad back, stopping just short of touching him. In a couple of days, they would cross the narrow seas back to England. She knew what she must do: she must reinforce as often as she could that they'd *had* to go back; that to go on after Ninian would have been useless and might well have cost both of them their lives. She must say, every day, *he is young, he is strong, he is resourceful.* And, more often than any of those phrases, *he will come back.*

Sending all the love that was in her heart out to this big, strong man of hers, Helewise closed her eyes and drifted into sleep.

NINETEEN

Ninian had reached his destination. He was a very long way from Acquin, and it was virtually impossible that Josse and Helewise would have found him, no matter how long and hard they searched. He was not at the address that Gervase de Gifford had given him. Nobody lived there now. The house, the street, even the town, had disappeared; burned and gone, along with most of the fifteen thousand who once had lived there, on the feast day of St Mary Magdalene more than a year before Ninian arrived.

Ninian stood looking down on what had once been Béziers. He found himself in the middle of a holy war.

The crushing disappointment of discovering that the place he had been heading for all those hundreds of miles was no safe haven but the burnt-out wreck of a town had rendered him all but catatonic. He had the sense to get out of the open and under cover in the remains of an outhouse but, once he felt reasonably safe, he gave himself up to his exhaustion and his grief and eventually fell asleep. By morning, however, he had made up his mind. He had come here to find someone, and find her he would.

Nobody in the Midi knew who he was. He had long ago realized that he was no longer being followed, and much of his former life back in England now seemed like a dream. His French had improved rapidly as he had journeyed, although down in the south they spoke a different tongue. He had already picked up a few useful words and phrases and, whenever he could, he struck up conversations with people, trying to discover what was happening.

The first time he plucked up sufficient courage to mention the name of the person he sought was almost the last. He was in a tavern, eating a large dish of a tasty bean and pork dish that the locals called cassoulet, and the man he was talking to grabbed him by the neck of his tunic and dragged him outside while he still had a mouthful of food.

The man had an arm round Ninian's neck. With his other

hand, he pressed a dagger into the exposed skin beneath Ninian's ear. 'How do you know that name, stranger?' he hissed.

They were in a dark alleyway that stank of urine and bad meat. There was nobody around. Ninian tried to wriggle free, but instantly the knife point dug into his flesh. 'Talk!' the man said.

'I have come from England,' Ninian began. 'The name was given to me by someone close to the man I call father. The person told me to come here. I have news of him, and of his wife and children.'

There was dead silence. Ninian thought the pressure on his throat had lessened a little.

Then the man whispered, 'Give me their names.'

Ninian felt there could be no harm in complying. He spoke five names. 'The girl is named for her grandmother,' he added.

He heard the man give a quiet laugh. Abruptly, he let go of Ninian, who almost fell. The man grabbed at him, still laughing. 'You are either a very clever spy, or you speak the truth,' he said, looking intently at Ninian. He was tall, broad, dark-haired and swarthy-skinned. 'Go and finish your dinner.'

Amazing for such a large man, he vanished as swiftly as if he had been swallowed up by the air. Ninian, eventually getting over the shock and returning to the cassoulet, thought he was lucky to have got off so lightly. He wolfed down the rest of his meal, drained his mug and was just vowing to himself that, next time he questioned someone, he would make sure they were nearer his own size, when the dark man came back.

He said simply, 'Come with me.'

Ninian barely paused to think about it before he stood up, put some coins on the dirty table to pay for his meal and obeyed.

The dark man was called Peter Roger. He rode a bay mare that, although smaller than Garnet, could easily match him for pace, and he led Ninian through the night on roads that gradually turned from wide, well-paved thoroughfares to tracks and paths which, climbing steadily, finally grew so hazardous that Ninian was forced to dismount. Peter Roger, on his sure-footed little mare, turned and grinned at him as he laboured ever upwards. From time to time Ninian caught the flash of white teeth in the moonlight.

They stopped just before dawn. Ninian had no idea where

they were. He did not much care. He was desperate for rest and fell asleep almost as soon as he was wrapped in his cloak and blanket.

He woke to the smell of new bread. Peter Roger offered him a generous chunk off the end of a loaf, spread with butter and honey. Ninian could not begin to imagine where he had acquired it. They seemed to be miles from anywhere.

As he ate, he looked around. They were high up in a long line of mountains, with green slopes falling away below and, behind them, tall, craggy peaks crowned with snow. They seemed to go on for ever, rising ever higher until their distant summits were lost in the hazy cloud.

Peter Roger noticed him staring. 'The Pyrenees,' he said. 'These mountains have always been a refuge. Few men know all their secrets, and that's the way we like it.'

'You – you're in hiding?' Everything began to fall into place. Ninian, kicking himself for not having realized earlier what now seemed so obvious, said, 'You're a Cathar, aren't you?'

The man grinned. 'I am,' he said happily. 'It's safe enough to tell you now, when it's only you and me, especially when I'm so much bigger than you.'

Ninian joined in the laughter. 'I know a little about your faith,' he said cautiously.

'You do?' The man seemed surprised. He smiled indulgently. 'Go on, then.'

Ninian gathered his thoughts and began to speak. 'You believe there are two gods: one who is evil and rules the earth and everything in it, and one who is good and rules the spirit world. You think you were once angels in the blessed realm, forced out of that existence to live in human bodies until the time comes for your death, when you go back to your heavenly forms.' He paused, trying to remember. 'You live simple, good lives. You don't eat meat or anything else that comes from animals. When you are ready, you undertake a special ceremony and after that you live as pure ones, without – er, without sharing a bed with a woman.' He thought he heard Peter Roger give a quiet chuckle. 'You don't have priests or a mother church, and you believe that everyone may speak to God directly without the intercession of the clergy.' He stopped. 'Er – that's all I know.'

'How do you come by your knowledge?' Peter Roger had got to his feet and was packing away his belongings.

'Where I come from, there was once a group of people who believe what you do. My mother helped them, as did my adopted father.' Ninian fastened his pack behind Garnet's saddle. 'I wasn't there when it happened, but my father remembers the people with affection. He says you shouldn't judge a man by what he believes, only by what he does. He also says nobody has the right to tell anyone else that his idea of God is any more valid than theirs.'

'Your father is a wise man,' Peter Roger pronounced. He took a scarf out from inside his tunic. 'Now, although I like you and I begin to trust you, I cannot disregard the rules of my people. You have to be blindfolded.'

Ninian only saw the terrifying heights to which he had climbed once the ascent was safely over. The scarf was removed from his eyes, and he found himself in an open space – perhaps a tiny village square – with modest buildings on three sides and, on the fourth, a low wall. Beyond the buildings, the mountains soared even higher and, immediately behind the little hamlet, a domed peak rose up shaped like an upturned cup. Beyond the wall, the ground fell away in an almost sheer drop to the valley far, far below. Whichever way Peter Roger had just brought them up here, Ninian thought, swallowing the nausea, they certainly hadn't climbed those dreadful, awesome slopes.

He was given little time to recover and was still feeling horribly vertiginous when Peter Roger, in the company of another man built on similar lines who had emerged to meet them, slung Ninian's pack over one shoulder and led him away across an open space and into a small dwelling. Within, a pale-faced woman dressed in black sat on an elaborate wooden chair before a hearth in which a fire blazed; it was very cold at that height.

Peter Roger pushed Ninian forward. As he approached her, the woman rose elegantly to her feet.

She smiled at him. 'I am Alazaïs de Saint Gilles, known in my previous life as de Gifford,' she said in a low, melodious voice. 'I am told that you bring news of my son.'

The details of that first extraordinary day in Alazaïs's little house stayed with Ninian for a long time. Peter Roger and his companion remained with them only for a short time. Ninian thought afterwards that Alazaïs had submitted him to some test, so subtle that he had no idea what it was, and, when he had passed it, the two men had felt it safe to leave.

Once he was alone with her, she fed him warm bread, goat's cheese and salty, herb-flavoured olives and gave him copious amounts of a rich, spiced drink. She built up the fire and made him sit down on a pile of animal skins placed close to it, spreading a sheepskin over his knees and putting another around his shoulders against the draughts. He tried to protest, especially since she wore only a thin, black robe and her hands were blue with cold, but she simply smiled, shook her head and assured him she was used to it.

When she had done all she could to make him comfortable, she sat down in her chair, fixed him with her light green eyes and said, 'Now, tell me of my son.' With a sudden, vivid eagerness in her face, she added, 'I believe he—' But she stopped whatever she had been about to say and nodded for him to speak.

Ninian paused to collect his thoughts. It was important, he realized, to say the right things. He could feel the heat of this woman's love for her son, and whatever impression he first gave her would be the crucial one, forming the picture in her head that must replace Gervase's living, breathing presence.

'He is sheriff of Tonbridge,' he began, 'which is a town—'

'I know Tonbridge,' she interrupted. Her comment greatly surprised him, but now was not the moment to question it.

'He is an honourable man and, although he has a reputation for swift judgement and sometimes severe punishment, he is widely regarded as fair and people respect him. Well,' he added, 'honest people do, anyway.' The woman's mouth twitched in a smile. 'My father regards him as one of his closest friends, and I respect my father's judgement.'

The woman nodded. Her face eager, she said, 'What of his private life? Is he happy?'

Reflecting that it might have been better to mention this first, Ninian responded quickly. 'He is married to a woman named Sabin who is a healer. He has three children: two boys called Simond and Benoît – he's called after Sabin's grandfather, who brought her up – and a girl called—' Only just realizing it, he looked up and met the woman's hungry eyes. 'Called after you, madam.'

An expression so poignant crossed her face that he was moved. Impulsively, he reached out and took her thin hand. 'They are good people, my lady,' he said. 'Their family is close and loving, and I would say that Gervase is blessed.'

There was silence for some time. Then she gave his hand a squeeze and released it. 'Thank you,' she said quietly. 'It is many years since I have seen my only son. Although I was married to a man of the north and went willingly with him to live in his country, I am a woman of the south and my roots here are very deep. When my husband died, I followed my heart and my conscience and returned to my homeland.'

'Your conscience?' Ninian was not entirely sure what she meant, although he had an idea.

'I am a Cathar,' she said, smiling down at him. 'Peter Roger tells me you have some knowledge of us and our beliefs.'

'Yes,' Ninian said slowly.

On the ascent to the village he had been thinking about what he had said to Peter Roger. One phrase in particular kept echoing in his head: *you don't have priests, and you believe that everyone may speak to God directly without the intercession of the clergy.* He recalled the terrible fate of Béziers and its inhabitants, and he thought he was beginning to understand what was happening down here in the south. 'The church cannot let you flourish,' he said now, speaking half to himself. 'You do not see the need for priests, and if everyone else were to become Cathars too, the clergy would lose their income and their homes. They must have persuaded the king of France to send his army against you, and the towns where your people lived are being destroyed.'

He looked up and met her eyes. She nodded. 'Yes,' she said on a sigh, 'in essence, you are right. Consider too that the lands of the Midi are fertile and contain many fine sea ports. Can you not see another reason why the king should join forces with the church to attack the Cathars?'

'He wants to increase his kingdom,' Ninian said. Kings always wanted that.

'Indeed he does,' Alazaïs agreed. 'Every knight who rides under his banner has been told in great detail of the glorious sunlit fiefs that will be his for the taking once the great Cathar families have been driven off. Religion is the excuse, young man,' she said, her voice suddenly harsh, 'but greed is the true spur.'

With a visible effort she made herself relax, leaning back in her chair and closing her eyes. After a moment, opening them again, she looked at him with a smile and said, 'I don't even know your name.'

'Ninian de Courtenay.'

Her eyes flicked from him to his pack, placed by Peter Roger on the floor beside him. Watching the movement, he realized that she had been doing it all the time they had been talking. He, too, glanced at his pack – it was Josse's old campaign bag and very precious to Ninian – and then up at Alazaïs. Her eyes were wide and, gazing into them, he felt momentarily dizzy, as if a memory of his earlier vertigo had returned. He was about to protest, but she spoke first.

In a soft, hypnotic voice, she said, 'What is in your pack, Ninian de Courtenay?'

'My – my father prepared it for me,' he managed to say. He was feeling very strange. 'He – he put in winter garments, a change of linen, a sharp knife and some food.'

'And have you unpacked your bag since you left home?' the soft but imperative voice went on.

He tried to think. Had he? Acquin was the last place he had stayed for more than a night, and he was almost sure he had not taken everything out of the bag then. While on the road he had only changed his linen once, stuffing the soiled garments down towards the bottom of the bag. 'No,' he whispered. He tried to think what she was doing, why she seemed intent on putting him into a trance; *what did she want from him?* Even as he formed the fearful question, it was as if her mind reached into his and swept it away.

'Look inside your pack,' she intoned. 'Take everything out. Lay your belongings on the floor where I may see them.'

With no will of his own, he obeyed. He reached out and dragged the pack towards him, unfastening the ties and taking out his leather water bottle – still half full – and his small knife. A shirt came next – very dirty – and then some mud-caked hose that stank of sweat. A lightweight tunic, a length of frayed and stained linen in which he had once wrapped some slices of ham, a filthy undershirt.

The bag was empty, and he turned back to face her. He thought she spoke to him, which was odd because her lips did not move. A voice said: *look again.*

He reached his hand right down to the bottom of the bag. To his great surprise, his searching fingers located a small, hard parcel wrapped in linen.

As he touched it, he thought that a jolt of some sort of energy flowed into his fingertips and up his arm. With a cry, he withdrew his hand.

'Take it out,' Alazaïs commanded.

He could not disobey. Nerving himself, he took hold of the package again. This time the shock was not so severe. Curious now – dear Lord, what *was* this thing he had carried unknowingly all those hundreds and hundreds of miles? – he pulled it out of the bag.

The parcel was rectangular in shape, about as long as a man's hand and two-thirds as broad. The linen that wrapped it was yellow with age and tied with a length of twine.

He held it out to Alazaïs, but she shook her head. Her eyes shining now, her face filled with such anguished yearning that he flinched from her, she whispered, 'You have brought it to me. You must unwrap it.'

He placed the package in his lap and with shaking hands untied the knotted twine. He pulled at the linen and it fell away. He stared down at what lay revealed.

It was a book, made up of several sheets of vellum, fastened together on the left-hand side with a leather cord woven into an intricate pattern. The covers were of board, bound in thick leather into which a pattern had been stamped.

'It's . . . it's a book,' he said stupidly.

'Open it,' she whispered.

He did so.

The first page was densely covered in letters. Ninian could barely read, but he understood enough to appreciate that the words made no sense to him. Whatever language they were written in, it was one he did not know. He turned a page, then another, and sumptuously-coloured illustrations seemed to leap out at him, so vivid, so alive, that he almost thought they moved. One showed a circle of black-robed figures, arms raised, their joy so palpable that he smiled with them. He flicked on through the book and saw a strange cross; another group of people, this time apparently singing; a beautiful scene of pink and gold clouds . . .

Then on the next page he saw a sight that made him gasp aloud. Two worlds were depicted, side by side. The light world had more of the fluffy, sunlit clouds, now inhabited by human-like figures that were vague and dreamy. The world of the dark, in hideous contrast, was a nightmare land of chaos and misery, its inhabitants wailing in torment as they tore at their hair, nature around them distorted and corrupt.

'Turn the page,' Alazaïs said sharply.

He glanced up at her. He wondered how she had known what he was looking at since she had her eyes closed and, anyway, could not have seen the book in his lap, for his shoulder concealed it from her.

He did as she commanded.

On the very last page, there was neither writing nor any illustration. Instead, there was a strange pattern of marks, odd little black dots, each with a tail that went either up or down. The marks were set out in careful lines, and the lines covered the whole page. Beneath the marks there were symbols. As he studied the lines, it seemed to him that somehow the symbols related to the marks . . .

He heard a snatch of music, if indeed music was what it was. Sounds, anyway, such beautiful sounds, in a pattern that stopped his heart and then set it beating in a different way. He was filled with a joy so vast that he felt his solid, earth-bound body could not contain it.

The sounds ceased. He gave an involuntary sound – a groan? A sigh of ecstasy? All strength left him, and he slumped to the ground.

He was awake. He did not know how long he had been unconscious. Tentatively, he flexed his arms and legs, trying to see if he had been hurt. Everything seemed fine. He opened his eyes and, very carefully, sat up.

Alazaïs sat in her high chair, dark, immobile, mysterious, like the statue of some ancient goddess from man's infancy. On her face was a look of bliss. As he looked more closely – for he wondered if she had died – he saw there were tears on her thin cheeks, glistening in the light from the fire.

After a while she opened her eyes and looked down at him.

'You have done it, Ninian de Courtenay,' she said softly. 'Against all expectations, you have found me and brought to me what I so desperately needed. May you be blessed with a long and happy life, for you have done a deed far greater than you can know.'

'What have I done?' he demanded wildly. 'I have never seen that book before, and I had no idea I was carrying it! What is it? Where does it come from?'

But she held out her hand, and abruptly he fell silent. 'Sleep,' she intoned. 'Sleep now, for your journey has been long and hard, and your heart is sore with sorrow. Sleep, be healed, and tomorrow we shall talk.'

Her hand waved above his head in a careful dance of precise movements. His eyelids drooped, and he slipped down on to the floor. His last waking awareness was of hands as gentle as a mother's tucking the sheepskins more closely around him.

TWENTY

Shortly after his return to the House in the Woods, and after he and Helewise had enjoyed to the full the family's relieved welcome, Josse set out for Tonbridge to see Gervase de Gifford.

He found the sheriff at home. With a glance at Sabin, occupied with her young daughter as she supervised the girl's efforts to grind some tiny seeds in a pestle, Gervase led Josse outside. He strode across to a stone bench in a corner of the courtyard and, under a weak late autumn sun, the two men sat down.

'Olivier de Brionne is dead,' Josse said. 'He died on the road south through France, and I surmise he was hunting for Ninian to silence him.' He outlined his reasoning, and Gervase nodded.

'You are sure that this dead man was in truth Olivier?' he asked.

'Aye, I'm sure,' Josse replied. 'The description fitted and, besides, the wounds matched those Olivier had. One was badly infected, and I guess that was what killed him.'

Gervase nodded. 'Poor Béatrice,' he murmured. 'Both sons gone, her daughter mistress of her own establishment, and a witless dotard her only company.'

Josse bowed his head. *Aye,* he thought, *poor Béatrice.* In the midst of his own worries and sorrows, he had forgotten hers.

'Ninian is safe, then, from pursuit?' Gervase said after a moment. 'The king no longer wishes to hunt him down, and Olivier is dead.'

'Aye,' Josse said heavily. 'I was for going on after him to tell him so, but Helewise—' Abruptly, he stopped. He had acknowledged she was right, but still his decision pained him.

'Helewise persuaded you otherwise,' Gervase supplied. 'Well, Josse, I have to say I agree with her. France is a very large country, and the south is in turmoil.'

'So I am told,' Josse said gruffly. Turning to Gervase and fixing him with an intent stare, he went on, 'And yet you sent Ninian to the Midi.'

Gervase looked down at his hands. He was silent for some time, then he spoke. 'Josse, there is something I must tell you. I deeply regret that I sent Ninian into danger, but hear me out, I beg you, before you judge me.'

Josse grunted his permission. Gervase was, after all, an old and trusted friend, and Josse was a fair man.

After a short pause, Gervase began to speak. 'You may not remember, Josse, but once before, years ago, I spoke to you of my mother.'

Josse tried to remember, and soon the few facts he had been told came to him 'Aye, I do recall that you mentioned her. She—' Suddenly, his head shot up as the details of that long-ago conversation flooded into his mind. And he thought he began to understand.

Deliberately lowering his voice, he leaned closer to Gervase and said, 'Your mother is a Cathar. She lives in the Midi with others of her faith, and you told me she wished you would join them, although that is not your wish. You heard what is happening to the Cathars of the Languedoc, and your burning need was to send word to your mother. I understand that, but, Gervase, it sticks in my throat that you used Ninian as your messenger.'

Gervase bowed his head. 'I accept your rebuke, Josse,' he said humbly. 'May I, though, finish what I have to say?'

'Aye,' Josse grunted.

Again, there was a pause as Gervase sought for the right words. Then: 'The Cathars are besieged down there in the south, but the wise among them knew what would sooner or later happen and made plans. They organized a network of . . . agents? Spies? I do not know what you would call them. These brave men and women are by no means all Cathars, at least not overtly; many are, as I understand it, merely friends and supporters who do not believe that the crusade is right or just. Despite their isolation, the southern Cathars manage to send word to the outside world, via this secret network that conveys messages in and out of the Midi.'

'And you received such a message from your mother?'

Gervase smiled. 'I did, although I already knew both that she needed me and what she wanted me to do, for she had – oh, Josse, you will, I fear, find this hard to believe.'

'I'll do my best,' Josse said wryly.

'I heard her voice,' Gervase said in a whisper. 'I was asleep, or possibly on the point of waking, and I thought I heard her speak. I was at first afraid, for I know she is hundreds of miles away, and then all at once wide awake. And in my mind there was just the one thought, which, no matter how unlikely it is, I believe my mother put there.'

Fascinated despite himself, Josse breathed, 'What was the thought?'

'She was in dire need of a certain object, whose whereabouts she was aware were known to me. She wanted me to locate it and send it to her.'

'A magical object?' Josse asked. 'A weapon? Something to help them in their struggle to defend themselves?'

Gervase shrugged. 'I do not know. I do not think so, unless this thing has powers that it keeps hidden.' He turned to Josse. 'But you know of it. You tell me.'

'*I* know of it? But—'

Then he remembered.

He recalled how, long ago, a worried young nun had brought to him an object of mysterious origin that she had found somewhere it had no place to be. He recalled looking at it with her, both of them full of wonder. And he remembered what had happened to that object.

And memory swiftly brought another realization.

'There is no band of robbers, is there, Gervase?' he asked softly. 'You requested the meeting with Dominic because you thought the thing you sought so urgently was still at New Winnowlands, where I told you I had hidden it. Having somehow ascertained from him that his valuable possessions included no such thing, you turned to me. When did you take it from its hiding place? When you pretended to hear voices and sent me hurrying off?'

Gervase made himself meet Josse's eyes. His were full of shame. 'Yes.'

Slowly, Josse shook his head. 'Did it matter so very much, Gervase, that you had to lie to me and trick me?'

'I am sorry, Josse, but it did. And, before you ask, I could not take you into my confidence, for already I suspected that Ninian might have to flee because of the crime he was accused of. Had I revealed the secret to you, you'd have known why I suggested my mother's house as a destination for Ninian and you would have protested.'

'I wouldn't if I—'

'You would, Josse. You would have said, quite rightly, that I was using Ninian's desperation for my own ends, making use of the fact that he had to run for his life to get this precious book to my mother.'

Gervase was right, and Josse knew it.

After some time, Josse said, 'Why does your mother want the book?'

'I asked myself the same question to begin with,' Gervase replied, 'before the full message reached me. Once I had her written words, I began to understand.'

'She wrote to you?' Josse could scarcely believe it. 'Did she not fear to put you and your family in danger? This war against the Cathars may well spread, and if you were known to be sympathizers—'

Gervase laid a hand on his arm. 'She wrote in code, Josse. I would be surprised if anyone not knowing the key would ever break it.'

'I see. Go on, then. Tell me about this book.'

Gervase looked up into the pale blue sky, as if searching for inspiration. 'It – as far as I understand it, the Cathars believe they were brought to earth out of their spiritual existence, and that they will return to that paradise when they die. They try to recall what it was like to live in spirit, but it is difficult. Some of them claim to remember a magical, heavenly strain of music, which they say is the sound of angel song. One or two men with a rare ability wrote down this music, just as a monk writes down plainsong.'

'And that – that music – was in the book?'

Slowly, Gervase nodded.

Josse was confounded. 'But I still do not comprehend the importance of it!' he protested. 'What difference can a snatch of music make to people who face being hunted out of existence?'

Gervase's face worked, but he kept himself under control. Belatedly aware how tactlessly he had spoken – Gervase's mother was one of those preparing for a terrible fate! – he began to apologize.

'No, Josse, you speak the truth,' Gervase said heavily. 'As to why the music means so much, can you not guess?'

Josse thought hard, but he could not. 'No,' he said shortly.

'They are probably going to die,' Gervase murmured. 'Perhaps it is simply that they wish to remind themselves that, beyond the sword, or the flames, a beautiful, perfect world is waiting for them.'

Josse put a hand to his face and rubbed hard at his eyes. Then, clearing his throat a couple of times, he said, 'Ninian agreed, then, to take the book?'

'He doesn't know he bears it. That day I came to warn you that the king had ordered me to hunt for Ninian, I spoke to you in private outside and then I went into the stables alone to fetch my horse. Ninian's pack stood ready, as you had told me it did, and I slipped the book right down into the bottom of it.'

'If he doesn't know he carries it, how will he be able to give it to your mother?' Josse demanded.

Gervase smiled. 'She will know he has it, even if he does not. Besides –' he lowered his voice until it seemed to Josse he was speaking more to himself – 'the book wants to go home.'

Postscript
Deep winter 1210–1211

Ninian was fast becoming a mountain man. The snows were deep in the Pyrenees, and the fugitive population had consequently relaxed a little. Not entirely – never that – but enough to spend the short days out in the open air, speaking to each other in normal voices rather than skulking in corners and whispering, always afraid that enemy eyes and enemy ears were near.

The village, like all the mountain villages, was cut off and would remain so until the snows melted in the spring. Simon de Montfort's army was far away, and it was very unlikely that even the most fanatical of his spies would find a way up the treacherous slopes.

Ninian had done his best to put his homesickness and his yearning for his loved ones aside. It was easier here than it had been on the road, for many of his new companions were also far from those they loved. Many were separated from their parents, spouses and children by something far more permanent than mere distance, for so many had already been killed that most households mourned at least one kinsman.

These Cathars were *good* people; there was really no other word that described them better. Their lives were hard, and they worked long hours; many of them were weavers, working at looms set up in their own tiny homes. There were few luxuries, and the winter was cold and deep, but Ninian never heard anyone complain. Far from it, for the people in the main were light-hearted and quick to laugh.

Their faith was clearly a fundamental part of them. It filled them with a quiet joy and gave them the strength to put up with hardship. He did not understand the nature of the book he had brought with him, and he was at a loss to understand how it had got into his bag. Had Josse put it there? He did not know. What he did know, because Alazaïs had told him, was that it somehow reminded them of the bliss from which they had come and to which they yearned to return. In that time of danger, when all their lives were under threat, he thought he could begin to appreciate what that meant.

Despite their eagerness to answer his questions, nobody tried to make him join them. Not all of them were what they called Perfects, by which they meant those 'pure ones' who had taken the ultimate vow. Many referred to themselves as adherents, which seemed to mean people sympathetic to the Cathar faith who did not yet feel ready to give up the earthly things of the flesh.

Ninian was fast growing to respect the Cathars. Some of them he thought he loved. Alazaïs continued to treat him like a son, and, lonely for his own kin, he responded. And there were others to whom he swiftly grew close because they had known Josse. One of them, a woman, had even known Ninian's mother.

He met her one day when she made the difficult journey through the snow to Alazaïs's village specially to meet him. Pointing to a barely visible scar on her forehead, she told him that Joanna had rescued her from an unspeakable fate and, at grave risk to herself and to her little girl – Meggie, Ninian realized with a pang – had cared for her and helped her to safety. He thought the woman said that Joanna had even killed a man to save her, but the woman spoke the language with a strong accent and he might have been mistaken.

When the woman got up to leave, she took Ninian in her arms, hugged him tightly to her and said, 'Your mother I love. You, too, are good, like her.'

He understood sufficient about the general situation to know that war was coming and that the Cathars would be relentlessly pursued all the time the king and the pope had men to send after them. The elders – both men and women achieved respected elder status in the community – had explained to him how the people were defending themselves, and as far as Ninian could tell, their plan consisted mainly of constructing strong fortresses high in the inaccessible upper reaches of the mountains.

Nobody said much about fighting.

Ninian knew how to fight. He had spent his youth learning the skills of a knight. Now, at last, he began to see a purpose to those long years in training. He had tentatively suggested to

Alazaïs and the other Perfects in the village that he could teach the men the things he knew, and they had accepted his offer with grave thanks.

'We do not want to kill,' one of the Perfects, a tall, skeletal old man had said sadly to Ninian. 'It is not right. But if armies come against our womenfolk and children, intent on burning down our homes and sending us into the flames, it is best that some of us at least can fight them off.'

The long winter was now passing more quickly for Ninian, busy as he was with his school of would-be warriors. Just like young men anywhere flung together for any length of time, there was plenty of fun alongside the serious business of learning to kill. Ninian found he was enjoying himself and, often at the end of a satisfyingly hard day, he would be aching with laughter as well as sore from physical work.

For hours, even days, at a time he would have said that he was happy. Little Helewise came to him in his dreams, and sometimes he woke longing for her so acutely that the fierce desire spilled out of him. He told one of his trainee fighters about her; the young man could not manage the English version of her name and thought she was called Eloise. Gradually, Ninian came to think of her by that name too.

The other person who seemed to haunt him was Meggie. On occasions he thought he heard her call out to him, and once he had a vision of her desperately trying to tell him something. He told himself it was probably his imagination.

There was nothing to be done but stay where he was. He could not have left the mountains yet even if he wanted to, for the ways down to the valleys were still impassable and the community was cut off. Besides, he had left England because he was wanted for murder and would probably hang if they had caught him.

Sometimes, in the midst of his new life, it was quite hard to recall what had driven him out of the old one.

Despite his feelings for his new companions and his deep respect for their faith, he knew he did not want to join the community. He would defend them if the enemy came, for they were his friends. But if he was honest with himself – and Josse had always taught him he must be – then he had to admit that their fight was not his fight.

One afternoon, when the ice and snow began to ease their iron fist, Ninian went off by himself up the track that led out of the village and towards the peak that rose up behind it, where he now knew there was a fortress. The day was fine, and the sun was out, glittering on the snow and making such brilliant reflections that it hurt the eyes. Ninian needed to be alone, for he had to think.

For some time now he had been wondering what to do. There were no easy answers, and the future was a mist. He still heard Meggie calling to him – he had heard her that morning – and now, as he stood by himself on the mountain-side, he tried to send back the message that he was alive, well, and – for the moment – safe with good friends.

But when spring came and the crusade against the Cathars began again, safety would be gone. Ninian did not want to die, for he loved his Little Helewise – his Eloise – and he had promised he would return to her if it was in his power. There would be fighting; there would be danger. Ninian knew his own nature and, even loving Eloise as he did, he knew he would not be able to stand back and watch when his friends battled for their lives.

So, he thought, I will fight.

Perhaps he would fight his way out of the mountains; he did not know.

He thought of Eloise. He imagined marrying her, taking her home to some simple dwelling, lying with her, planting his seed inside her so that she bore his child. The pictures in his mind were so vivid that he believed they must be a true prediction of what lay ahead.

Before the vision could come true, though, he would have to fight.

He cleared the snow from a rock and sat down on it, gazing out across the endless mountains. He stayed there for a long time. Finally, growing cold, he realized it was time to return to the village.

He stood up, squared his shoulders, took a deep breath and said aloud, 'I'd just better make sure I stay alive, then, hadn't I?'